I0603686

ABOUT THE AUTHOR

Kellie Cox is an Australian writer indulging her love of fiction and prose. With qualifications in psychology, she relishes writing about the human condition and the vulnerability of the psyche. A therapist, clinical trainer, creative coach and conservationist, she enjoys a dream life on the beautiful Gold Coast.

Wanting to see a change in the narrative of gender roles in storytelling, Kellie has created her publishing and production enterprise, Strong Female Protagonists and encourages others to write and produce work that challenges our preconceived notions of societal values.

Most days Kellie can be found working with artists in the creative industries or writing her novels. When not writing, Kellie will likely be saturating her social media accounts with photos of her adorable dogs.

Follow Kellie on social media as KellieCoxWriter and KellieMCox.

www.kelliemcox.com
www.strongfemaleprotagonists.com

WRITTEN BY KELLIE M COX

Fiction
Murderous Intent (2019)
The Last First Kiss (2020)
The List (2020)
The Reef (2020)

Short Stories
Death by Trident (2018)
Short Yarns for Big Imaginations, GCWA.

THE LIST

Book One

KELLIE M COX

THE LIST

This book is a work of fiction. Names, characters, places and incidents are the product of the author's imagination or are used fictitiously. Any resemblance to actual events, or persons, living or dead, is entirely coincidental.

Published by Kellie M Cox
and

Strong Female Protagonists

www.KellieMCox.com

www.StrongFemaleProtagonists.com

ISBN 978 0 6484767 2 6 (paperback)

ISBN 978 0 6484767 3 3 (ebook)

Author - Kellie M Cox

Cover Photo – Georgina Winters

Cover Design - Blair Renwick

Logo and Website Design – Connor Renwick

DEDICATION

To my beautiful mother who fell in love with this story and has waited years for it to be published. Thank you for your endless encouragement of my writing.

and

To those hoping to meet their soul mate, may your heart burst and your mind discombobulate when you finally meet the one.

Enjoy the read.

ONE

THE SWIM

Kasie dove into the water. Her flowing blonde locks cascaded behind her as she pierced the smooth surface. The sea, a bright turquoise colour, erupted at the intrusion to its serene peace. A shockwave of ripples permeated the ocean as Kasie's body quickly descended. Visibility was high. She kept her eyes open searching the clear waters for her beloved friend. She glanced down to the darker depths below her, the lightly coloured sands of the ocean floor clearly distinguishable. She hoped she hadn't missed him. She prayed that she wasn't too late.

The engine above her was silent. The voices of the crew quietened by the heaviness of the dense salt water which surrounded her on all sides. She felt a pressure in her chest. That familiar feeling of the air inside her lungs withering away to nothing warned her of her limited capacity beneath the surface of the water. Her breaths were laboured. She needed to concentrate. She needed to control her emotion. Choosing not to use a tank, for fear that the bubbles from her exhaled breath would potentially risk all hope of a successful rendezvous, instead she had chosen to free dive.

Kasie needed to surface briefly to once more fill her lungs. She looked skyward to quickly calculate the distance between her and the oxygen her body now suddenly craved. As she began her ascent, a shadow stirred the current beneath her. Her friend, he was close, she could sense him. With graceful strokes her fins encouraged her to the surface. Her arms dangled beside her body as the buoyancy of her own muscles and the propulsion of her long black fins ferried her to the ocean's surface.

She felt him close and needed to find him. Her head broke through the warm waters as she exhaled the last of her breath. She wasted no time and inhaled the warm air to fill her lungs once more. She hoped she would dive down to be greeted by him. Luck was on her side and her wish was granted immediately. As she submerged into the clear waters once more, he presented himself to her. Her friend had wanted to find her too. He was the largest and most elusive male great white shark on the reef, there for his biannual visit to the little town of Coral Cove and she was lucky enough to jump in the water just in time for a close encounter.

He had been nicknamed Bruce and it was well suited to him. Swimming slowly and with obvious intent, he too, was curious about the diver sharing the waters with him. Meeting only a handful of times before, the two were friendly but not yet familiar. His huge body swayed gently from side to side. His eyes focussed, watching with purpose, swimming with immense grace as he slowed and circled the mesmerised Kasie.

Without fear she swam toward him. He ascended to meet her and as the two joined Kasie gently placed her hand on his huge dorsal fin. The strength of the massive creature immediately pulled her body along. He didn't submerge nor make any effort to surface but instead continued his slow graceful meander through the crystal waters.

Forgetting all thoughts of oxygen Kasie relaxed into the moment. She felt blessed beyond belief to have this time with Bruce alone. She took the opportunity to look over him quickly. He looked well. He seemed healthy and possibly larger than their last meeting earlier in the year. Wherever he was going to feed must be plentiful. Kasie was secretly pleased that Bruce had managed to so far elude any attempts at placing a tracking device on him. This created for her the illusion of mystery. Her handsome friend staying quiet on his whereabouts during his long stints away from Coral Cove.

Unlike the other great whites that were tracked, Bruce was free to come and go without warning. No obvious pattern to his movements except the promise of a visit every six months or so. Her ride with the beautiful creature had to come to an end. He was without intent perhaps taking her further and further away from the boat and the crew waiting she imagined, with bated breath above them. She placed her one free hand onto his massive back and gave a gentle stoke to say her farewell. She wished him luck and released her grip on the front of his fin. *Goodbye Brucie,* she said silently as she swam away from him.

She allowed her body to float effortlessly to the surface so as not to disturb the peaceful creature below. Bruce didn't look back but continued on his way swimming further offshore. She hoped his time in Coral Cove wasn't coming to an end already and planned to listen out for further sightings in the hope for another rendezvous.

She once more broke the surface of the warm waters and searched for the boat. It wasn't long before they saw her and turned their engines on to slowly steer the boat in her direction. She bobbed in the water, not removing her mask. Not needing to kick, she just allowed her body to float taking in that addictive feeling of weightlessness.

Kasie was quietly confident that she had the best job in the world. Having been contracted to work on restoring the reef of this gorgeous costal town after a devastating tsunami wreaked havoc only a few years earlier, Kasie was more than grateful at the opportunities given to her. It was a dream job born from a natural disaster that had taken lives. Lives of people she would never meet. Yet a grief of sorts, a grief she felt very deeply had formed at the loss of those very lives.

There was silent fist pumping into the warm air as the crew came into view. They too were well aware of the impact that any loud noise had on the shy Bruce and had until now been silently waiting for Kasie to emerge. As the boat reached her, Marco stretched his strong arm down to offer Kasie a hand up. He was soaking wet. His naked torso glistened in the sun, the salt water still damp on his skin. He too must have made the peaceful vigil to try to catch a glimpse at Bruce.

"I got it," he smiled at her. "I got the footage."

Kasie hadn't even been aware that Marco had been in the water with her. So intently focussed on finding Bruce she hadn't even looked to see Marco too, dive into the blue waters right behind her. So secretive is the ocean that depth and perception are mind-blowingly altered once beneath her. Keeping her secrets to herself the ocean enjoys toying with the senses. Kasie was so tuned into Bruce she hadn't even realised Marco had filmed the entire surreal encounter.

"That was amazing!" he chimed in once more as he lifted her body effortlessly on board the vessel. "What made you think to do that?" He was intrigued.

"I don't know. I wasn't thinking. I just wanted to say hello up close I guess," she sputtered, not really sure her answer adequately described the unbelievable moment.

"Kasie," Aretha, the conservation society's assistant, immediately walked toward her, mobile phone in hand, a worried frown on her young face. "You have a message from the boss." She handed Kasie her phone.

The message was concise but direct.

"Kase, I heard about your dive. Don't ever enter the water like that again without me beside you. Understood?"

"Control freak!" Kasie replied under her breath just enough to be heard by Marco. She turned her phone to face him, which allowed him to take in the message from their employer.

"How did he know already?" she asked Marco accusingly.

"Don't look at me!" he laughed. "He knows everything. It's his town remember. Don't fight it," he tried to reassure her. "Just reply, yes boss, to appease him and keep doing what you want to do. That's worked so far hasn't it?"

Kasie felt the feeling of frustration well up inside her. She knew that her employer meant well. He really did look out for her but this constant micromanaging of her day to day work life had gotten to ridiculous extremes lately. She made a mental note to have a chat with him about it. But not that night. That night she had even more pressing agenda items to discuss with him. And she was not looking forward to it at all.

"Want me to share the footage with our boss?" Marco asked his companion.

She paused and thought about it for a minute. Not sure how he would take the scene, she wasn't convinced it was a good idea but also very certain that he would insist on seeing it. Control freak was an understatement. This man managed every aspect of his small town with detailed and passionate precision. He knew everyone and everything that happened. It exhausted her just thinking about what he must get up to everyday. And with all of his endeavours, his projects and goals, he still found ample time to reprimand Kasie while she was on her impromptu reef dive.

Marco stood waiting for an answer that didn't come. "You could give it to him as a birthday present," he jokingly suggested.

"Damn!" Kasie said as she realised she had forgotten to get her employer a present. She didn't want to walk into the party empty handed but had no idea in the world of what to get the most established man in Coral Cove.

"What did you get him?" Kasie questioned Marco hoping for some inspiration for a gift idea.

"My presence is his present," Marco laughed with her. "Nah, he gets nothing from me but my friendship. And he is lucky to have that with the way he behaves," he added with a grin on his gorgeous face.

"I completely understand. What is with him lately?" Kasie hoped her employer's best friend might hold the key to his out of character bad mood of late.

"Let's just say he has a lot on his mind at the moment," Marco hinted without giving anything away.

"Do tell?" Kasie's curiousity was peaked. She needed to know more.

"You know already. I don't have to tell you what happens at the party." He added the vague response in an attempt for Kasie herself to piece together the answer to her own question.

"Do you mean that stupid list?" Kasie couldn't have guessed at a more unlikely reason for the increased stress for the birthday boy.

"It's a big deal for him Kasie. You have no idea. Well you should, considering you are on it. But you don't seem to have given that a second thought until this very week. What's with that?"

Kasie recalled the conversation with the intimidating Doctor Phoenix, experienced psychologist and trusted friend of her employer. The therapist had approached her nearly twelve months ago informing her of a structured process he had put into place for potential women to date her employer with the long-term goal of marriage. Kasie remembered shirking off the suggestion of her actually dating anyone while working abroad for a few years but nevertheless her name was taken down and The List was created.

She had tried to forget about it. It seemed an outrageous concept, but the women on this small island paradise mentioned it often. She had never really taken it that seriously, she barely understood the entire custom and traditions that accompanied island life. Never in her wildest imaginations had she thought she would be asked to go on a date. It just didn't seem right to her.

This normally very generous and caring man, her employer had given her an incredible opportunity to work on the restoration of the reef. She had during that time formed quite a friendship with him. He too sharing her love of the water and her passion for conservation. These reasons combined meant that for her at least, there could be nothing more than a strong friendship and a collaborative working relationship between the two of them.

"Marco," her thoughts interrupted with a question that needed an answer. "Is he really serious about announcing this list? Is this dating and potential marriage thing actually going to happen?"

Marco laughed at her choice of words. "Potential marriage thing Kasie?" he let his head fall back in laughter. He threw his strong arm around her and squeezed tightly. "You are beautiful and intelligent, but naïve. Of course, Kasie, he is one hundred per cent serious about this plan. He wants to get married and start a family and sooner rather than later I might add." He paused before playfully teasing her some more. "Are you ready to be a mummy?" He roared with laughter again at his joking with his friend.

Kasie tensed up and released herself from Marco's now vice-like grip. The thought of her becoming anyone's wife, let alone mother, was ridiculous. She was no closer to getting married than she was of becoming the next Nobel Prize Winner. In all of her thirty-four years she hadn't even gotten close enough to a man to think about taking marriage vows and because of that, she had imagined her hopes of ever becoming a mother were equally as unlikely. Kasie had just been happy to live for a short time in this island paradise concentrating on the work she was born to do.

She loved Marco but right at that moment, she didn't appreciate being the brunt of his teasing. She should have been used to it by now but this was a little too much for her to just laugh off. She had planned to meet the birthday boy later that day to let him know that she needed her name taken off The List but then had second thoughts imagining it wasn't a real threat anyway. Now, on hearing Marco's teasing and realising the serious nature of their employer's intent to marry, she knew she needed to meet with him and straighten things out and the party night was the night she planned to do it.

TWO

THE LIST

As she looked once more into the mirror that adorned her bedroom wall, Kasie bowed her head in exhaustion. She felt tired from the day's adventures and knew that it showed on every pore of her sun kissed face. She had been feeling increasingly overwhelmed by the dilemma that had been ruminating in her head for weeks now and she had no idea why this ridiculous plan she found herself caught up in was causing her so much unrest.

She had signed off on the agreement to be on The List with little thought as to the consequences of her actions at the time. It seemed harmless really. There was no way she could have imagined herself, now twelve months later, losing sleep over it. This truly was the most insane idea she had ever been talked into. At the time she hadn't imagined it would ever actually amount to anything. Why would it? She thought to herself, really, how could it?

Kasie had her own plans; she knew she was in Coral Cove to work for a few years before returning home to Australia and to her family and friends. Coral Cove, just that name alone conjured up immensely comforting feelings of contentment within her. It was such a beautiful name for the small coastal town she had instantly fallen in love with.

Coral Cove reminded her of her very own home back in Australia, in Far North Queensland, her birth home that she missed so much. She had grown up in a gorgeous little place called Port Douglas. So very similar to her temporary home, similar, except in Coral Cove the amazing reef system could actually be seen in part from land. Port Douglas on the other hand required a short but scenic boat ride to view the reef.

Such an unusual and delicate ecosystem was the reef, her reef as she was starting to think of it. Her home away from home was Coral Cove sitting just an ocean away from Australia nestled in a cosy little chain of islands in the South Pacific. So very close but still so far away from where she grew up. It had become for the time being anyway, her own perfect part of the world that she had trouble leaving.

She looked at herself again in the mirror. Her long blonde hair straightened to perfection, her make up applied with the brush strokes of a fine painting. She had been trying her hardest tonight of all nights to look her best, but yet something was failing her. The stress of the conversation she knew she needed to have was causing her immense worry, and worry for her always lead to physical symptoms. For the last while, she hadn't been sleeping well or eating properly. She had literally bitten her nails down to the core. She needed to talk to her boss and have her name taken off The List. She knew this was the only possible solution but it had been too hard to do up until now.

She stared deeper into her blue eyes, normally sparkling with the brightness of a person who enjoyed a healthy lifestyle. The reflection of her blue eyes looked dull and a little bloodshot like someone who desperately needed a good eight hours sleep. She had woken constantly during the nights that preceded her. She recalled stirring several times as her mind worked overtime trying to sort through this dilemma. Looking at herself, she nodded as if in agreement with the image before her in the mirror. "I need to ring Dee," she said to herself.

She laughed out loud. "I have gone insane, talking to myself in the mirror," she again spoke the words out loud to the empty room. Kasie picked up her mobile phone and rang her lifelong best friend back home in Australia.

"Hello home!" Kasie excitedly yelled at Dee as her friend answered her call.

"Well hello stranger, tell me you are ringing to come home, please?" Dee yelled enthusiastically back at her.

"Not yet, but one day soon, I promise. When are you coming to visit me again?"

"Visit you again in tsunami city?" Dee replied with more than just a hint of sarcasm.

"Please don't call it that. Actually, you wouldn't know the place. A lot has changed since you were last here. He has developed much new infrastructure within an incredibly short timeframe."

"Oh yes, really? Has he?" Dee added the appropriate sarcasm only a best friend could conjure up. "I imagined it wouldn't be long before his name popped up in the conversation. How is your handsome Prince Charming anyway?" Dee cheekily questioned her friend.

"Ha! You are so funny. You know he is not that to me. We are just friends and I work for the man, nothing more but actually he is what I wanted to talk to you about"

"Oh, sounds interesting," Dee teased her once more.

"OK. But this is going to sound really strange, so you have to promise to not make any judgements until you hear me out. I've been reluctant to share this with you but I need your advice."

There was silence on the other end of the phone as Kasie imagined Dee's head racing with possibilities. "Promise?" Kasie repeated her demand, waiting eagerly for agreement from her friend before continuing.

"Yes, yes I promise. This is sounding more and more delectable by the second. What is going on between you and your Mister Handsome then?" Dee's tone was sincere with just a hint of concerned curiousity for her friend.

"Ok, so here goes. It's his birthday today, and there's a huge party at his house tonight to celebrate."

"Oh, I wish I was there now. Why didn't you invite me? I'm so jealous. He has the most decadent parties!" Dee interrupted her.

"You know how the parties go. Always so much fun! But this one is a bit different," Kasie hesitated.

"The suspense is killing me Kasie, what's happening tonight?" Dee responded with growing impatience.

"Well, tonight he literally turns into a prince as you like to call him."

Dee paused for a second as even more possibilities raced through her head. "Oh my God, is he proposing to you?" Without waiting for a response, her wild assumption was now turning into its own reality. "Oh Kasie, that is so exciting, but you can't live there with him. You have to bring him back here."

"Hold on Dee," Kasie pleaded with her friend to stop. "You are incorrigible! It is nothing like that. Well actually, not nothing like that...it is a bit like that...but not," Kasie tried to explain with little success.

"If you don't tell me soon, I swear I am hopping on the next plane to Coral Cove to ring your scrawny little neck," Dee yelled at her.

"Alright, but this is complicated. Your aptly nicknamed Prince Charming is actually going to announce that he is ready to settle down."

"That will make every woman of Coral Cove all very hot and bothered won't it? I can't even imagine the lengths some of them will go to, in an attempt to lock down a mega wealthy husband."

"I don't want to imagine it. The only thing is, there are actually only a select few who will be jumping with joy," Kasie explained.

"Why?" Dee was genuinely confused.

"Well he has made a kind of a deal with some of the women of Coral Cove. This sounds so ridiculous."

"Go on…" Dee paused, waiting for the rest of the story to unfold.

"There is more to him than you already know. He is sort of island royalty and there are some generations long traditions and rules about who he can and can't marry. Not to mention he owns most, well nearly all of this little town, so the stakes are pretty high for the right partnership."

"Are you kidding? I knew he was wealthy, but are you kidding Kasie?" Dee yelled with excitement.

"No, I am not exaggerating. His family settled this town generations ago. So, he literally owns most of the township and nearly all of its surrounds. And the way he has managed the properties since his parents' death has led to massive returns. You would have no idea of the celebrities and entrepreneurs who are rushing to secure pockets of land on the island. And traditions states that only locals can own land, so these wealthy foreigners are leasing their piece of paradise at exorbitant costs."

"Wow, that is some serious cash but how do you fit into any of this?" Dee let out an envious sigh as she spoke.

"He made a kind of a pact that he would not date anyone seriously until he turned thirty-five, which of course is now. That meant that the pressure was off him to get married and he could spend his time really just looking after his businesses, which already keeps him incredibly busy."

"That makes me feel a little sorry for him," Dee responded with a tinge of empathy.

"Oh, please don't. Regardless of his plan, he is virtually hunted down every time he steps into town. Women are continually throwing themselves at him," Kasie continued.

"So, the expectation is that at his party he will announce that he would like to be married and start a family in the next few years," Kasie elaborated on the plan even further.

"How do you know all of this?" Dee demanded to know.

"Everyone knows. It is all the town has been talking about."

"So, what is the problem? So far it is sounding very appealing. I am packing my bags as we speak."

"Dee, you are more than welcome to come for a visit, but you can't date him cause you're not on The List."

"What List? Why is there a List? Who is on the List? Oh my god, please tell me you are on The List?" Dee pleaded with her friend.

"Well, actually yes I am. For some ridiculous reason, I am on The List," Kasie replied.

"That's great news Kasie. I knew the two of you would start dating sooner or later."

"When he came up with this plan that he wouldn't date exclusively until after his birthday, he also came up with a bit of a list of women who might be eligible to marry him, that is taking into account the ancestral family rules regarding marriage for someone in his position."

"I knew it. I knew all along that the two of you had something brewing between you."

Kasie couldn't share Dee's enthusiasm. From what she had pieced together, a number of women had been in discussions with Doctor Phoenix. He asked the women if they would consider spending time with eligible bachelor and only the women on The List qualified to date him.

"Sounds like some crazy, nasty, reality show," Dee said with slight disgust at the idea.

Dee still had no idea how complicated the scheme actually was. To get onto The List, a woman had to have been born in Coral Cove or living there long enough to be considered a local. That was the reason why Dee herself wouldn't be eligible. The women could only be chosen if they too, like their bachelor had a desire to live in Coral Cove forever. Kasie's mind remained stuck on that last thought.

As if reading her mind, Dee yelled at her once again. "Kasie…this better not be your way of telling me that you are staying there for good."

Kasie sighed, "No, not at all. I am coming home," she tried to comfort Dee before continuing. "The woman who does marry him has to want to live here and work towards rebuilding the town and the reef after the tsunami."

"This isn't making any sense. How did you make it onto The List when you are not local and definitely not staying around?"

The answer to that question didn't actually make much sense to Kasie herself either. Doctor Phoenix had made some argument around her conservation role and how long she had already been working in Coral Cove to rebuild the ecosystem off the coast. He went on to explain how important this work was and somehow this made her eligible. Kasie explained the loophole to Dee in detail.

"Well, he has a point. You said you were going for twelve months and how long have you been there now, three years? I guess they figured you were staying," Dee added with a slight sound of resentment in her voice.

Kasie replied, "I feel a bit guilty about it, I had agreed to go on The List not really thinking about the forever part…or even the marriage part for that matter. I think I was just flattered that I would even be considered. And Doctor Phoenix was very persuasive I might add."

"That sounds ever so slightly unethical for a psychologist. And Kasie, this just sounds absurd but I am still failing to see the big problem here though? You are living in what you describe to me in your emails as a paradise, enjoying parties most weekends in a billionaire's mansion and now you are telling me that you might actually have to go on a date with this gorgeous, sexy man. Who by the way I might add, worships the ground you walk on and thinks you are pure genius for the conservation work he is paying you great money to do. Work I can also add, you are unwaveringly whole heartedly passionate about."

There was long silence by both women as they attempted to take in the enormity of what Dee had said.

Kasie broke the silence. "Before he makes the announcement tonight that he is finally going to start dating, I was thinking of taking my name off The List."

Kasie could hear Dee about to explode. "That makes no sense Kasie. You two belong together."

Kasie knew they were great as friends. She agreed with that observation. But she had never thought about them being anything more than that. That just was too strange for her to even imagine.

And staying in Coral Cove was never part of her plans. Never to live on the island permanently that was.

"Sounds to me like you need some time to think about this a little bit more Kasie," Dee added as she broke through Kasie's thoughts.

"I don't have time. This all kicks off in a couple of hours. I have made an appointment with the psychologist beforehand. He can take my name off The List for me."

"So, have you made up your mind then?" Dee asked with a mixture of gentle enquiry and empathic concern.

"I think so," Kasie hesitated. "But it has helped to talk about it. Hearing the words out loud made it sound even more ridiculous than it did in my head."

Kasie glanced at her watch. "Oh god, is that the time? I have to run to make my appointment with the Doctor."

"Ok Kasie, you take care babe, call me tomorrow and let me know how it all went. Love you babe!"

"Love you too sweetie, miss you!" Kasie replied as she ended the call.

As Kasie grabbed her bag and keys she did one final check in the mirror. The relief of finally making the decision showed in her face. Her eyes were brighter and she felt the beginnings of a smile at the thought of the fun that lay ahead. After of course, the tough conversation with the party host had been had first.

Kasie felt a strange mixture of relief at finally making the decision and yet a looming sense of dread which she wasn't quite certain about. She knew she needed to do what was right for her. At the same time, she worried about how he might respond to the news. It was only fair to tell him before anyone else and that was her plan, to grab him for a few quiet minutes before the party to tell him that she had removed her name from The List.

* * *

Arriving at the mansion, a mere fifteen minutes later, Kasie couldn't help but smile at the festive decorations and party feel that were already resonating through the house. None of the guests had arrived and fortunately he wasn't home yet either but she knew who would be inside the house and waiting for her early arrival. Marco, best friend, confidant and loyal employee to the mansion owner and the man she was here to see, Doctor Phoenix himself, the specialist with all the questions.

Kasie had met Doctor Phoenix a number of times before; he seemed to have a habit of being in the right place at the right time to gather the necessary information for his role. He appeared to always be in full time assessment mode, listening to every conversation, watching body language from the corner of the room, asking curious but very purposeful questions. It was, as if his role all along had been to provide his client with the wealth of advice to get him to tonight's big announcement.

She didn't know quite how she felt about Doctor Phoenix. She got the sense that he was always judging, always analysing every word that he heard. She also had been told that he had an incredible memory. Recalling even the slightest detail he had learnt years earlier. This made him a man to be feared or at the very least a man to be cautious about. But her friend, her employer trusted him explicitly.

She had known that he sought his advice on many areas of his life and that he trusted the guidance that the Doctor so generously dealt out. She wondered how much of a role the Doctor was actually playing in providing guidance as to potential marriage partners. It started to feel all very clinical to Kasie. She wondered how much passion and attraction could feature in a marriage that has been so carefully planned and orchestrated.

Kasie knew one thing. She knew she believed in instinct and in that physical attraction and spark between two people. She had read somewhere a Buddhist saying that when you meet your soul mate, there would be no spark, no electricity; just an amazing sense of calm and that is how you know you have met the one. Kasie wasn't sure. She guessed she might find out one day. Well at least she hoped she would find out one day.

As Kasie walked up the front stairs of the old mansion, the wide glass and timber door swung open. Stood there to greet her with a grin from ear to ear was Marco. As always looking absolutely gorgeous, arms outstretched ready to envelope her into his strong tight embrace. A girl could get lost in his hugs. She held him tightly, taking the time to breathe in the warm manly scent of his cologne as he placed a delicate kiss on her cheek. It would be one lucky girl who finally got Marco to settle down, she thought as she returned the greeting with a kiss on his cheek.

She stepped back and took a good look at her attractive friend. His dark hair and brooding brown eyes set against his deep chocolate coloured skin. Standing there in a pair of lightly coloured shorts, a crisp linen shirt and deck shoes, he looked like he was ready to step foot aboard the nearest boat and sail away. He was definitely in off duty mode tonight and ready to party like the couple of hundred or so other guests due to start arriving within the hour.

"Good evening, most beautiful girl in the world. How are you tonight?" Marco greeted her.

"You can't say that Marco. Aren't you meant to be his unbiased best friend there to offer advice and guidance in the dating world? Given that you have so much experience that is," Kasie responded with a cheeky grin.

"I would offer unbiased advice, if he ever asked me for it. Hell, I give it to him just because I can, whether or not he wants to hear it. And you my beautiful Kasie, do you want my advice?"

Kasie hesitated, she knew she didn't, but figured she was going to get it anyway whether she wanted it or not. "Um, do I have a choice Marco?"

"Smart girl and no, not really. My advice would be, to not do this. There is no need to take your name off The List. I don't think you have really thought this through," Marco pleaded with her.

"Actually, that is what got me into this mess, I didn't think about it, I just went along with it and said yes to this ridiculous potential marriage plan."

"Ridiculous? You do realise you are currently in the lead according to the women's tally that is. I haven't been keeping score myself."

The women's tally was a horrible scoring system that someone was keeping of how much time each woman was logging with the attractive bachelor. The competition had been getting more intense as the big night approached and the women were keeping tabs on one another. The tally was their way of trying to work out who stood the best chance of scoring the marriage proposal. Kasie was currently in the lead but that was due to a technicality. The technicality that she not only worked with the man of the moment, but she was also good friends with him and Marco and spent time with both of them alone at the mansion.

How anyone had that much time to waste on tallying superficial details was beyond her. But as much as she tried to ignore the ridiculousness of the behaviour, it did at times bother her.

"Yes, well that is part of why I am doing this. This is crazy! The women are going to hate me for taking his time away from them when really it is all very innocent. You know that. You are with us most of the time when we are together. Do these women realise that? It is often the three of us watching a game of football or going for a surf. I think they imagine some romantic candlelight dinners for just the two of us that simply aren't happening"

"So, what?" Marco scoffed, "Let them think what they want Kasie. Don't worry about them."

"I have to live in this town too Marco. It isn't pleasant being watched and questioned all the time and after tonight I will just be able to spend time with the two of you without all the scrutiny."

Although this made sense to Marco, he suspected there was more to Kasie's decision than she was letting on. Everything she had said was true. It was mostly the three of them doing normal everyday things like playing pool or spending time in the ocean. But he also knew that as time went on he was fast beginning to feel more like the third wheel around the two of them.

If anything was to happen between his two friends, he couldn't be happier. He loved them both and secretly thought they would be perfect together. It made him briefly consider his own future and the prospect of carving out a life with someone special. He had fleeting visions of it from time to time but as yet, hadn't met a woman who had managed to keep his attention for anything longer than a few months. For Kasie and his boss though, he suspected things might be very different.

He hadn't been told as much but from what he knew of his boss and best friend he could tell that something had definitely changed between them. Whether Kasie herself had recognised this or not he wasn't so sure. "Is that really the reason Kasie?" He looked deep into her blue eyes as he asked for her honest response.

"Yes Marco. I don't want to be part of this craziness. I just want to spend time with him as friends. And you of course."

Marco laughed, "Yeah you don't have to explain it to me. I know that every man in this town comes a distant second to our local Prince Charming."

"Oh no, not you too! Dee has been calling him that as well," Kasie laughed.

"Well, if the name suits…you know what they say. Isn't that every woman's fantasy? You know a fairytale with the glass slipper and all that?"

Marco paused as he consulted his watch. He knew there was only a small window of time to get done what had to be done before his boss returned home to start the festivities. "So then, sounds like you have made up your mind. Are you ready to meet again with Doctor Phoenix?"

"Let's get this over with already," Kasie replied as the two friends headed through the grand entrance of the opulent mansion.

No matter how many times Kasie had been in the mansion, she remained in awe of its sheer size and luxury. The marble tiles that lined the entrance carefully placed to create a sense of formality but at the same time felt comforting in a strange sort of way. The warmth of the colours of the tiles were in line with the natural surrounds of the grounds. The beiges, the soft greens and the warm browns of the interior of the house welcomed in its guests. Each time she stepped foot inside its walls, it was as if she was stepping into a sacred dwelling of an impenetrable fortress. The home was understated and welcoming.

She imagined the lucky woman who would one day call this place her own and wondered how much she might want to change it and make her own mark on the huge home. Kasie wondered what it was like for the current resident to live there without a partner. She guessed that the sheer size of the mansion would make for a lonely existence. She was a little curious as to why he hadn't married before now and started a family of his own. There really was nothing holding him back.

A tinge of some strange emotion rose inside her. Sadness possibly, grief maybe at the loss of what she currently enjoyed. She had built a wonderful friendship with the mansion owner but imagined that would change once he was married. Her regular visits to the mansion wouldn't be the same once he had a wife and possibly children to occupy his time. Gone would be the carefree existence he enjoyed with Marco and Kasie, replaced instead with a new-found sense of responsibility to dedicate his time to his young family.

"Kasie, are you ok?" Marco interrupted her daydream. "You were miles away. Having second thoughts maybe?"

"No Marco. Not at all. I was just thinking of how much things will change when he gets married. It won't just be the three of us anymore, will it?" She added with sadness in her voice.

"Well that kind of depends on you now, doesn't it Kasie?" Marco teased her. His smile lit up his stunning face as he looked her straight in the eyes waiting for the realisation to hit her.

"Don't be stupid Marco! You can't seriously believe for a second that I could possibly be someone he would consider marrying." Kasie was quick to respond and if she was honest with herself slightly annoyed at Marco for suggesting that she would even consider such a thing. "Let's get to Doctor Phoenix, shall we?"

As Kasie followed Marco up the stairs to the top floor, little did she realise it would not be the last time that night she would enter the sacred third floor of his private residence, the area off limits to guests most of the time. It was their host's very own house rule to allow him and his staff privacy and space within the normally busy mansion walls.

And fair enough Kasie thought. The ground floor of the enormous mansion seemed steadily busy much of the time, flooded with friends, distant family and more staff than she imagined it was even feasible to employ. It was understandable that guests shouldn't have access to the entire house. It made sense that there remained private areas in his home, only accessible to a few trusted employees and a couple of close friends.

At the top of the stairs, at the entrance to a small but elegantly decorated office stood Doctor Phoenix. As he shook her hand, he appeared to want to get right down to business. The psychologist ushered her into the room. "Please sit down Kasie. It is lovely to see you. You look stunning," he greeted her.

"Thank you, that's very kind of you to say Doctor."

"So, is this the attire to wear for breaking a man's heart?" The psychologist questioned her immediately.

Slightly taken back by the seemingly inappropriate comment, Kasie didn't quite know how to answer at first.

"Breaking a man's heart, may be a bit of an exaggeration don't you think Doctor? And this is a pool party, so a guest has to come dressed for the occasion."

"You do indeed, you do indeed," the man relented.

Was she detecting a hint of sarcasm? Or was he purposefully trying to get a reaction out of her? It was hard for Kasie to tell. Not knowing the psychologist that well she wasn't sure what to make of his inappropriate line of questioning.

Kasie did a quick scan of her seemingly unsuitable attire. She was wearing her favourite red bikini. A string bikini with a glittering pattern of embroidery and Swarovski crystals beneath skinny white jeans and a red linen shirt. She glanced down at her top buttons. Ok, well maybe she had left one button too many undone she thought to herself, but it was hardly scandalous.

She imagined what the other women would be wearing to the party. Most would enter the house wearing very little, a tiny-mini, or skin-tight shorts, and they would lose more and more layers of clothing as the party progressed until most if not all of the women were in their smallest of bikinis.

And the men, they would be wearing fitted shorts and enjoying cocktails and music in the pool or spa. She couldn't help but feel slightly angry with the professional for his judgemental comment.

Doctor Phoenix seemingly eager to get the meeting over with began with his line of inevitable questioning. "So, I am led to believe you want to remove your name from The List."

"Yes," Kasie replied with some irritation forming in her voice. She wanted this all to be over with already and didn't want to waste any more time discussing this with anyone else but the birthday boy himself.

"And have you discussed this with him?" The psychologist paused and waited for her response. His strong jawline fell down and into the palm of his hand as he looked straight into her eyes from over the top of his dark rimmed glasses.

Kasie felt her irritation grow inside her with a slow burn. She didn't know how much of this questioning she would be able to remain polite for.

"No." She paused as she thought carefully about her next words. "And I didn't feel I had to. It is not as if I need his permission to do this."

"No, you are correct, you don't need his permission, but I assume he will have questions as to why you want to do this."

"I understand that and I am planning to talk to him tonight before the party to let him know my reasons for this," Kasie replied, now feeling a sense of strength and certainty that this was the right thing for her to do.

"Ok." The Doctor seemed unwilling or without energy to question her any further. "I will take your name off The List. But I do implore you…" he paused again mid-sentence. "Please speak to him before the party. Before he makes any big announcements."

"I will, I promise you. I will chat to him as soon as he arrives home," Kasie assured the Doctor.

The Doctor appeared convinced that Kasie would honour her promise and turned to gather his things.

"And he will be home in about ten minutes Kasie, so we had better get you downstairs in time to catch him," Marco warned her.

Kasie turned her attention back to the Doctor. She was relieved this part of the conversation was over and thankful that she didn't have to think about anything more now than letting her friend know. "Thank you for your understanding Doctor Phoenix."

"My pleasure, Kasie. It is always a pleasure to speak with you." The Doctor reached out to take her hand in his and with that, he leaned in and whispered in her ear. "I do hope you change your mind though, Kasie. Good night."

Kasie leaned back and searched the psychologist's face for some clue as to his intent. What a strange thing to say, she thought, but did not say out loud. "Thank you again Doctor, but I can assure you, my mind is made up."

With that, Marco gently grabbed Kasie's hand and led her back down the impressive staircase to the entrance. Kasie was fuming. She could not believe the unprofessionalism of the psychologist. How dare he suggest she was behaving in any way that would cause harm to her friend. She stomped down the stairs behind Marco now more convinced than ever of her decision to remove her name from The List and be done with this ridiculous scheme. She wanted her friend, her employer to be happy and knew she would be there for him in whatever capacity he wanted until things changed permanently for him with his impending marriage.

Marco broke into her thoughts once more. "Do you want to wait here for him?" he asked.

"No thanks, Marco. I might go and see the birthday cake, if that's ok. I hear it is stunning, five layers tall and mouth watering."

"No problems, Helen is in the kitchen, I'm sure she will be more than happy to show off her handiwork. She is most impressed with it."

"Great. And Marco, could you please let him know I am in the kitchen and I want to grab a couple of minutes with him before the party starts?" Kasie requested.

"Sure, will do. I will send him in when he gets home."

"Thanks Marco and thanks again for today. For the video of Bruce and for organising the meeting with Doctor Phoenix. I hope I don't get you into any trouble for going behind his back like this."

"Happy to help Kasie. And don't worry about him, he won't be happy, the control freak that he is, but he is just going to have to live with it, isn't he?"

"Absolutely, and I am sure it won't bother him. He probably just had my name added so as not to hurt my feelings. He knows we would never be anything more than friends and colleagues," Kasie giggled quietly to herself as she headed for the kitchen.

Marco watched as Kasie exited the grand entrance, speaking quietly to himself, just under his breath, his eyes followed her from the room.

"I don't know about that Kasie. I just don't know how he is going to take this."

THREE

THE KISS

"So, Helen, is this the birthday cake I am hearing so much about? It is absolutely gorgeous. Has he seen it?" Kasie asked the older woman as she entered the enormous commercial sized kitchen.

"Do you like it? No, he hasn't seen it yet. Do you think he will like it?" Helen replied. The excitement on her face was contagious.

Kasie smiled at Helen. "He will love it. You take such great care of him. I hope he appreciates it."

"He does, he really is the most generous person. Did you hear that he has given me a holiday to Tahiti to take next week? He said that he recognised all my hard work and that I deserved a special holiday. Isn't that just so sweet? Would you like to come with me?" Helen added with a laugh.

"I haven't been to Tahiti. It looks absolutely gorgeous. I would love to. Do you think he would buy me a holiday too?" Kasie joked with her.

"Do you want me to ask? I am sure he would say yes," Helen giggled again.

"Maybe next time Helen, I have a specialist crew coming soon advising on the rehabilitation of the coral, so I can't get away just at the moment."

"Your work sounds fascinating Kasie, I would love to come out and see it sometime."

"I would be honoured to take you out to the reef, how about when you return from your holiday?"

Helen was about to respond her mouth was open and ready to form the next words when the two women spun around to catch a glimpse of the birthday boy himself as he entered the kitchen. His arms outstretched looking from one woman to the next as if unsure who to greet first.

All eyes in the kitchen were on their host, the mansion owner, Kasie's trusted friend and employer. The most charismatic man Kasie imagined existed. He knew how to command a room and he looked as if he enjoyed every second doing it. His wide glistening smile erupted as he entered the kitchen. Looking similar to Marco in his colouring, their host shared the same dark hair and dreamy chocolate coloured skin.

His physique, tall, a good several inches taller than Marco but with the same athletic build, strong square shoulders and a body most men would kill for. The striking point of difference was their host's eyes. The most stunning dark green eyes that came alive and sparkled like emeralds whenever he engaged with someone. He had the most mesmerising eyes Kasie had seen.

"Well, well, what have we here?" he began, "Two of the most beautiful women that ever lived, side by side next to what I am going to assume is the birthday cake to marvel all birthday cakes. It looks amazing Helen. You really are a goddess in the kitchen. What have I done to deserve you in my life?"

"Well thank you, kind sir. I do my best to please" Helen teased him back as he enveloped her in an enormous heart felt hug of gratitude.

Releasing Helen from his embrace he then turned his full attention to Kasie. "And what have we here? The gorgeous Kase in my kitchen, and barefoot?" He smirked as he glanced at Kasie's bare feet on the kitchen tiles.

Slightly embarrassed by the unwanted attention, Kasie blushed.

"Well, your kitchen tiles are extremely slippery and I have new super high shoes, you know how clumsy I am, I didn't want to fall and embarrass myself. I am planning on putting them back on for the party though if you were concerned about my lack of foot wear."

His smirk widened and with a glint of a smile in his wicked eyes, he turned to Helen with a serious and inquisitive tone and asked. "Helen, what is that old saying? Something about a woman being barefoot and, in the kitchen…there is more to it...how does it go? Remind me please."

All too quick to assist with the impromptu comedy sketch, Helen quickly replied. "Well some men, very sexist men I might add, have been known to say that a woman's place is barefoot, pregnant and in the kitchen. Is that the phrase you were searching for boss?"

Helen looked toward Kasie with a smile plastered from ear to ear. She enjoyed her employer's wicked sense of humour and she knew Kasie well enough to know she could take care of herself when the playful banter between them began. Helen was all too willing to be an active participant in their witty exchanges when called upon. Being around these vivacious young people kept her young at heart too.

Kasie felt the need to defend herself and quickly negated the outlandish suggestion. "Well I can assure you both that I am not pregnant, so two out of three will have to suffice for you very funny people tonight."

Looking straight into Kasie's bright blue eyes, his face instantly lit up. He beamed widely, showing his perfectly aligned and glowing white-toothed smile. His wicked glint shined like light bulbs in his eyes. He reached out and placed his fingers very gently under Kasie's delicate fingertips to raise her hand up to his mouth.

Placing a lingeringly sweet and tender kiss on the back of her fingers, his bowed head then turned slightly upward, just enough for his eyes to meet hers once more.

"Well my beautiful Kase, may I offer you a visit to my bedroom upstairs to see what we can do to make that three out of three?"

Without hesitation and in absolute shock at what she had just heard Kasie jerked her hands back which released them immediately from her boss's hold.

"That is so inappropriate. You can't say something like that to me!" she challenged him. She yelled the words to him as she responded to the unusually sexually charged comment from her employer. She was shocked and taken by surprise with her friend's behaviour.

Her pleas fell on deaf ears as she realised that not only Helen but the entire rest of the kitchen staff were now in fits of laughter at her very righteous and indignant response to their boss's extremely public and sexy foreplay.

Helen contained her laughter just enough to say. "Oh my, you are a naughty boy on your birthday, aren't you?"

"Not funny Helen!" Kasie interjected sternly. "He doesn't need your encouragement to act inappropriately."

Kasie was more than just a little embarrassed. She felt her hands get damp and her stomach twist as she looked again into his bright green eyes. There was absolutely no sign of remorse as he beamed his delicious smile back to her.

With that, Kasie grabbed his hand and began to lead him back into the grand entrance. "I need a few minutes to speak with you alone please," She instructed him. Not giving him time to argue, she began to drag him from the kitchen area and away from the still giggling staff busily preparing for the night's festivities.

"Of course," he willingly responded before turning to Helen on his hasty retreat from the kitchen to add one final humorous addition to his impromptu performance.

"Oh Helen, if Kase does decide to take me to my bedroom, please inform the guests to start the party without me. We may be a little while."

"I certainly will do boss," Helen giggled to herself. She loved being in the company of her host and his effervescent friends. And she especially loved Kasie, the young woman she had begun to know extremely well from the time she spent at the mansion. She stood and watched as the two friends finally excited the room.

She chuckled to herself once more at Kasie's shocked response to her boss's flirtation and couldn't help but wonder what was behind her startled reaction. She had never seen Kasie so rattled before at the scandalous behaviour that she had more than likely become accustomed to from spending time with Marco and their boss.

As Kasie and the birthday boy approached the entrance to the house, Kasie looked around and decided that the office was the most appropriate place to speak in private. She dared not risk more public humiliation tonight and knew that the topic of conversation was one she needed to address with just him alone. Walking into the office, she turned to him, and motioned for him to take a seat. She ensured the door was closed and locked behind her before she took a position standing but perched ever so slightly on the edge of the huge wooden and leather desk that took central place in the impressive book lined office.

"Well, this feels like that time back in school, when I was in the headmaster's office and about to get told that my parents were going to be called," he joked with her. He seemed in a particularly joyful mood tonight, obviously ready for his party and chance to celebrate this birthday with friends. It was a stark contrast in mood to the firm and annoyed sounding text from earlier in the day.

"Please, this is important," Kasie pleaded with him. "I need to talk to you so I need you to be serious for a few minutes. I promise I won't take up too much of your time." She nervously waited his response.

"I am all yours!" he replied with a wide grin that wouldn't stop. His deeply tanned face was alight tonight. He was in fine spirits, playful and eager to celebrate this special night. He watched Kasie as she nervously settled into position ready to make her important speech. He looked at her long slender legs in her skinny white jeans. He could just make out the outline of her red bikini bottoms beneath. He secretly wondered if he had seen them before or if she had bought a new pair, just for the party…just for him.

He glanced further up her body and saw just the bright string of her bikini top fastened tightly around her neck. The thin and delicate material of her linen shirt allowed him to view the sparkling crystals etched into the small red bikini underneath. He felt his body temperature rise and hoped that he wasn't blushing. Being friends with Kasie had meant they had developed a certain comfort in each other's presence but he wasn't sure how she would feel if she knew he was scanning her body with his eyes, etching every inch of her into his memory.

Kasie took a deep breath before beginning, "Ok, well. I wanted to talk to you before the party to let you know that…" Kasie hesitated, suddenly feeling very unsure about how he might respond to the news.

"Kase, before you start, I need to talk to you about today." He was quick and to the point with her. "I don't ever want to hear you have taken that level of risk again without informing me first. I need to be present in the water with you any time you enter with the great whites. Do you understand me?"

Kasie was taken back. She had almost forgotten about her day's adventure and the conversation she knew would ensue once he saw her. She stood open mouthed, unsure how to respond. He had taken control of the conversation and steered it in a direction she wasn't quite prepared for.

The handsome birthday boy stayed seated in his chair, but just barely. He needed to make Kasie understand once and for all, that she could not take these insane risks, anymore. He had too much at stake to lose her now. Loss and grief had become his permanent filter in which he viewed the world and he was determined to do whatever he needed to not lose anyone he loved ever again. He hoped she would respond. He needed to hear her say that she would stay safe for him.

Kasie felt the blood flood to her cheeks. She felt immense anger at his attempt to control her. "There were no risks to me. You know that as much as I do."

He shook his head. He wanted to jump from the chair and take her in his arms. He wanted to not let her go until she promised him that she understood want he needed from her.

"Kase, there is always a risk. Every time you enter the water you take a calculated risk. Yes, it is small but you can't deny that it exists. It's a hazard we live with every day and I agree with you, neither of us would have it any other way, but to stand there and blatantly deny this fact to me is incomprehensible." He paused as he shook his head in frustration at the woman in front of him.

"Kase, if you can't make this commitment to me to keep me informed every time you plan on entering the water, you will leave me no choice but to have you accompanied each time you leave the shore."

"What?" Kasie screamed back at him. "I am a professional. This is what I do for a living. This is what you pay me to do. If you want to hire a babysitter for me…well…" She didn't know what the next words out of her mouth were going to be. The level of control her employer demanded of her work life had reached unmanageable levels. She looked at her friend and forgot for a moment what they were fighting about. His eyes looked sad, beneath the obvious frustration, she could see hurt. She didn't understand what the conversation was actually about anymore. She blurted out the next few words to him. She needed to take back some control over her life.

"I need to tell you that I have taken my name off The List."

Without hesitation and with an innocent and unconcerned expression he asked her quietly, "What List?"

"Your List," she added for clarification. "The list of potential wives that you and Doctor Phoenix have painstakingly prepared. I met with Doctor Phoenix today and he has taken my name off The List."

With all of the final shreds of lightness now leaving his gorgeous face, he responded with just a few words, "With Marco's help, I assume?" His mood had suddenly shifted back again. His cheerful tone from earlier in the kitchen replaced with one of accusation and businesslike formality.

His words were part question, part statement and Kasie wasn't sure if she needed to answer, but did anyway. "Yes, Marco helped me to contact Doctor Phoenix, but that is all. I haven't talked in depth to him about my decision, I wanted to talk to you first."

Moving with slight unease in his chair to re-position himself, he seemed to be thinking very carefully about his follow up question. His face wasn't giving much away and Kasie felt nervous about what he might say next.

"And can I ask, why you would do that?" His voice was deep, his tone serious. He had definitely lost all of the playfulness of only moments earlier.

She thought carefully before responding, "You know me." She paused for just a moment trying to match the right words to her thoughts. "You know that I am a hopeless romantic. I have imagined many times how I might meet the man I might one day marry. I envisaged I would meet a stranger's eyes across a room and we couldn't resist introducing ourselves and sparking up a conversation. That we would start talking and I would know instantly that he was the one."

He looked somewhat concerned as a slight frown formed over his gorgeous green eyes. He began to question her further, "Are you suggesting our first meeting wasn't romantic?"

Feeling confused by his response, Kasie tried her hardest to reassure him. "Our meeting was well, more business-like, than romantic, we met at the research facility if you remember correctly. You were checking on the running of the research project that I had just been appointed to."

"And I saw you and thought you were the most beautiful woman I had ever met." He sounded as if he was almost begging for understanding, for reassurance from her. Kasie felt an ache in the pit of her stomach as she realised that this conversation was not going as well as she hoped it would.

Kasie looked at her stunning friend. His expression was one of confusion and at the same time disappointment. She stared into his deep green eyes and thought she saw tears forming. She tried to regain her concentration but as she looked at his gorgeous face it was hard for her to remember why it had been so important for her to tell him what she thought she needed to tell him.

She took in the view of this near perfectly formed human being in front of her. His dark tanned skin enchanted her; it was glowing tonight. Having been born in this part of the world, she imagined it was his ancestral heritage that provided him with the gorgeous dark colouring of both his skin and hair. His face was the perfect backdrop for the gorgeous smile that he wore most of the time and the deep green eyes were highlighted on what she imagined was the most perfectly sculptured face.

It wasn't hard to see why every woman in Coral Cove wanted to marry their handsome landowner. And she of all people somehow got lucky and quickly became one of his most trusted friends in just the short few years she had been living in his hometown.

Kasie realised she needed to draw on all of her strength to continue this increasingly awkward conversation. "That's not all though," Kasie tried to explain. "I feel like I am on the set of some weird dating reality show. This is not how I pictured the start of any relationship, yet alone, the start of a possible marriage."

Taking advantage of his unusual silence, Kasie continued. "And the other concern for me is, that I can't promise anyone I am staying here in Coral Cove. I signed on for twelve months here to work on re-establishing the reef after the tsunami. It is going on three years now and I am not sure how much longer I can stay. I really have to think about heading home sometime soon."

He paused for a moment, his strong squared jawline hiding what appeared to be clenched teeth. She glanced at his disappointed face and saw tiny frown lines etched on his forehead. His normally sparkling eyes a sad mixture of hurt and confusion. He raised his strong masculine hand and swept it through his dark hair, leaving it looking like he had just hopped out of bed. Kasie was struggling to stay focussed.

Even without the wide smile and glint in his eyes that she had come to know, he was still by far the sexiest man she had ever laid eyes on. She knew a man of this calibre would never truly consider her as anything more than just a playful but loyal friend.

He started to move from his chair toward her as Kasie quickly motioned for him to stay seated. The last thing she needed right now was to feel his soft, warm and familiar touch. This was hard enough without the challenge of resisting the temptation for a reassuring hug from her friend. "Please sit, I need to finish this!" she directed him without hesitation.

He interrupted before Kasie could finish. "Kase…is there someone else? Have you met someone?"

"No, of course not. It is not about that at all. And it isn't a matter of someone else anyway. There can only be a someone else if there is a someone to begin with. You and I are friends remember.

We have never been anything more than great mates hanging out and enjoying each other's company. Marco, you and I, we are great friends. And besides if I had met someone that I was interested in romantically, you would be one of the first to hear about it."

He looked somewhat relieved by this declaration of honesty, so much so that his frown was replaced with smile lines around this gorgeous mouth, his eyes glistened again, lighting up once more his perfect features.

He couldn't help but stand from his chair and make his way toward Kasie, who remained firmly perched on the side of the desk. Feeling relief that he was understanding of her decision and the interrogation was over, Kasie didn't stop him as he moved slowly toward her.

"Are you really giving me the friends speech Kase?" he asked with a show of genuine interest.

"What is the friend's speech?" She enquired with an innocent and honest air of uncertainty.

He smiled as he responded, still slowly making his way to her. "You know, it is when the woman tells the man that she likes him but just wants to be friends or doesn't want to risk his friendship by entering into a relationship."

She smiled, feeling as if he was truly understanding and was accepting of her decision. "Well yes, I guess that is partly what I'm saying. I don't want to lose our friendship. And think of how helpful

I can be to you when you are dating and need a female perspective on where to go for dinner or what flowers to send after a date," she tried eagerly to encourage him.

With a noise that sounded like a slightly sarcastic scoff, he replied. "You really are a hopeless romantic aren't you Kase?"

"Yes, I am! I am so glad you understand," she replied with relief. "You have some big decisions ahead of you and as your friend," she continued, with an emphasis on the words, your and friend, "I will be able to help you work out which of those gorgeous women you should date. You could talk to me and I could offer a non-judgemental and listening ear." Kasie felt hopeful that he was beginning to understand her perspective. She felt the tension start to leave her body.

He continued to move closer to her until she found him standing directly in front of her, his legs close enough to be touching hers. Uncomfortably close for some strange reason.

The two of them had spent many a night cuddled in front of the large screen adorning his living room watching her favourite scary movies. He was one of the few friends she knew who would stay awake and keep her company and ensure she didn't get scared while they enjoyed late night movie marathons of trashy, poorly made B grade horror movies, the old classics, her favourites.

She, like many of the other girls had spent time with him in the pool. Enjoying being physically close while playing around in the pool or soaking quietly in the spa. Kasie had never felt uncomfortable before in his presence. She had never felt anything more than at ease with the physical contact they had shared.

A safe and familiar sibling comfort was what their contact had always felt like, but right now, sitting trapped between the edge of the desk and his tall, strong, warm body, Kasie felt ever so slightly uneasy. Had the offhanded comments about taking her to his room had some impact on her tonight? She wondered to herself.

It wasn't like him to make such sexualised comments. He had made an extreme effort to keep his conversations with all of the women he knew polite, conservative and always very appropriate. He once said that was the only way he could ensure that every woman felt respected and honoured, as they should feel.

Was this, the new thirty-five-year-old version of him - the flirty, inappropriate, dating bachelor? Kasie wasn't sure she liked this new version quite so much. There was something unsettling about the changes but she couldn't quite work out what.

Finally, after what felt like an eternity of watching him walk toward her, he was close enough for his face to be inches away from hers. He smiled at her with a confidence that unnerved her. As he stared directly into her eyes, he asked her.

"How about a birthday kiss then, friend? I don't believe you have even wished me a happy birthday yet?"

Relief flooded her body. All he wanted was to point out that she had missed his birthday well wishes. This is the friend she knew well, always wanting to get one over her, holding her for ransom, having her owe him some debt for some random ridiculous excuse he had conjured up. This was the playful friend she felt comfortable to be around.

"You are correct as always," she whispered. "I didn't get a chance in the kitchen to wish you a happy birthday." And with that she reached up and planted a gentle peck on his lips. Her lips closed and her eyes opened, she looked directly into his eyes and briefly touched her lips to his lips for a quick but friendly kiss. "Happy Birthday," she added as her confidence around him slowly began to return.

As she started to lower her head, he placed his hand ever so gently under her chin, again bringing her eyes to meet his. "You call that a birthday kiss?" he smirked.

Before she knew it, his lips were on hers, one hand still under her chin, holding her head in position, trapped and unable to pull away. His other hand now making its way to her lower back. His right leg gently sliding between hers and parting her legs while his body pushed against hers until she found herself forced backward and sitting on the edge of the desk, her legs now dangling and unable to reach the floor. If she felt trapped before, she was now well and truly unable to move.

His left hand was applying enough force to her lower back to support her but at the same time pushing her body closer to his. Somehow feeling like a perfect fit, her body moulded like a glove to his. Her once closed lips were now parted as her body began to give way to the sensual taste of his delicious lips on hers for the very first time.

Ever so gently but with increasing urgency his mouth moved over hers, one lip and then the next. The warmth of their skin together was intense as she began to feel his body push against her upper thighs. Was her body responding involuntary? Was she actually moving closer to him? Was she pushing her body into his?

His warm lips left hers for just a second as she heard him whisper, "Shh."

She realised she was actually mumbling out loud? She knew her mind was swimming with questions and her mouth was uttering the words that her brain couldn't comprehend.

As if by command, her body and mind, a willing and eager volunteer to him immediately responded with silence. Her head suddenly void of any thoughts gave way to the pleasure of her body. Allowing her lips to respond to his sweet touch. Her arms no longer needed to hold her upright, released the edge of the table to envelope his hard, hot torso, leaving him to support the full weight of her body with his embrace.

His right hand, once navigating her face to meet his was now sliding slowly across her face until his strong thumb was softly caressing her left cheek and the palm of his hand was burning with heat on the side of her neck. His body, every part of his body was hard and firm and so very hot. The heat radiating from his skin seeped through every fibre of their clothing until her skin was virtually on fire.

Just as quickly as it began, the kiss was over. His eyes once again meeting hers but this time with the soft, sleepy look of a man content. She could only describe the look as a man taking what was his and enjoying every second of it.

Could this be what some would call the look of love? She had never seen it before, but imagined this is how it could be described. His strong right thumb was still caressing her cheek. His legs still pressed firmly against hers. She noticed her own arms still wrapped around his body, unable or unwilling to be moved.

He moved his face slightly to the right of hers, his mouth now next to her ear as she heard him whisper to her. "I could stay, kissing you all night."

Her heart stopped.

She pulled her body back, her hands returning to the desk to support her as she attempted to look him straight in the eyes, attempting to make logic of what she thought she had just heard. This isn't happening, she thought to herself. How could this be happening? Her mind raced with questions again.

He looked straight into her eyes once more, as he said. "I really must go and shower before our guests arrive."

Did she just imagine it? Surely, she imagined what he had just said. Then without a moment's hesitation, he again moved his mouth so close to her ear that she could feel the warmth of his breath against her skin. He said quietly, slowly and with intent, "And no, I will not permit you to remove your name from The List."

With this he released his once tight grip on her and made his way to the door, not looking back for a second.

It happened again. Surely, she was hearing things. What did he just say? Did he just say that, she couldn't take her name off The List? Her hesitation to move from atop the desk gave him enough time to reach the door, and exit the office.

"Wait!" Kasie yelled as she finally jumped down from the desk, her bare feet firmly landing on the carpeted floor. Extremely light headed she felt as if she had just woken from a deep sleep.

Obviously intent on getting away from her as fast as he could, he was already making his escape up the elegant staircase she had descended only a short time before.

"Wait!" Kasie yelled again only this time he stopped, mid step. His left hand had firmly grasped the thick marble banister as if, he himself, was in need of its sturdy support.

His eyes meet hers, but only just, with a sheepish look on his now boyish and guilty looking face, Kasie wondered if he was already regretting what he had just done.

"You can't just say that and then walk away. Hell, for that matter, you can't just do that and walk away as if nothing happened!" Kasie yelled at him.

His eyes shifted from her to the person standing in the corner of the grand entrance. Unaware that they had company, Kasie turned to see Marco standing only a few metres from her, a look of concern on his face. His mouth was partially open as if about to speak, or perhaps in shock at what was evolving in front of him.

"I am sorry Marco," Kasie apologised. "I didn't see you standing there."

Without hesitation Marco replied. "Are you ok Kasie?"

"Yes...yes, I am fine, thank you Marco. We just have something we need to discuss," she replied, tilting her head to motion that she needed to continue the conversation with the escapee on the stairs.

Just as she caught his stare again, the smirk she witnessed minutes ago, returned to his face. He paused for effect. "Well can I suggest we continue the conversation while I shower and get dressed...friend?" An almost evil glint appeared in his eyes as he dared her to join him on the stairs.

Kasie didn't quite know what to do or how to respond to the flirty suggestion. She couldn't work out what was going on with her friend tonight. His behaviour was so out of character, so unrestrained and now so very confident and challenging. She couldn't let him feel as if he had gotten the better of her. She knew he was challenging her to prove she just wanted to be friends. He must have felt her body give in and her lips respond to his touch. She felt embarrassed at her behaviour, her lack of restraint around him. She felt naked and exposed. The little confidence that she had gained in the lead up to her conversation had all but been stripped away. He now held the upper hand and he was wielding it like an axe. Ripping away shred after shred of her resolve leaving her helpless to do anything other than what he commanded of her.

She held her breath and looked quickly at Marco. His concerned expression did little to reassure her. Something had suddenly changed between the three of them. Three years of friendship, never a hint of anything more and then this eruption of passion. Kasie knew she needed to regain some control over the situation. She needed to talk further to her boss, to make him understand that they would never be anything more than friends, colleagues and great mates.

"Sure," she replied with a confidence that surprised even her. She needed to continue this conversation even if that meant being alone with him in his bedroom. She needed to end this insanity tonight. Here and now, they had to discuss whatever was going on between them and promise that they could return to being themselves again.

"Kasie..." Marco began before being interrupted by his boss. He didn't quite know what was going on but could see that Kasie wasn't feeling completely comfortable with whatever had just happened between the two of them. He knew his boss well and could see that he was taunting her. Testing her to her very limits. He loved them both dearly but didn't see any good coming from this power play.

"Marco, don't you think you have interfered enough for tonight?" His boss bellowed at him.

The tone was stern and with a hint of annoyance that sounded to Marco as if his employer had much more to say to him later about his actions intervening. Marco knew his boss meant business. He couldn't do anything more then to stand down and let whatever this was play out as it had to.

Not wanting to see her two friends battle it out in front of her and feeling ever so guilty for even involving Marco in this mess, Kasie spoke, taking charge once again. "It's fine Marco, we just need to talk in private for a couple of minutes. I will be straight back down, ok?" She wanted to reassure him that she was able to manage this on her own. She needed to, but she feared her faintly covered words were of little comfort to the overly protective Marco.

"Ok," Marco hesitated, knowing that he didn't really have a choice but to allow her to go. Marco turned and left the grand entrance and retreated once more to the kitchen.

FOUR

THE SEDUCTION

With a beaming smile and a newfound confidence, her handsome friend waited on the staircase for Kasie to join him. He reached his hand out to take hers and proceeded to lead her up the wide staircase and toward his bedroom. Once upstairs, the nervous self-talk began again for Kasie. *What the hell am I doing here? This isn't wise, not after what just happened. I can't control this. I am kidding myself here. What the hell am I going to say?* Her mind was manic with thoughts and worries about the difficult discussion she imagined lay ahead.

Just as they reached the entrance to his room and he turned the handle opening the door to the most exquisite bedroom, her mind once again went blank. As her now very unstable legs entered his room, she tried taking in the beauty of every inch of rich, colourful fabric and sparkling mirrors complimenting the largest walk in robe every made. Lounge settings, not one but two adorned with coloured, textured cushions that made her just want to run and jump into their soft plumpness.

And then she saw it, the bed...his bed. Her head was spinning, her whole body went weak as she realised he was leading her straight toward his bed. *Stop! Stop!* Her head was yelling at her and just as moments earlier, his mere physical presence beside her deemed her body unable to respond to what her mind was commanding her to do.

As they approached the bed, he placed both hands on her upper arms, motioning for her to take a seat on the edge of soft duvet. As if folding a stiff old board, she eventually got her legs to free enough to bend for her bottom to place itself very hesitantly on the edge of the bed. *Oh no!* Her mind was screaming at her. *Now what are you going to do?*

Kasie was shocked back to the present moment, by his fast and purposeful about turn away from her and into his wardrobe. She watched as he disappeared into the enormous changing area.

Ok, she thought, this is going to be ok. He is just getting ready. He must just be going to choose some clothes for the party. Ok, so I had better start talking then. She tried to instruct herself. She wanted to sound calm and in control.

"So, do you want to explain yourself?" She yelled across the bedroom and into the adjoining dressing area. She hoped the right amount of irritation in her voice would help her regain control over the conversation.

"For what exactly?" The curious lightness in his voice suggested a resounding tone of innocence that made her doubt her accusations of indecorum for just a moment.

"For that downstairs" She was hesitant. None of tonight was making any sense to her.

"You might need to be a little more direct in your line of questioning," he instructed her. "I am unsure as to what you are referring to." Although she could only hear and not see him, she could picture that smart little smirk on his face as if he was teasing a cute, little kitten with a ball of yarn.

"Stop being so evasive. You know what I…" But that was all she could manage to articulate as her eyes caught a glimpse of the near naked god that emerging from the walk-in robe. He smiled as he strutted toward her.

"What's wrong, cat got your tongue?" he joked and with the air of confidence that only someone that stunning could muster while wearing nothing but a pair of very sexy, small white briefs.

Oh my god, she thought to herself, does this guy not have any tan lines, surely, he would have tan lines, he was nearly naked and a perfect colour of dark honey brown all over. Kasie's fixation with tan lines would only make sense to those who like her, spent their life in the sun for work and who constantly found their arms and legs to be shades darker than their more covered body parts.

Thoughts of tan lines, quickly faded, as this perfect creature continued to make his way toward her as she could do nothing but remain motionless, frozen with anticipation, still sitting firming perched on the edge of his bed. Kasie had never seen a man before more perfect in every way.

Kasie had seen his body before of course. Many times, before. After all they were living on one of the most gorgeous coastlines ever created and the three friends spent many hours in the water together. She had seen her friend's amazing body before, but not like this. Not while she was sitting on his bed in his bedroom alone with him as he walked toward her wearing nothing but the smallest of sexy briefs.

As if the universe itself was concerned that she had seen all that she could handle of viewing of the world's most perfect torso, he turned and walked toward the bathroom. Now displaying what could only be described as the most firm, delicious, masculine arse ever witnessed.

"I need to jump into the shower, won't be a minute though," he explained. He needn't have bothered, there was no way she was going to be able to force speech from her now trembling body in order to respond to him.

Kasie felt a rush of relief as she heard the shower turn on. *I have a few minutes to pull myself together,* she thought to herself. *What the hell is going on here?* It was as if she was Alice in Wonderland, thrown down the preverbal rabbit hole into some insane nonsensical land with whimsical creatures there for the intent purpose of screwing with her mind. She was able to finally find her legs to stand and make her way to the mirror opposite her to check out the damage to her lipstick, carefully applied and re-applied what now felt like a lifetime ago.

"Hey Kase?" the masculine voice from the bathroom yelled.

"Yes?" Kasie hesitantly responded.

"Can't hear you," the distant voice yelled back.

"I said... yes?" Kasie replied again.

"What? I can't hear you, come to the door," the voice from beyond continued.

Kasie slowly approached the nearby bathroom door to again reply to the voice in the shower.

"Yes, what is it?"

"Would you like to scrub my back for me?"

The cheeky, almost laughing voice offered. He was toying with her once more. She was the innocent little kitten and he was the playful owner, dangling that ball of string just within her reach forcing her to play along.

What is going on? Kasie pondered in her head. *Why does he think he has this over me? I'll show him.* She thought, as she made her way around the bathroom door, stepping just ever so slightly into the tiled bathroom and into full view of the steaming shower. She swallowed hard and tried to stop the obvious trembling in her voice long enough to respond to his lewd suggestion.

"No thanks, I wouldn't want to get wet and ruin my hair," Kasie replied, mustering all the confidence she could gather in an attempt to outwit her skilful opponent in this daring game of bluff.

Kasie could just make out his smiling, gorgeous face through the steaming glass shower screen, not daring to glance beyond his face for fear of seeing more than she needed to tonight.

"Oh ok, would you like to scrub my front then?" The now chuckling voice from inside the shower asked her as he turned completely around, forcing Kasie to view for the first time in what seemed like a really, really long time, a man standing in full view directly in front of her and completely naked.

Half stumbling, half falling backwards out of the bathroom door, Kasie made her way back to the mirror for a quick time-out and some deep breathing to calm herself.

"Round two to the birthday boy, but I'm not giving up there," she said quietly to her reflection in the mirror. Kasie was determined for the game playing to end and to end immediately. She didn't know why her friend would be behaving like he was with her. She couldn't comprehend what had changed between them for him to be able to affect her in this way. She didn't know what had happened to their friendship that now saw him determined to tease and taunt her in with his sexually charged flirtations.

Kasie was so pre-occupied with her thoughts that she didn't realise the shower had turned off until her once trusted friend stood directly behind her. Hoping he had at least some form of clothing on, Kasie took one last deep breath in. She glanced at her reflection to see his tanned, freshly shaven and slightly damp face right behind hers in the mirror. She was relieved also to find that although it wasn't much, he was at least wearing a large white towel draped tightly around his toned stomach.

With his best attempt at innocence, he moved toward her until his body was again pressed firmly against hers. This time from behind, where he took great pleasure in pressing his hard chest against her back.

"What cologne would you like me in tonight?" he asked her with the sweetest of sweet tones. His play at the harmless words only betrayed by the sexy, wicked glint in his eyes suggesting something more than just a meaningless question about a fragrance.

He reached past Kasie grabbing the furthest bottle from him he could find. Any excuse, she imagined, for him to force his body against hers. The cologne bottle looked like Poseidon himself had crafted it. If the ocean could be shaped and blown into a glass representation of itself, this would be it.

"This one smells like the ocean. You love the ocean Kase. You should like this on me tonight," he cheekily teased with breathy whispers into her ear.

He squirted the fresh and delicate fragrance onto his chest. He watched her in the mirror to ensure she was catching his daring display. His eyes remained locked firmly on hers. He took one step back and with a quick flick of the wrist, released the towel from his body allowing it to fall on the floor at his feet. He smiled at her as he positioned the bottle at his lower torso and slowly sprayed the fragrance once more this time in the direction of his manhood.

He watched Kasie's reaction as she strained to speak. She was obviously feeling very uncomfortable. He didn't want to push her too far too soon. He took one small step forward, once more pushing his body against hers as he leaned around her to replace the cologne bottle onto the dresser. He hesitated just a moment, ensuring his whole body contacted with hers. He closed his eyes for a second to feel the warmth of her against his nakedness.

He opened his eyes quickly, turned to his right and headed away from the now visually trembling Kasie.

Making his way into the dressing room near the wardrobe, Kasie had just a minute or two to assess her next move. *That was crazy!* She thought to herself. *What is going on tonight with him?* She had never seen her friend behave like this, not to her nor any other woman. Why was he teasing her in this way? Why was she reacting as she was? Why had she no control whatsoever around him?

Her mind and body had betrayed her, as she became a whimpering, shaking, nervous mess under his sexy mind taunts. She didn't understand the game he was playing at with her and what brought it all on? The one thing she knew for sure was that he was winning, two to zero at least, she had calculated. Whatever she did next, she needed to do it with certainty.

She looked around his bedroom and wondered what he would do if he walked out to find her laying on his bed. A couple of extra buttons on her red linen shirt undone just enough to catch a glimpse of the sparkly red bikini top. It was the psychologist who gave her the idea, somehow hinting that she was dressed to impress rather than dressed to talk seriously with her friend tonight. Only one way to find out, she thought to herself. *Here goes nothing. Let's call his bluff.*

Kasie positioned herself on his bed, channelling her inner supermodel diva in her best come hither pose. The waiting was excruciating but not long as he emerged from the walk-in robe, jeans on but not surprisingly with the top button still undone and his shirt on but only one button done up. He had his head down, concentrating on buttoning up his shirt and didn't notice straight away, Kasie's new position in his room.

Just as he raised his head to speak, he saw her. Without a second's hesitation, he ripped the shirt from his strong, square masculine shoulders and picked up the pace as he headed straight to Kasie's position on the bed.

Without a word, without a doubt, without flinching, he launched himself at her. In the process rolling Kasie onto her back. Within milliseconds he had placed himself between her legs, his body pushing down on hers, his lips locked onto hers, his hands finding the buttons on her shirt and skilfully undoing each one after the next.

Gone were the gentle caressing kisses of before. Replaced instead by the skilful manoeuvring of his hands on her body, the careful prying open of her entwined legs as he positioned himself between them. The urgency with which his body was responding to hers suggested something more to Kasie than just a game of bluff.

His strong large hands, which had now finished unbuttoning her shirt, found their way to her breasts. Her mind was starting to race a thousand miles an hour…*he's not stopping…he's not stopping*…she repeated to herself in her head.

Buzz… they were both stopped still by the sound. Shocked by the rude interruption. They were frozen, listening to the shrieking of what appeared to be a communication of some description alerting them to company. The unmistakeable voice of Marco could be heard through a hidden smart device near the bed.

"Guys, your guests are wondering where you are. Maybe you should come down stairs and join us all," the somewhat hesitant voice of Marco over the device informed them.

Her friend furious at the interruption muttered to himself. "Marco, I swear if you weren't my best friend, I would…"

Thankfully, he didn't finish his sentence instead keeping his punishment for the sudden intrusion as a mere ideation of threat in his head.

He took a deep breath as he tried to centre himself. Still firmly positioned on top of Kasie, their bodies once again joined and unwilling or unable to uncoil.

"We might have to continue this later," he said as he regretfully brought his body to a standing position and placed a hand out to help Kasie from the bed.

Quick to begin dressing, Kasie began working on rebuttoning her shirt. He walked the few steps, grabbed his discarded shirt from the ground and pulled it over his bulging, tanned biceps.

Kasie felt the frustration rising inside her at the knowledge that this situation between the two of them was still not yet resolved.

"You do know, if this is just about sex, then this has nothing to do with me taking my name off The List, which by the way you can't stop me from doing," Kasie began to state her case once more. She felt as if she wanted to cry. Things had gotten completely out of control between them and she feared they may have both taken things a little too far.

He glanced up and looked her in the eyes. There was no mistaking the look of hurt, a hurt she had obviously caused him.

"How could you say that?" he began, his voice trembling with obvious emotion.

"I just don't get any of this, we have been friends for ages, where has all of this come from? What has gotten into you tonight?" Kasie asked with genuine concern. "This feels to me like some sort of pent up sexual frustration. Has this been going on between us…have I been oblivious to this?" She continued. "Have I led you on in some way?"

He reached out for her arm and with delicate procession, swung her slender frame across his until her back was hard against the wall in front of him. His body again found a way to push hard against hers until it felt to her like their two bodies had actually become one. His lips found hers once more and with tenderness and passion, they kissed.

His frustration was evident as he slowly stopped kissing her lips, lowered his head and took a deep sigh. Without again glancing into her eyes, he began to speak, softly, slowly and with heart felt emotion.

"Kase, I'm sorry, I know there is some frustration here but I never meant for this to happen, not like this."

Kasie felt deflated. All the fear and the self-talk in her head that Kasie had struggled with earlier in the evening had come flooding back.

"We have made a terrible mistake." She managed to say the words out loud. "Please say this hasn't ruined our friendship?" she pleaded with him. She couldn't imagine life in Coral Cove without him as her companion, her strongest supporter and her best friend.

"Of course not, Kase, I couldn't imagine being without you." He paused, thinking carefully about his next words. "But that is why you need to trust me when I say to you..." He looked deep into her eyes as he uttered his next words carefully.

"Believe me, when I say, that the next time I have you in this room, that I have you in my bed, I am never going to let you leave again."

His eyes burned into hers and she detected what appeared to be tears welling in his dark emerald eyes.

This wasn't a threat nor was this some sort of evil, vindictive game. This was genuine. What was he saying? What did all of this mean? Her head was spinning trying to make sense of it.

Her silence allowed him to continue. "All I ask is that you please keep your name on The List, please do that for me," he begged her.

Without hesitation, she replied. She knew what her answer was. She long knew that her life in Coral Cove would need to come to an end. "I can't, you know I can't stay here forever, I need to go home. Plus, you know what you mean to me. I don't want to ruin that for anything."

Defeated and deflated he released his grip and again the two of them began to dress. Kasie left the bedroom first and ran down the stairs not waiting for her friend, not wanting to look back, not daring to look back.

FIVE

THE PARTY

It didn't take long for the sounds of serious partying to echo through the house. The pool and surrounding landscapes were awash with gorgeous twenty and thirty somethings there to celebrate what promised to be a landmark occasion. The birthday of their beloved island prince and the much-anticipated announcement of his impending plans for marriage.

Every girl was primped, pumped, and straightened to within an inch of their lives. Kasie often wondered why the women went to so much effort when without an hour or so most of them had stripped down to their bikini to sip cocktails in the heated spa. She realised the hypocrisy in her thoughts and decided she shouldn't be so judgemental considering the efforts she herself went to tonight for the big party.

Kasie had found a few familiar friends and was hearing their playful banter about the rumour that she and the birthday boy had engaged in a bit of a fight.

"Lover's tiff?" one partygoer teased her. She glanced toward their host, who was laughing and seemingly enjoying the attention of a few mates. One placing the first of what she imagined would be many drinks he would consume that night into his hand. She continued to watch as they toasted him. A roar of cheers rose amongst the boisterous group of mates.

"Do you know when he is going to make the announcement?" one eager and absolutely stunning brunette asked Kasie. "Is that what the two of you were fighting about?" she continued to question Kasie in the hope for some helpful information or advice.

"I'm sorry. I don't know anything," Kasie replied. "And we didn't have a fight, we just had words. Nothing really. We sometimes disagree. That's what friends do." Kasie felt the need to empathise to people again that her and the birthday boy were really nothing more than just good friends.

Although if she was to be honest with herself, she felt more than a little confused about the exact state of their relationship. She was still unnerved by the declaration whispered into her ear in the bedroom. She couldn't seem to shake his sexy words of promise from her head.

"If he was mine, I couldn't imagine anything we would disagree on," the hopeful brunette stunner disclosed.

"You might be surprised," Kasie informed her. "He is a very stubborn man when he wants to be and incredibly controlling. I can't imagine he would be that easy to live with."

"I like a man who knows what he wants," the woman replied. "As long as what he wants is me and only me!" she continued. "I would more than give in to whatever he wanted any time of the day or night. Don't you agree Kasie?" She added the last few words with a sexual hunger and innuendo hard to miss.

Kasie looked on as the brunette stared eagerly at the birthday boy. Kasie followed her ravenous glare to also take in the sceptical that was the guest of honour in action. He really was in fine form. Laughing with his friends, confident to be the centre of attention as if he didn't have a doubt in the world as to his place and purpose in it. Possibly, feeling their eyes on him, he turned and glanced around to Kasie and her companion. He shot them his megawatt smile and gave them a cheeky and knowing wink. Kasie felt her face blush with embarrassment as to the intent behind the sexy gesture.

"Did you see that?" the brunette squealed. "He just winked at me."

"I did, lucky you!" Kasie sung out in excitement for her. She had only hoped she had added the right amount of tone and pitch for her enthusiasm to sound genuine enough to be believable.

"I might cruise over there and give him a birthday kiss." The brunette hadn't needed much encouragement to plan out and make a move on their attractive single host. "You never know. He might be waiting for me to go and say hi so he can ask me on the first date." She was beaming with excitement at the possibility.

"Yes sure, you never know," Kasie added, this time without even attempting the right amount of enthusiasm for her friend's cause.

Kasie didn't know how to feel about any of the events as they unfolded. She had never felt even the slightest twinge of jealousy at the overwhelming attention the girls paid to her wealthy bachelor friend. But upon hearing the brunette's hopeful words a strange feeling of discomfort rose in her chest. She had imagined that when he started dating the obvious difference would be that he would probably have less time to spend with her but she wasn't really worried about that.

She always had Marco. And Marco was and she imagined always would be the eternal bachelor of Coral Cove. She hadn't envisaged him settling down anytime soon. Even if Marco did settle down she always had a hoard of girlfriends she could spend time with. Life was anything but dull in Coral Cove. From the constant parties and clubs at night to the gorgeous beaches and reefs to explore during the day, it really was the perfect location to spend a few years of her life.

Kasie realised they were all at the age where most people were if not already coupled, at least thinking about marriage and children and creating a future with someone special. She hadn't thought much about any of that for herself lately. But then again, she hadn't had much luck in the relationship arena to date and didn't see that changing anytime soon. Not as long as she lived in Coral Cove anyway. Maybe, she had hoped, things might change when she returned home to Australia. Maybe there, she might meet someone special and get her chance to settle into some form of domestic bliss.

Kasie's thoughts of future relationships were interrupted when she heard the crowd cheer as a new guest joined the party, the absolutely breathtaking Tiffany.

Kasie watched as Tiffany entered the pool area. Always the one to make an entrance, Tiffany knew that every set of eyes at the party were on her and that was just how she liked it. That's not to say that Kasie didn't like Tiffany, she actually did. She enjoyed her company and embraced the girlie chitchats they shared. She had just never met anyone quite like her, so confident, so demanding of attention, so high maintenance as Marco would describe her.

Tiffany looked particularly gorgeous, wearing a tiny white lace dress barely hiding beneath it a turquoise bikini, heels that were sky high, nearly matching Kasie's own in artistic glory and mind-blowing aerial engineering.

Kasie watched Tiffany cross the pool area, headed straight to their birthday boy and his group of merry mates. Without hesitating, she reached her destination and dropped her white crystal encrusted bag at her feet. The crowd stared intently as Tiffany reached up and grabbed the birthday boy, who stood towering above her. Her two hands stretched up and pulled his face down to hers, as she pressed her lips against his. She held him tightly as her tongue performed what appeared to be a search and recovery mission in his mouth.

Obviously aware he was now being watched by every person in attendance, the birthday boy appeared nervous as he gripped the neck of his beer. Not putting the beverage aside to fully embrace Tiffany in his arms but not actively pushing her away either as the crowd mesmerised by the floor show watched on. Kasie felt a rising sense of some strange emotion in her body and felt uncomfortably voyeuristic but still not able to look away.

The kiss lasted forever. Kasie couldn't take her eyes off the live and impromptu floorshow. She couldn't bear to witness his lips on Tiffany's for a second longer but she was powerless to do anything about it. Tiffany finally released her vice like grip and allowed the birthday boy to once again return to a full standing position. Kasie watched as she noticed him slowly release his clenched fist around his beer. Tiffany wasn't yet finished as she held his glance just a moment longer, before giving him a playful slap on his rear.

It was as if the crowd simultaneously and suddenly turned into a bunch of wild teenagers, the party guests witnessing the shameful scene let out a collective "Woohoo!" The birthday boy's mates around him, being the most playful of them all, congratulated him with manly slaps on his back.

As soon as Tiffany released him from her glare, Kasie noticed the birthday boy search the room with his eyes. She wondered who he was looking for until his stare met her own. Kasie smiled at her friend, but he didn't smile back. He immediately turned away.

Kasie tried to guess at what was behind the glance. He appeared shameful, guilty almost, as he once again raised his face, turned in her direction and allowed his eyes to meet hers across the room. His mates continued their celebration with loud claps and cheers and slaps on his back. Kasie broke the stare. She didn't know how to feel about it and didn't really want to work it out tonight either.

Kasie knew that she needed to spend some time apart from the birthday boy, figuring she had probably monopolised more than enough time alone with him for one night anyway. He had many, many women to share his time with tonight not to mention his masses of male friends, some colleagues, some business partners, but most long-time friends from childhood. Guys that he had grown up with, played sports with, shared his first drinks with, guys like Marco.

Kasie didn't get to witness the discussion between Marco and their mutual friend following the bedroom interruption incident but she assumed there was one and if not already, surely a conversation would follow about Marco's meddling.

It was a strange kind of friendship the three of them had, like three souls who were destined to meet. They got along as if they had always known each other, well the boys of course had, but Kasie slipped into the friendship triad effortlessly.

It was probably their love of the ocean which bought them all together. Their passion for conservation and their joint goal to rebuild Coral Coast and repair its reef while replenishing its dwindling ecosystem. It was this work that they debated passionately; they worked tirelessly and with everlasting enthusiasm to complete.

Kasie found comfort in the fact that she knew Marco was looking out for her, but wasn't looking forward to the barrage of questions she knew she was about to face as she watched him track her down and close in on her as she was attempting to order a much-needed cocktail from the bar.

"What the hell Kasie? What was that all about?" Marco started in without hesitation as soon as he reached her at the bar. He had been more than a little concerned for his friend and needed answers.

"Well needless to say, he didn't take the news very well," Kasie informed him.

"No shit, he was like a man possessed. What did you say to him?" Marco asked with genuine concern for his friend. He didn't give her time to respond before the interrogation continued. "So, did he manage to change your mind? Are you keeping your name on The List?"

"No, I'm not. I can't Marco! You know that. I really can't commit to being here forever. I respect what he has to do. I want to help out as much as I can, but eventually I need to go home. I can't stay here permanently." She pleaded with her friend for understanding and hoping for some form of support, some confirmation maybe that she was doing the right thing.

"What is at home for you that you can't get here? You have made a life here, great friends, important work, you have me?" His downturned frown turning into a wide smile as he added the last comment.

"I love you Marco and I even love him as much as he frustrates me at times. I love my friends here but I have a life back in Australia that I am not willing to give up just yet," Kasie added, trying desperately to help Marco understand her predicament.

Marco paused sensing he wasn't going to get much further with his attempts at convincing her to stay. Not tonight anyway.

"How about we agree we have endured enough serious conversation for one night, let's celebrate and get this party started. It's not every night that your best friend turns thirty-five and pledges to marry one of the girls in the room," Kasie encouraged him.

"Yeah, well it is not just any girl in the room, is it Kasie? It is one girl in particular isn't it now?" Marco challenged her throw away remark.

"Please Marco, not you too! Can we please forget it all for just one night? I want to dance, swim and spend time with my best friend."

"That's me, right?" Marco grinned.

"It is as long as you dance with me," Kasie added as she dragged Marco onto the dance floor.

Keeping Kasie never too far from sight the birthday boy didn't seem at all impressed as he watched Kasie and Marco whispering in hushed tones near the bar. They appeared to be trying to have a very private discussion and he could only guess that he was the topic of conversation. Less impressed was he to watch Kasie drag Marco onto the dance floor with Marco playing along as the only too willing victim.

What was happening to him? He felt increasingly frustrated with himself and his lack of emotional control. He really did lose the plot earlier, a saying Kasie had taught him from Australia. Years of keeping it under control finally flooded to the surface like the rush of exploding lava from a bubbling volcano.

Maybe Doctor Phoenix was right. This was going to be harder than he imagined. He felt a flush rise in his face. His emotions again not far from the surface as he watched Marco and Kasie dance arms wrapped tightly around each other.

He looked toward the DJ angered at his current choice of slower ballad amidst the high energy beats that he had hoped would continue playing throughout the night.

"That's enough!" he mumbled out loud to himself. "I can't handle watching this a minute longer." With that, he slammed his drink on the nearest table and marched directly over to his two best friends.

Kasie was pleasantly unaware of the birthday boy's impending arrival to cut into their very cosy little dance for two. Marco, with the sixth sense that only a best friend could have, sensed the birthday boy long approaching before he saw him. As he looked up at his friend towering over him, Marco guessed it wasn't worth fighting him. He knew what the determination on his face was saying. It was giving him a clear message to not mess with him anymore tonight. Marco knew that he could do no more, he relinquished his dance partner to his best mate - he was the birthday boy and special guest of honour after all.

Kasie watched the quick and silent interaction between her two friends and could only imagine what was coming next. The birthday boy had that look on his face again. The look she was very quickly coming to realise was the look that had one hundred per cent pure 'do not fuck with me' determination written all over it.

It was kind of sexy too, especially when she seemed to be the target of these incredibly intense emotions. A girl could get used to that kind of passion. As Marco silently left the dance floor the birthday boy held out his hand to chivalrously request Kasie's permission for a dance. Obligingly, Kasie grabbed his hand and he pulled her close to him. The position she found herself in, their bodies joined together was starting to feel a little too familiar for her.

"Are you trying to make me jealous on purpose?" he asked her as he held her tightly in his arms swaying to the music together.

"I didn't know you were the jealous type," she responded with a wry grin.

"Me neither, but I am learning a lot about myself tonight" He replied with his gorgeous upturned smile. Kasie was appreciative of the lifting of the mood. This was the friend she knew and loved, cheeky, playful, entertaining, witty and charming. She could spend hours talking just like this together. In fact, so many times they had. They had gotten to know each other well after hours of getting lost in this kind of conversation.

"Actually, I am learning a lot more about you tonight as well, really getting to know new parts of you," Kasie giggled, both of them knowing she was referring to the earlier naked exhibition. She couldn't help but flirt just a little. It seemed to help develop the positive energy between them, friendly and playful. She wanted to avoid another argument for now.

With his gorgeous smile lighting up his intense eyes he replied, "Well I have learnt that I don't have as much self-control as I thought I had when it comes to you."

He paused. He felt some relief to be able to finally share his recent reflection with Kasie. He had just begun to realise himself that he couldn't wait much longer to let her know how he was feeling. He had hoped it would happen under much more romantic circumstances, but he needed to say now what he had been unable to admit before. He paused to add one final request.

"So please, don't make me jealous again. It's not a feeling I am comfortable with."

Looking around quickly to see who was within hearing distance, he quietly whispered in her ear. "But, if you do make me jealous again…I might just have to take you back up to my bedroom, take down those tight, white jeans of yours, put you over my knee and spank your bare bottom."

Holy fuck, were the only words that Kasie's brain could manage. This man was the real deal and she saw a side to her friend that she would never again be able to un-see.

Kasie felt the intense heat rise in her body once more. Here they were, not alone in his room, but on a dancefloor surrounded by a couple of hundred or so of their friends and this effect he was having on her, it was uncontrollable.

He took her moment of distraction as the time to pounce and without asking permission, placed his lips on hers once more. He pressed his warm mouth tightly on hers as his strong grip on her body prevented her from struggling. Not that struggling was something she was contemplating doing at all.

Kasie felt a somewhat smug sense of superiority as her lips moved with his. She compared this moment to his earlier kiss with Tiffany. Completely different, she thought to herself, he is kissing me. He has his arms wrapped around me. Not the other way around. He instigated this, not me.

He did not allow her to move away, not letting her go until he was completely satisfied that he had tasted every inch of her mouth once more.

With her eyes closed, Kasie didn't see Alice and the other girls walk toward them. Nor did she notice at first as the guests let out a collective sound of approval.

"Woohoo!" the guests yelled as they witnessed the steamy interaction between the two friends.

"Hey what about us?" She heard the voices around them demanding his immediate attention back to the surrounds of the party.

Kasie opened her eyes and looked up toward the perfect face in front of her. To each side were attractive bikini clad female guests now pulling their birthday boy away from her by attempting to release his arms from around Kasie's waist.

Each girl grabbed at his limbs, slowly prying them off Kasie. As they giggled with satisfaction they began to lead her friend backward and away from her. Unable to resist against their playful banter, he surrendered and allowed himself to be dragged away. He kept his eyes firmly on Kasie's. Her eyes fixated on his as he puckered his lips and blew her a cheeky kiss farewell across the widening gap between them.

The girls collectively manoeuvred their new plaything to the pool edge and laughed flirtatiously as they pushed him in. Playing along he grabbed two of them as he slipped into the warm clear blue waters of the enormous pool.

Kasie felt her hand move to her mouth. Her delicate fingers touched her soft lips ever so gently. Her mouth was tingling. Every nerve ending felt as if it was on fire. What was this reaction she was having to this man?

How and what had transpired for him to be torturing her in this way? She didn't know what to make of what was happening to her but she knew for sure that the party was not the right time to get any clear answers from him.

She continued to watch as one by one each of the women from the staged abduction jumped into the pool literally on top of the birthday boy. She watched as the beautiful Alice threw her arms around his broad now bare shoulders. Throwing her slim toned legs around him, she wrapped her body over him before finally locking her lips on his.

Kasie couldn't watch a second longer. She turned and walked toward the bar. With any luck a drink or two would help to ease the visual memory of the image of her friends and their playful and flirtatious game playing in the pool.

SIX

THE PARTY ENDS

The birthday party to rival all birthday parties had neared its end. Kasie looked forward to getting home and crawling up into her warm, soft bed. Her feet ached and her head felt blurry. She practiced her best cat burglar impersonation as she attempted to sneak away from the party without being noticed. Not wanting to risk another encounter with the birthday boy tonight, she snuck through the house and out the front door seemingly undetected.

As she walked down the stairs of the impressive mansion her mind wandered back to those dreamlike, unbelievable moments alone with him. She was still wondering to herself if it was indeed really just a daydream. She questioned whether it was even possible for her to simply imagine all of it. Her mind trailed back to the sensual and soft first kiss in his office.

She remembered clearly the sight of his magnificent body in the steamy shower as he called for her to join him. She could almost feel the warmth of his body launched on top of hers on his bed. She closed her eyes momentarily at the memory of his hands running furiously over her breasts, trying desperately to touch her bare skin.

She shook her head to try and dislodge the unnerving imagery from her brain.

It was a huge, fun night filled with laughter, music, dancing, pool games and cocktails... many, many cocktails, so those few stolen moments seemed long ago and just a little unimaginable. Her mind once more drifted back to his lips.

"Oops!" she shrieked.

"You scared me!" she yelled out as she ran directly into his now familiar hard body. "What are you doing out here?" she demanded to know. "Why would you sneak up on me like that?"

Actually, I have been standing here watching you from the time you came down the stairs Kase. You seemed a little preoccupied. "Want to share your thoughts?" His face had twisted into that cheeky smirk she had seen several times already that night. "Thinking of me perhaps?" he playfully teased her.

"Of course not. Not everything is about you!" Kasie replied, trying desperately to sound as casual as possible as she attempted to redirect his line of questioning. "Oh, of course what am I thinking? Everything in this very town is about you, isn't it?"

"Do I detect a hint of sarcasm in your voice?" he enquired, his face lit with the same flirty smile. "Or is that a little bit of jealously coming from my favourite friend now?" He laughed to himself at the thought of it. He wondered if he was getting to her in the same way that she had gotten under his skin tonight.

"Absolutely not!" she replied almost too quickly for it to be believed.

"You know I didn't ask for that kiss from Tiffany," his joking persona replaced with a seriousness tone.

"You don't have to explain yourself to me," she interrupted him. "I know how this works. You have your list."

"No, Kase, no it's not like that at all," he tried by way of explanation. "I didn't kiss her, or anyone. The only woman I kissed was you."

"Goodnight birthday boy!" Kasie said as she attempted to brush past him, feeling slightly uncomfortable and more than a little irritated with the direction the conversation was taking. She really didn't want to hear another word about Tiffany nor Alice nor anyone else for the matter.

Kasie headed toward the waiting car - an essential provided at all mansion parties, cars complete with drivers to transport all of the party guests safely home.

"No goodnight kiss then?" he said as he grabbed her arm and pulled her mouth close to his gorgeous face once more.

"No!" she almost screamed back at him.

"That's not very friendly for a best friend and all," he laughed as he said the cheesy words out loud.

"I never said I was your best friend and I think you have already had your birthday kiss for the night…if you can recall!" Kasie informed him with a serious but playful tone.

"Oh yes, I do recall… I recall very well," he replied with his sexiest hushed tones. He licked his lips as a way to exaggerate even more the meaning behind his seductive words. "But it is a special celebration, I just thought you might want to show me a bit more birthday cheer before you leave me for the night."

"You have such a sense of humour tonight," Kasie teased him. "I never knew you were this funny," she added.

"Maybe that just shows that you don't know me as well as you think you do," he replied with a very matter of fact tone to his voice.

"I would have to say that is true. You have been full of surprises tonight!" Kasie agreed with her handsome host.

"Well how about you stay the night and see if there are any more surprises that pop up?" he looked at her wishfully. His eyes darting daringly down the length of her body.

Kasie felt a slight twinge in her stomach, perhaps nervousness she thought at the not so innocent offer. She was trying to convince herself that was what it was. But in reality, if she was being honest, she would more likely describe it as a mixture of excitement and sexual energy at the thought of his suggestion. Whatever it was she knew her answer, even without thinking about it. She knew there was no way she could stay for even a moment longer.

She looked into his glowing, gorgeous smiling face and knew she had to make her exit and make it soon. For some reason all wisdom and self-control had gone out of the window during the course of the last few hours and she knew it was wise to get back to the safety of her own little house.

"You know I am not going to stay. Friends don't do sleepovers," she finally replied, emphasising again the word friends for him.

"Really? I beg to disagree. That's exactly what friends do. And how many nights have you already stayed here. Falling asleep with me as you made me stay up to watch one dreadful movie after another?"

"Goodnight again. I will chat to you tomorrow." She began making her way to the car. She needed to get home while her resolve to do so remained strong. "We actually really do need to talk, but not tonight." She added before releasing herself from his strong arms.

"Yes, I agree. There is something I do need to talk to you about." With that, he pulled her close again and strengthened his bear like hold around her forming a tight warm embrace. She snuggled into his body and wrapped her arms around him. She felt his familiar lips reach down and kiss the top of her head.

He whispered as he kissed her. "I love you Kase."

"I love you too birthday boy," she replied.

"I really do need to talk to you, are you sure you can't stay?" he pleaded with her once more.

"You have guests to attend to. We can talk tomorrow," she assured him.

"How about you come back tomorrow night, just you and me? We can have some alone time and talk," he suggested. He really needed to finally say to Kasie what he had become increasingly sure about. He needed to let her know once and for all that she was the one.

Kasie didn't think it the best idea. She was struggling with what had been happening between them but knew that after the party being alone probably wasn't in the best interests of their friendship.

"So how about The Gaol, tomorrow night? We can have a post birthday cocktail and chat," she offered as a safer alternative for a meeting place for them both.

"Sounds great!" he replied, readily agreeing to what seemed like the most sensible thing he had heard all night.

"See you there," she replied, as she released herself once more from his arms and began to take a step toward the waiting car.

"I will pick you up from your house at eight," he said, making what should have been a question sound very much like a statement of fact. He wasn't ready to relinquish all control to her and wanted desperately to have some time alone with her at some point.

"No," she laughed. "I will meet you there, at nine o'clock. I have a few things to do at work first."

Always the gentleman he very gently placed his fingers under hers to bring her hand to his mouth and planted a moist, hot kiss on the back of her fingers, "Until tomorrow night then."

As he walked her to the waiting car, his hand snugly on the small of her back, she felt a slight sense of regret tinged with a tiny amount of relief.

Where was her head? she wondered. How easy would it be, to just give in, to turn around, look at his beautiful smile and let him know she had changed her mind and would stay?

Get in the car! Get in the car! The small rational part of her brain screamed at her. With that she jumped into the car as he closed the door behind her.

She couldn't leave without just a few more words. Her body was screaming at her to get out of the car, to embrace this man once more and to stay with him even for just a few more minutes. She pressed the button on the window and watched him lower his face to meet hers as the window slowly wound down.

"Happy birthday again," she whispered to him.

He leant in through the window and kissed her cheek. "Goodnight beautiful," he replied.

"Go back to the party and have fun," she demanded with a hint of lightness to her voice. She paused trying to think of the right words to say, "But not too much fun."

He laughed. "It won't be fun with you gone."

"Oh…" She started, before pausing again. "And don't make any big announcements without me there to hear them. Ok?"

"I wouldn't dream of it," he promised her.

Kasie continued, "And maybe don't go and get married without your best friend there to witness it."

He leant in through the car window and kissed her on the lips. "It would be impossible to get married without my best friend there," he whispered back.

She felt her breath leave her body and wondered if her heart had stopped. What was going on for her tonight? Who was she to make demands of this man? All she knew was that something had changed. She wasn't acting rationally. She wasn't thinking or acting like the friend she was to him. The word discombobulated came to mind. That was how she felt, totally and utterly discombobulated.

She watched as he removed his head from inside the car window and blew her a kiss. She turned her attention to the driver.

"Good night, could we please leave quickly?" She addressed the driver.

"Of course, Kasie, where to?"

"Home please Anthony. To my sane, safe and predictable little home. Thank you."

Kasie let her head fall back to rest on the comfortable leather seat behind her. She closed her eyes and let her mind take her back to those few stolen moments in the office. She felt her body respond immediately to the sensual memory of his body against hers. Pinned against the desk unable to move, an unexpected birthday kiss that began the passionate chain of events that unfolded throughout the course of the night.

Kasie felt more than a little ambivalent about meeting with the birthday boy the following evening. She knew on the one hand she wanted, no needed some answers as to his behaviour. But on the other hand, she quite enjoyed the surprise and spontaneity of this new connection with him. She wanted to know what was behind it all but she also feared that she might not like the answer.

She opened her eyes and looked out as the quiet, empty streets of Coral Cove passed around her. She knew she was only a matter of minutes from her house and she wondered how she would ever manage to fall asleep with the visual images of the night on constant replay in her mind.

SEVEN

THE RESEARCH FACILITY

It wasn't until midday the following day that Kasie had felt rested and re-energised enough to make it to work. And work for her was going to be a healthy distraction from the ruminating she had been doing since she woke. She couldn't persuade the memories of the night before to slow at all.

She had a myriad of tasks to complete. The prioritising of what to focus on first caused her concern. She glanced down at the recent research papers from Australia, one in particular from a well-regarded colleague from the University of Queensland. She had been extremely interested in the research behind the potential and as yet unknown damage that shark-tracking devices presented to the shark populations they were designed to protect.

She couldn't help but fear the implanting of these tracking devices could in some way permanently damage the shark's dorsal fin. For her it was a constant debate over the potential for valuable information that could save the sharks and the possible risk of any damage to the individual shark itself.

She wondered if the samples of the seagrass had been completed and whether she should go to the lab to see if there was any updated news on the health of the recently replanted vegetation.

On top of her urgent tasks, her emails were piling high and she couldn't ignore the number of urgent markers indicating those of special importance to someone. She struggled, as always, never feeling she had enough time to do everything she needed to do, read everything she needed to know to bring a sense of accomplishment to the very long-term work that she had undertaken.

This was most probably the reason behind her lengthy stay in Coral Cove. The initial one-year contact was not time enough to see the longer term pay-offs for the reef system. She felt she needed to stay on longer to ensure there was indeed some recovery to the reef and foreshore after the devastating damage done by both the tsunami and climate change.

As Kasie continued to toil at work later that day she was still struggling to get her normally clear and focussed mind to concentrate on the important work she had planned to tackle.

She wanted to give up, to just go home and call it a day. But at that moment there was a knock on the glass door of her office.

Looking a little sheepish at her office door were her two young research interns, Annie and Aretha.

"Um, can we talk to you Kasie?" Aretha asked.

"Sure, come in, is something wrong?" Kasie enquired.

"Yes, well, we think so," Annie added.

"I'm intrigued and a little concerned. What's happened?" Kasie prompted the two women to give her more information.

"We really don't want to cause any trouble, but we have both seen something disturbing and we need to let you know" Annie continued.

"Whatever it is, I am sure we can work it out, tell me more."

"Well it's the tracking devices, the ones used on the sharks, we think there is a problem with them," Aretha explained.

This was Kasie's greatest fear, that an issue with the newly developed tracking devices would indeed prove some destruction or harm to the population of sharks on the reef.

"It's more serious than that Kasie. The tracking devices have been changed. They weren't what was originally designed," Annie elaborated.

"In what way?" Kasie became increasingly concerned and she knew by the look on their faces that the girls were genuinely scared. She wondered what could have caused them to be so anxious.

Kasie had always and would probably always have issues with the use of tracking devices on sharks. It was an idea that somehow got turned into a reality at the insistence of the Chief Scientist, Doctor Chris Bartlett.

Doctor Chris Bartlett was the epitome of the mad scientist. He was a short man, not helped by his slumped-over shoulders, no doubt the result of many formative years hunched over books and computers studying to get him to where he was now, at the top of his field in ocean conservation.

To say that Kasie had never warmed to him was an understatement. He literally gave her chills. He was the type of person that if he brushed his hand on your arm, which he seemed to somehow do on a regular basis, the result would be a shiver up the spine and goosebumps the length of the offending limb.

Kasie always felt uncomfortable around him, never knowing if it was just his intensity for his work or if there was something more sinister to his behaviour around her. One thing was for sure. Doctor Chris hated their boss with a passion. Two greater polar opposites you could not find. The handsome town owner, with wealth, intelligence and breeding; the toast of the island, the envy of all men and the desire of all women.

Then there was Doctor Chris, unattractive by anyone's standards, not one to smile often or even engage in small talk really, except for some very uncomfortable conversations around his lack of romantic attachment. How their boss could have ever hired Chris to run the conservation society was beyond Kasie's rational understanding.

The repair and future development of the reef and the oceans around Coral Cove were a key priority for the town and he had placed the job into the hands of this very competent but very, very strange little man. Hating the thought of having to engage in another argument with Chris about the tracking devices but knowing that it would be her responsibility as second in charge of the research facility, Kasie knew she had to find out more.

"So, what is different?" she asked the young interns but not really sure she wanted to hear the answer.

"You are not going to believe this, but we think the tracking devices contain some sort of chemical deterrent," Aretha finally found the courage to divulge what they had learnt.

"How is that possible?" Kasie asked with growing concern.

"We think that Chris is using them to control the shark population on the reef. I know this sounds ridiculous, but he has been acting especially weird lately and extremely secretive," Aretha added.

Annie was next to share her theory. "We have been doing a bit of investigating. We wanted to make sure of this before we came to you. Chris has been receiving emails directly from Eric Cobalt. We also know he has met with him a few times already."

Eric Cobalt, another questionable man, the CEO of Reef Adventures, the company given the contract to promote tourism in the area. Eric was all about the money. Values inconsistent for someone who promoted holidays to connect with nature. Strange also, Kasie thought, for Eric to be spending any time at all around Coral Cove. It wasn't exactly his favourite tropical location. He had let everyone know that many times over.

Eric was all about the glamour and glitz of the big cities, not the quiet beaches and sparkling turquoise waters of Coral Cove. He looked more suited to a blackjack table inside a noisy, bright casino in Las Vegas than sailing a catamaran around the crystal-clear waters of the reef, swimming with the huge sea turtles, white tipped reef sharks and manta rays that Kasie loved working with. The mere thought of some collaborative working partnership between Doctor Chris and Eric Cobalt left Kasie feeling nauseous.

Knowing she needed to get to the bottom of the situation quickly, Kasie wondered if she should ring her boss first to give him the information or whether she should find out more and let him know later that night over drinks. After all, the conservation society, the promotion of tourism to the area, the rebuilding of the town after the horrific tsunami was all one man's vision.

And that man would not be happy to hear that someone had deviated from his grand plan, especially a plan that would involve any harm to the creatures he was so adamant to protect. Seeing that is was already three o'clock, Kasie decided to investigate further herself and share her findings with her boss when they met later.

Kasie followed up with a few more questions. She wanted to find out how the young women had gathered the information and whether they had asked Doctor Chris about any of it. They had both admitted they didn't feel safe going directly to Chris and had therefore made the decision to speak instead with Kasie together. They asked Kasie if she could keep the source of this information to herself for they feared what Chris might do if he learnt about their prying.

Kasie thanked the young assistants for their courage and gave them the rest of the afternoon off. She could tell they were both visibly shaken from what they had found out and it wouldn't be helpful to them to hear her and Doctor Chris battle it out again over their differing values on the project. Kasie took a deep breath and a long sigh and headed to the laboratory to find her colleague.

As she had predicted, Doctor Chris was at his microscope, presumably peering at his latest find of some algae, seagrass or seaweed that supported the local sea turtle populations. The support of the regrowth of these plants after the damage to the reef was a major focus for the scientist. Kasie didn't hesitate with pleasantries today, instead bounded straight in to the lab.

"Chris, we need to talk!" she demanded his full attention immediately.

As he raised his head from the eyepiece of the microscope, Chris looked surprisingly pleased for the interruption. This is what Kasie couldn't quite grasp with Chris. She knew they didn't see eye to eye, that their core values around conservation and the study of the ocean couldn't be further apart.

Chris viewed the ocean as a meal ticket for human populations. A resource that needed to be protected to further enhance the financial growth of companies and individuals alike that might want to make their living from the ocean and its inhabitants.

Kasie on the other hand, felt that the conservation of the ocean was for the benefit of the creatures, the billions of sea life that needed humans to not continue destroying the oceans to ensure its future growth and well-being. Kasie fully embraced her values and the role she played in ocean conservation and she found confidence to stand toe to toe with anyone who wanted to challenge her views.

"Well hello Kasie," Chris replied, seemingly not concerned about the intent and obvious directedness behind her entry. "What can I do for you today?"

There it was, that sliminess, that creepy stalker vibe she often got from Chris. Was it just his obvious social awkwardness that made her uncomfortable or was it something else? Chris wasn't one to attract a lot of female attention or any attention for that matter. Doctor Chris hadn't regularly engaged in the local social gatherings in town. Kasie never once saw Chris at a party at the mansion, which didn't surprise her, knowing his hatred for the mansion's owner. Kasie wondered for a minute what he did do with his social time when not at work.

Looking a little worse for wear, the obvious result of long hours in the lab, Chris wasn't getting any more attractive by the day. He appeared a little more pasty than usual, surprising for a town that's centred around its beach, gorgeous ocean front and outdoor lifestyle, but not surprising for a man who spent the majority of his life engaged with technology inside the confines of a laboratory.

He appeared not only paler, but a little more bald than normal, his face aged perhaps. It was hard to tell exactly what it was, but whatever Chris was scheming was talking a toll on his body and his looks.

As she snapped herself out of her thoughts and hoped that she wasn't staring too much, Kasie finally replied, "Chris, I need to find out what is happening with the tracking devices for the sharks."

"No, not this again. We have been over this a thousand times. The tracking devices are just to protect the tourists, give them piece of mind when they are in the water. The boats will know what sharks are around and when and if they need to get people out of the water if they have some not so friendly visitors."

"I don't need you to rehash your reasons again Chris, I want to see the devices," Kasie demanded.

A stunned Chris replied. "Why?"

"Do I need a reason Chris? Do you have something to hide? It is my right to see. I am second in charge here and I want to see the devices…now!" Kasie felt her anger grow at Chris's obvious hesitation.

Doctor Chris rose from his chair and adjusted the glasses on his face as he started to walk toward the secure cabinet situated at the back of the room. Kasie followed, feeling hopeful that this would all be over in a matter of minutes and that there would be some simple explanation for what the interns had believed they discovered.

Chris stalled, "Oh, the key, let me grab it, here look at this one in the meantime Kasie," he said, handing her one of the prototype tracking devices she had inspected many times before in her debates with the doctor.

Kasie turned the device over in her hand, looking closely at the intricacies of this small black box no larger than an USB and no heavier than a small remote control. Although she hated the idea that this artificial manmade device would be attached to a shark, she couldn't help but marvel at the genius of the invention. She was a scientist after all and could appreciate the innovation of the simple and highly effective design.

Kasie was satisfied at least that this device was the one that had been approved, without her full agreement, but she wasn't the one making the final decisions.

Looking with such intent at the device, Kasie had nearly forgotten that Chris was in the room with her. Wondering where he was and what was taking him so long to return with the correct key, she found her frustration begin to rise again. She raised her head to call his name, "Chris…"

And then there was nothing, no further sound escaped her lips. No further thoughts entered her brain. There was nothing but a dark black fog which fell over her eyes and her mind. Her loss of consciousness, similar she imagined to the closing night's curtains on a stage play, fell like a heavy weight dragging her to the floor. Kasie dropped silently to the ground.

EIGHT

THE DEVICE

Kasie's eyes felt heavy, her eyelids barely able to be lifted. The room around her was out of focus as if she was looking through a cloud, through a dream. But this was no dream. This was a nightmare beyond her worst imagination. As she struggled to open her eyes the room slowly came into focus and she began to recognise some of the features around her. She distinguished the dark wooden wardrobe, the one that housed the extra clothes that she, Annie and Aretha had put together as a result of too many lab tests gone wrong.

Someone, somehow often managed to spoil the clothes they wore to work that day so they decided to keep some spare clothes around. There was a joint decision after so many mishaps that the women would keep some clothes nearby for a quick and easy change. It didn't matter so much what was in the wardrobe as much as the fact that it was there, if they needed it.

The wardrobe for some reason was the comforting vision in the room. At least she could distinguish where she was. The rest of the room and the reason she was in it was a nightmare in the making. As Kasie started to feel more in focus as her vision and her cognition began to clear, the strongest and only emotion she could decipher was anger.

What the hell had that little creep done? She asked herself, recalling that her last memory was being in the lab alone with Doctor Chris. What has he done to me? She questioned herself out loud.

Kasie had become more and more curious of Doctor Chris's strange ways. In her head she ran through the various and numerous reasons that had flagged her own concerns about him. There was of course his inability to be socially competent around others, his lack of social discretion, and his incredible unease anytime their boss was around. These to her were all signs of a man not to be trusted. Also concerning were his sudden outbursts of rage at the inanimate objects or the technical failing of the equipment around him.

Kasie had started to think that Doctor Chris was not a healthy and well person to be around, but never had she thought that he would harm her in any way. But here she was, waking up in a room she hadn't entered herself and knowing that Doctor Chris was the only person who was present in the laboratory and the only person who could have put her there.

As her strength grew and her focus cleared, Kasie began to realise that she wasn't in the same clothes that she began the day in. Not a huge fan of setting out her wardrobe for the week, she instead just chose her clothes day by day and today she remembered she had worn her favourite comfortable blue and white dress. Some would say it was a dress that looked more appropriate on the beach, but Kasie would wear it on the days when she didn't feel like wearing anything too tight or restrictive. Kasie knew the reason for the dress today. It was the party the night before, the party at the mansion to end all parties. It was the food, the amazing cake and those delicious cocktails.

In a less busy working world Kasie would have arranged to take the next day off work after a party as special as the one at the mansion. After all it was a Saturday, but she knew there was far too much work to be completed for her to take a day off. Instead she went to work and ended up here, in this little room, in clothes that she hadn't dressed in that morning and actually had never seen before.

Her thoughts started to race... the party... her employer... the promise to meet him at The Gaol. She wondered what time it was. As she raised her head from the bed, ready to make sense of this madness, Kasie was startled by someone at the door.

Doctor Chris stood at the door. He was the last person she had spoken to. He was the last person to see her conscious so it made sense that he was the person who put her in this room and in the clothes she now wore. That meant that the reality was, Doctor Chris was the one who had changed her clothes and that opened the possibility for so many other, more concerning violations.

Chris was without doubt the one who saw her naked as he undressed her. Of all the people, why would it have to be him? Especially after she had just spent the night before trying to not get naked in front of the most gorgeous and most eligible man on the planet.

"Good afternoon my darling Kasie, I hope you have had a nice rest," Doctor Chris directed his attention to her as he entered the room.

"What the fuck?" Kasie started to reply before she was rudely interrupted by the creepy Doctor and his open palm hand gesture signalling her to be quiet.

"Shh" he immediately ordered her. "Not that anyone is around to hear you, but shh, because you are being far too loud for my liking, Darling."

"As if I give a fuck about your liking," she continued to protest.

"Well it is not as if you have any choice now, is it Kasie?" Doctor Chris replied.

"Screw you!" she screamed at him once more.

"Well only if I let you," Doctor Chris's mouth formed a smarmy grin that sent Kasie into a rage.

"Fuck you and your self-serving, money hungry grab at power. You wait until he finds out about this! And he will find out. I am on my way to meet him now and I am going to tell him everything that you have done!"

"Oh my! Please don't! I'm so scared," Chris responded with the heaviest flavour of sarcasm he could muster.

Kasie couldn't believe what she was hearing. "Well, I am late already, so if you do excuse me, I have a meeting to attend."

"Yes…well…about that. It's not happening," Chris replied.

"You can't stop me, I am walking out of here," Kasie protested, certain that she had had enough of his insanity for one day.

Chris stood in front of her, not moving an inch. Suddenly more confident and more defiant than Kasie could ever have imagined he was capable of being. "Of course not. I can't stop you. You are free to go wherever and see whomever you want."

"No doubt!" Kasie retorted as she headed for the door.

"It's just…" Chris continued, "that your tracking device isn't exactly one hundred per cent accurate yet and I can't promise that it won't arm itself."

For the first time since Kasie had raised herself from the bed she began to feel the pain in her right shoulder, the pain of a bite, an injection or a break? She sensed the pain of an injury of some description, possibly as a result of her fall. Then she realised. He had done something to her. He had harmed her in some way. There was something feeling very wrong with her right shoulder blade.

She reached her hand behind her to feel the hard, plastic object embedded in her skin. The shape was familiar. The function of the device was well known to her. She had only seen this latest design in the lab but it was easily distinguishable now as it sat raised over the muscle in the right shoulder.

Suddenly it all became clear. She screamed with rage at the evil spineless monster in front of her.

"No way. There is no way known that you could justify implanting a tracking device in a human! This one isn't tested for use on humans. I don't even believe animals should suffer from the implant. How would you think you could use this on a person?" Although Kasie was still capable of rational thought her emotions were starting to overcome her cognitive processes.

She started to feel teary as the pain in her right shoulder become more apparent. "You cannot do this. I am leaving. I am getting this thing out of my shoulder. Get the hell out of my way," she screamed at him.

"I wish I could," Chris replied smugly, but there is more to the tracking device than you understand."

Suddenly Kasie's face turned a ghostly shade of white as the realisation hit her that Annie and Aretha were right. Dr Chris had his own evil plans and she had now found herself caught unexpectedly right in the middle of them.

"Chris!" she screamed at him. "Whatever you have done, you need to undo it right now. Which begins with getting this thing out of me!"

"I wish I could my darling Kasie. You know how much I have wanted to work with you. How I have tried for us to be closer. How many times have I asked you to share lunch with me or to come out on the research boat to the reef with me? How many times have you turned me down?"

Chris continued as Kasie looked upon him in horror,

"How many times have I tried to make you part of my world, part of my plan for this town, but instead all you seem to do is spend time with him! How can he fulfil your desire to save the reef, all he has is money, no knowledge, no sense, no research or qualifications behind him!"

Kasie felt powerless as his rant continued. "That is why he hired people like you and me…me and you, my darling Kasie. We are the same Kasie. We are the scientists, the researchers, the smart people. He is just some lucky, rich prick whose parents died and left him a fortune, a whole town even."

Kasie stood in shock unable to process what she was hearing. "So that is what this is about?" Kasie asked. "You are jealous of his wealth? Jealous of his family and his friends and yet you are happy to let him pay your salary, pay for your accommodation, your lifestyle and your research?"

"As if he pays me nearly what I am worth!" Chris spat back in response.

"I've heard enough," Kasie screamed back as the pain in her shoulder became unbearable. The initial shock was wearing off and the realisation of the pain was intense. "I'm leaving."

"You are free to leave, of course," Chris responded. "Just know this," he paused. "I can control your every move, it isn't just a tracking device that you have in your shoulder. I have given you more than that. You are after all my research partner and for that reason I have shared with you my latest invention."

"Chris, what the fuck? I have seriously had enough of you today. Either tell me straight up what you have done or I leave the room now. And you know where I am going. This is ending right now!"

"Kasie, I love you. I don't want to hurt you. Please don't make me hurt you!"

"Chris, I can't stand to be around you a moment longer. You are pure evil! I have to go!" Kasie demanded as she walked toward the door and turned the handle on her way to freedom and some sense of normality.

Without even a sense of remorse, a sign of regret, Chris turned to Kasie and very firmly, very confidently said. "If you turn the handle on that door, you will die."

NINE

THE GAOL

"Enough Chris!" Kasie screamed at him. "Enough of your threats, what are you going to do? Stab me? Shoot me? This is not rationale, what you are saying to me is not rationale? Do you understand that?"

"I'm not sorry," Chris stammered. "What is done is now done. You have the tracking device. I don't need knives or guns. All I need is science."

"Chris, you better tell me right now what you have done, what is in this tracking device?" Kasie demanded to know.

His vile little face lit up as he answered her. He took his time to allow the words to truly sink in. The reality of Kasie's situation was becoming more desperate with each word of reply.

"What is in the tracking device my darling Kasie? You want to know what is in the tracking device?" Chris paused again prolonging the agony for Kasie just a second longer before finally responding. "Enough toxins to kill a great white shark," Chris replied quite matter of fact.

"Oh my god Chris, what have you done? Why would you? We are here to restore the ecosystem. We are here to save the reef, to save the great white population. What have you done?" Kasie pleaded with the madman.

"It's not enough anymore to just restore the reef Kasie or to save the great whites. What purpose does it serve to do that and for no one to come? Have you ever thought about what actually pays our way? It's not wealthy young socialites, it is big business and, in our case, it is the tourism business. Your little boy wonder can only pay us for as long as we take to restore the reef but our friendly tourism corporations, they are the ones who can promise us dollars long term."

Kasie looked on in total disbelief unable to take in Doctor Chris's philosophy of world economics as her increasing concern for her own wellbeing became paramount.

"Chris, you need to answer me now. What is in the tracking device?"

"Can't say, won't say," was Chris's unsympathetic and unemphatic response to her.

"That's enough, I'm leaving!" Kasie screamed at him.

"Kasie, I'm sorry but I can't let you leave, not now and if you try I will detonate the tracking device. You will be dead in seconds. Enough toxins to kill a great white shark, only a fraction of those toxins is required to kill a lowly marine scientist like you."

Kasie wanted to scream, cry, yell, hit out, even stab this man in the heart but she realised none of that would do any good. None of that would help her live past a few seconds of him pushing the detonation button he was holding in his hand.

"What do you want from me?" she asked with a new-found resolve.

"Well I am glad you asked. I did have something in mind and it seems to fit perfectly with your little man about town's poor excuse for a party last night. I heard that you have taken yourself off that stupid list of his? That ridiculous list of stupid young girls who have nothing better to do than to get married to some rich prick and play house. Why your name was ever on that list I will never understand," Chris continued.

"How did you know that?" Kasie questioned him.

"I know everything," Doctor Chris replied to her. The corner of his mouth turned upward in an attempt to form a sadistic smile.

Kasie interrupted him. "I took my name off The List because I am going home Chris, not because I think anything negative of him or for that matter of any of the women on that list. I just know that I can't stay here indefinitely, that I always planned to go home. I am not staying here and I am not getting married here."

"That is what I wanted to hear," Chris replied. "And in response to your question about how you are going to stay alive Kasie, it's that simple. You continue to tell people that you want to go home, that you don't want to be Mrs Rich Prick, part of the founding family, wife of the wealthy owner of this town and instead you will tell your friends and in fact, you will tell him, that you have chosen me."

Kasie couldn't believe what she was hearing. Her head felt foggy. Every muscle was stiff and sore. The pain from her right shoulder was searing through her body. She felt the heat of a possible infection begin to throb through her shoulders. She found it hard to focus on the words being spoken. They made no sense and her body was doing her no favours by failing her right now.

She stood by helplessly as the evil scientist continued his list of demands, "You will tell everyone that you want to be my wife, that you will live with me wherever I decide our next venture to be and that you are excited to be part of my life, my world, and that you will follow me to whatever corner of the globe I choose to go because you never want to be apart from me."

"You want me to lie and then throw up in my mouth?" Kasie spat back at him.

"Why are you so uncouth?" Chris demanded of her.

"Because we call it as we see it where I come from, Chris. Because you make me sick Chris, that is why! I would never say those things. I would never feel those things for you and you are insane. Do you understand that Chris? You are insane and I would never say those things to anyone!"

Without a hesitation, without a flinch, without a breath, Chris replied, "If you don't do as I ask Kasie, I will detonate and you will be dead within seconds."

Chris continued, "Now finish getting ready. We are going to The Gaol for you to make your announcement to the world."

Kasie was beyond shocked. She could see no way out of the horror that she found herself trapped in. Unable to move, all Kasie could feel was a deep, dark hole forming underneath her feet. Unable and unwilling to move she just wanted to stand in place and let the blackness consume her.

Chris left the room and Kasie took a few moments to adjust to the reality of the seemingly disastrous situation she found herself in. She looked at her makeup bag placed on the table next to the wardrobe. She looked further to find what she presumed to be pain relief medication and a glass of water. A present from Chris she imagined to try to get this increasing pain under control. She was hesitant to take the unknown drug but desperately needed some relief.

She slumped down on the bed, sitting upright, her head fallen into her hands. She allowed herself to shed the tears she had been fighting. Unsure of how long she sat silently, Kasie looked around the room again and with a newfound sense of determination, decided that she needed to be strong to get herself safely through this.

Ever resilient, Kasie snapped herself from her waking nightmare to begin to plan her escape. Having been dressed in the royal blue monstrosity Chris called evening wear, Kasie had then applied her make up to the best of her ability given the current circumstances, taken the two tablets for the pain and obligingly jumped into the waiting car ready to face the crowd at The Gaol. She knew who would be there. Absolutely every single person in Coral Cove would be there.

She had known this because the events of the birthday party the night before, as amazing as they had been, had failed to determine a future date for their town bachelor. Every woman on the list felt as if they had a chance of being the first date, to be the first potential relationship for him.

They all thought the same thing, that the first date would be his last, that they had the beauty, intelligence and sex appeal to win him over. That after the first date he wouldn't need to look any further, that he would fall madly in love and propose.

Kasie felt that she knew a little more than the other women, having been so close to their object of affection, given just as friends. She felt that he had been able to open up to her far more than any of the other women. On top of that, his behaviour at his birthday party and his insistence that she stay the night with him clued her into his potential feelings towards her. In thinking this, she was trying not to be arrogant. It wasn't about that.

She just knew that there was obviously something between them that they both needed to get to the bottom of. She had promised to meet him at The Gaol at nine o'clock for drinks to discuss the events of the night before. Kasie was actually counting on it, counting on him being there. She was relying on being able to tell him that her life was in danger and that he was her only hope of getting her out of this predicament alive.

Kasie's most pressing concern was that she had no idea what time it was. She knew that when she had walked into the laboratory to confront Doctor Chris it was just after three o'clock. She also realised she had no idea of how long she had been unconscious. She knew when she woke, Chris and her had argued for some time before she agreed to finish getting dressed and come out and face the crowds. She only imagined that it was well after nine, her scheduled time to meet her friend, the person who she believed could save her.

When she presented herself dressed and made up, Chris led Kasie to the waiting vehicle. Feeling disheartened and disempowered, Kasie looked out the window of the company car that was driving her to her destiny. She felt a total loss of power and control over her current situation. The pain in her shoulder was beyond belief but she was determined to not let him see her anguish. She wasn't going to give him the pleasure of seeing her suffer.

* * *

Meanwhile unknown to Kasie, her boss was also in his car. It was unusual for him to not drive himself to a personal engagement but he wanted to take the mansion car, along with Marco because he felt as if tonight was going to be a special night. He didn't want to be tied down to driving, who knew he thought, what the night might hold in store for them. He hadn't exactly worked out what he wanted to say to Kasie, word for word that was, but he knew the general message he wanted to get across.

After his party ended and for the duration of what felt like a long and thoughtful day, he had done a lot of soul searching. He had come to realise that the thought of losing the one woman he had ever loved was too much for him to bear. He knew that he didn't want to wait a day longer, he needed to tell Kasie that he loved her and that he wanted her to become his wife.

He needed to tell her that he didn't want to go on and date and get to know the women on The List. That he knew from the moment that he saw her amazing smile, her sparkling blue eyes and heard her infectious laugh that he had only ever wanted her.

So many times had he felt like telling her, when she was watching the game on TV with him and Marco, all the other women already left getting bored when they weren't the centre of attention. Or when the three of them were playing games of pool and sinking beers like they were all long-time friends from years before. The times that he organised dinner parties inviting people that he hoped wouldn't attend just so he would have more time on his own with her.

He couldn't tell her before. He hadn't been able to tell her how he felt. He had made a promise that he wouldn't get into a relationship, that he would take the opportunity to get to know all the women on The List, but how could he do that with all honesty. He knew and he never doubted that she was the one; that she was his one.

After the madness of the night before, his birthday party, he knew he needed to see her, to apologise for his strong-arm tactics and to explain to her that he only did it because he feared he was losing her. As he waited at his table by the window of The Gaol, he feared it was all too late. After all it was now ten o'clock and she was already an hour late for their drinks date.

He hadn't been an ungracious potential suitor to the women who had chosen to join him for a drink at the club that night. He wondered what the women thought he was doing there. He joined them if they wanted to have a drink with him but at the same time, he remained distant, ready and available to greet his special guest as soon as she emerged from the elevator.

His obvious preoccupation didn't stop most of the women from trying to entertain him though, from buying him drinks, complimenting him and flicking their hair and puckering their lips in a vain attempt to accentuate their best features. Marco had found suitable company and was enjoying chatting to the crowd and laughing at the highlights retold of the party the night before. The two men had waited patiently for their special guest to arrive.

By ten thirty, he was getting ready to hop back into his car, Marco by his side. He had by now resigned himself to the fact that Kasie wasn't coming to meet him. That maybe and understandably so, she had changed her mind. He couldn't blame her. He had come on to her pretty hard and heavy the night before. He had pushed the limits to the boundaries of their friendship and in all reality, he really didn't know how she actually felt about him.

He knew he loved her and that she was the only woman he wanted to be with. But her feelings, they were still a mystery to him. He just didn't know how she might respond to his declaration of love. Having tried to phone her mobile several times already with no answer, he guessed that she wasn't ready to talk about any of this with him.

How horribly did he regret his behaviour of the night before? If only he could apologise. If only she would answer the phone, meet with him, talk to him and give him a chance to say how sorry he was for his out of character actions.

Having convinced himself that she wasn't coming, he found Marco and the two men made their way back to the car. From the seat of his vehicle, he checked his phone once more and when he hadn't heard from her, he sent her yet another text message:

Kase, I am so sorry if I have upset you.
Please call me. I need to speak to you urgently. Xx

* * *

Unknown to Kasie, Doctor Chris's car pulled in to The Gaol car park only a short time after her boss had left. If only, Kasie thought to herself, he is still here. He would know how to help her. She would confide in him and only him and let him know that her life was in danger. Not only that, she needed to let him know that Doctor Chris was endangering the life of the reef's shark population, potentially destroying the sole reason for her being here in Coral Cove in the first place.

Kasie's heart stopped as she felt the vibration of her phone in her bag. Having thankfully kept it on silent while she worked, she realised that Doctor Chris had failed to check her bag and inadvertently left her with the one tool she needed to escape him, her mobile phone.

The car had barely stopped before Kasie pushed open the door and felt her shoes on the hard, dark car park surface.

"Wait there, dear!" Chris was all too quick to alight the vehicle himself stopping her dead in her tracks. "Don't you think we should make our entrance together, hand in hand that is, displaying for all, the loving couple that we are?"

Kasie honestly felt like she was going to pass out again every time Chris spoke. She had never felt so trapped in her whole life. The still throbbing pain of the tracking device, even after she had taken substantial pain relief, a constant reminder that she had limited options here. It was a painful token of the havoc that he was prepared to unleash if she didn't do as Chris asked of her, to keep her alive. She made her way toward him and with much distaste held her hand out to gently clasp his.

Her hand in his made her feel even more nauseous. Unlike the strong, warm grasp of her boss, Chris's hand was small, weak and cold. She detected an unpleasant sensation of moisture on his palms. A sign she hoped that he was feeling as anxious as she was. Chris's touch on her skin sent a shiver through her arm. She had never had such a strong negative reaction to another person's touch in her entire life.

Together they made their way to the lift entry to meet with what she expected were the excited crowds. If only he is still there, she closed her eyes for just the tiniest of seconds to make a silent wish to the universe. She prayed that he was inside the club. Please be there, she hoped to herself.

* * *

"Marco?" he interrupted the stony silence of the thoughtful drive home. "Was that the Conservation Society car that just passed us?" It was unlike the user of the car, Doctor Chris to ever be seen this late at night. He wondered who could be using the vehicle and heading for what it seemed to be the direction that he had just come from.

Shaking his head, Marco apologised. "Sorry about that, I really didn't notice. Who do you think was in it?" Marco asked.

"It was too dark, I couldn't actually see," his boss replied.

"Do you think it was Kasie?" Marco was curious to hear what his boss was thinking.

"I don't know, maybe? But possibly it was Chris," his employer replied.

Would you like to go and check it out, it shouldn't be too hard to locate, it's a small town you know. Not much can go on without someone seeing it around here," Marco chuckled before he added, "And normally that person seeing everything is you."

"I wish I had seen more, trust me Marco, if ever I had wished to know everything, now would be the time."

"We are turning around to investigate further?"

"Yes, thank you Marco. I just have a strange feeling about it."

"Are your senses tingling boss?" Marco laughed. "Has Kasie taught you how to trust your intuition too?"

Instantly, at the mere mention of her name he was reminded of the overwhelming grief he had been feeling.

"Actually, that is exactly it, Marco. I have no reason to be curious and no reason to even care why Doctor Chris might be out, but you are correct, something just doesn't feel quite right."

"Ok, boss," Marco replied. "We are turning around now. As Kasie says you should always act on your instincts. So, where do your instincts tell you to drive to?"

"Actually, you won't believe this, but I think we should head back to The Gaol. Let's see if his car is there."

"ETA, five minutes boss," Marco replied in strict military fashion as if suddenly assigned to some secret mission to save the world.

"Are you enjoying this Marco?" he asked, silently wondering if Marco's humour was sarcasm in disguise but secretly thankful that his loyal friend was with him tonight, no questions asked.

"No, of course not boss," Marco replied in all sincerity, "it's just the first time you have really spoken in hours and I thought this would be a good distraction. Don't stress about Kasie. She is probably just annoyed by you and all your control issues. She will most likely call you in the morning and all will be good in your world again," Marco was eager to reassure his best friend.

"I sincerely hope you are right Marco. I really do."

Marco sped up ever so slightly, thankful for the concentration required of getting his boss to his destination with haste. It also added a much-needed distraction from his current concerns about Kasie's absence from the club.

* * *

At The Gaol, Kasie headed across the car park and toward the lift entry. She felt as if she was walking to the electric chair. She was reminded of the survival shows she and Dee had enjoyed watching together on their lazy nights in.

On the nights when they couldn't be bothered to get dressed up and meet friends out, they instead relished one of their secret little pastimes, reality television and home delivered pizza. She remembered how many times survivors of horrific plane crashes or near-death experiences spoke of the minutes or seconds leading up to the disaster.

The survivors recalled everything playing out around them in slow motion. As if almost to give the victim every available chance to stop what was about to happen or at the very least prepare for the inevitable. If this was the case, and this was her very own seconds before disaster, she felt disheartened that she didn't have a single clue on how to prepare for or overt her impending demise.

Any plan or hope she had of coming out of this alive was that he was there. That he would see her walking in and instantly know something was wrong. That he would, without her saying a single word, know how to help her and wouldn't hesitate for a second to do whatever he needed to do to keep her alive.

So much for being the strong, independent, educated, worldly woman she thought she was. When it came down to the most important decision of her life, her survival rested solely on a man. She came to Coral Cove, pleased to be away from the dating scene for a while, to avoid relationships and concentrate on her research and this is what it had come down to. A love triangle, if you could call it that.

The sound of the lift arriving brought her swiftly back to reality. *Here we go,* she thought to herself again. *It's all down to you,* another silent wish in her head. *I just hope you are here. Please be here.* As the lift started to ascend to the club floor, the heavy beat of the music made her stomach drop and she became acutely aware of the sweaty, clammy hand of Doctor Chris squeezing hers just that little bit too tightly.

"Here, we go my lovely fiancé, this is our time to shine," Doctor Chris beamed to her.

Was it possible, she thought to herself, that this man was getting more and more unwell by the minute? He actually looked like he was thoroughly enjoying her pain and torture way too much for her to feel anything but utter terror in his presence. How he now imagined them to be engaged was beyond belief.

* * *

As if by instinct again, Marco sped up the shiny black sedan he drove for his best friend. Unsure what to make of the night and aware that although his employer had complex thoughts rushing through his mind, he didn't want to push to ask for more details. He was sure of one thing and that was whatever had happened, it involved a certain woman. A woman who was also one of his closest friends. A woman he himself cared for very much.

Marco just hoped that whatever was happening that Kasie was alright. It wasn't like her to stand anyone up, let alone the man all women desired. Beside all of that, beside the fact that he was the most eligible bachelor any woman was ever going to meet, they were great friends. Marco knew that whatever was happening in her life she would find a way to phone them, or to somehow let at least one of them know that she was going to be late.

He knew that if she was held up at work or decided that she was too exhausted from a busy research day on the reef that she would call or message and let them both know. Never wanting to play favourites, she had always treated the two men the same. Not like the other women, who only had eyes for their wealthy bachelor, Kasie seemed to enjoy spending time with Marco as well. And he had always enjoyed her company too.

Unlike the female friendships, Marco always felt a real sense of comfort and ease around Kasie. They say that Australians are a friendly, unpretentious bunch of people, but with her it was absolutely true. She was honest, open, giving and generous, and fun to be around. The other women could be fun too, but generally more so in smaller doses.

The other women quickly tired if they didn't get the bachelor's full attention and in doing so were often dismissive of Marco. Only ever engaging in conversation it felt to find out more about his boss. When did he plan to marry? How many children had he said that he wanted to have? Or who did Marco think he liked best of the women? Marco soon tired of the relentless questions and instead enjoyed the company of the other guys; his long-time mates from childhood, and of course Kasie.

Kasie was the woman who was just as comfortable playing volleyball in the pool as shoe shopping and lunching with friends in some trendy new restaurant in town. His boss was perceptive, Marco thought to himself. Something just didn't feel right and with that he put his foot down on the accelerator with even more force and headed for The Gaol.

Their now speeding black sedan drove quickly into the nightclub car park at The Gaol and with a grinding holt pulled alongside the Conservation Society's company car. This now confirming what Marco and his boss had somehow already guessed.

He knew that something was wrong, just what and how bad it was, still remained to be seen.

Marco looked at the rear-view mirror and directly into his boss's worried eyes. Without needing to say anything more the two men knew that they had each other's support tonight. Silently they both stepped out of the car and made their way to the lift entrance, the entrance they had departed from just a short time earlier.

Marco walked behind his boss, but only a step behind as he always did. Some old-fashioned sense of respect he felt that this was his place beside the man who paid his wage. He looked at his friend, trying to read the thoughts behind the frown on his downturned head. Marco attempted to make sense of this feeling of unrest and he also knew that was exactly what his boss was doing.

His employer could feel Marco's stare almost burning a hole directly through the back of his head, as if trying to read his mind. He was trying desperately to make the links in his head. Why would Doctor Chris be here and why on the one night that Kasie had failed to show for their date? Could the two oddities be in any way linked? His concern had intensified as he felt the speed of the car increase and he guessed that Marco too must have a growing concern for the events unfolding.

"I can feel you trying to read my mind," he said to Marco as they walked toward the lift. "If you want to know something, you should just ask."

Marco didn't hesitate to ask the question that was at the forefront of his mind. "What's your theory boss?" Marco asked as instructed.

"I don't know. I truly don't, but I am worried that Doctor Chris's car and Kasie's silence may be linked. Human nature suggests that people don't often deviate from their normal behaviour and tonight both of them have acted out of character. Do you think that could just be coincidence?"

"For some reason, I truly hope so," Marco replied.

"Me also."

His thoughts returned to Doctor Chris. Why would he be here tonight? He knew that he would be the only person to be driving the car. He had let Doctor Chris know that as part of his contract package, that he had a car at his disposal. He had offered this to most of the people on his payroll, feeling not only that it was a decent thing to offer but also that fewer privately owned cars in the town reduced the town's carbon footprint.
Both good reasons he thought to ensure that staff had access to vehicles when they needed them. He knew for sure that Doctor Chris would be the only one in the car because although he had suggested that Chris allow other staff in the laboratory to access the vehicle, Chris had politely declined.

Doctor Chris's philosophy with staff was something along the lines of treat them mean, keep them keen. In other words, the more you do for them, the less they want to work hard. On the other hand,

and probably the polar opposite of the Doctor, he himself thought that good people deserve to be treated well.

He believed that people with real passion give far more than their required forty-hour working week, so why not reward their passion with little extras, like use of the car or surprise bonuses.

How worlds apart he and Chris were, he thought to himself, as he neared the elevator. He couldn't imagine for a second anything really that the two men would have in common, no middle ground for them to join together and get to know each other. To be honest, he really couldn't tolerate his company for long at all.

He was eternally grateful that he had Kasie working with Doctor Chris. He imagined that her influence in the research and conservation was the reason they were achieving such great results and progress in the rehabilitation of the reef. He couldn't imagine how the two of them worked together really at all, come to think of it.

He put it down to Kasie's easy-going nature and assumed that she managed Doctor Chris in the same way that he himself somehow found himself doing when meeting for regular updates on progress.

If only Kasie was running the conservation and restoration project herself, he thought, then he wouldn't have to endure those awkward debates when he and Chris couldn't agree. Kasie would not consider herself experienced enough to handle the project on her own, but he had faith in her. Besides that, it was a growing field and there were plenty of young passionate people out there who really wanted to make a difference in sustaining the ocean's ecology who could work alongside Kasie.

His thoughts again turned back to Kasie and her absence tonight. If only he had some word from her. His head was racing with possible explanations for her sudden disappearance. Each option was becoming more and more worrying as he let his concern for her reach unimaginable heights.

Now inside the elevator and headed toward the sound of the music and the noisy crowds, he reached into his pocket for what seemed to the thousandth time that night to check his phone for any new messages from her. Just as the doors of the elevator opened a welcomed alert sound came from his phone. He lowered his head to see his mobile alight with the news he had been waiting for all night, a message from Kasie.

Without looking up, he stepped from the elevator with Marco only a foot behind him. He opened the message he had been waiting to read for hours. A sense of relief washed over him as he let out a sigh, thankfully she was ok, he thought to himself. Only a second later his relief was washed away, replaced by a stabbing pain in his chest as he read the message. One word only, the message from Kasie. It wasn't the message he had hoped for.

It simply read:

HELP

TEN

THE TOAST

He looked up at the waiting crowd as if needing to consolidate his bearings. He felt nauseous and hot as the sudden pain in his chest was causing a searing heat which was quickly rising to his face. Sensing something was wrong, Marco stepped beside him and scanned his boss's face for any clues as to what he had just read. As if unable to speak he simply handed Marco the phone. Now free to properly scan the room, his immediate thought was that he needed to find Doctor Chris.

Whatever was going on, he knew Doctor Chris had something to do with it and he wouldn't stop until he told him what he was doing here and where Kasie was. He scanned the room and it didn't take long to find him, his greying balding head stood out amongst the crowd of the thirty something beautiful people who frequented the club. He could only see the back of him until he began to turn slowly, a bottle of champagne in his hand. The silver ice bucket filled to the brim with ice, two crystal glasses placed precariously on top.

* * *

Kasie felt a sense of relief for the first time in what seemed like hours since she had entered the laboratory to speak with Doctor Chris. Her actions had been very slow and careful as she had reached into her bag and pulled out her mobile phone. Thank goodness, she thought to herself that her mobile was still working. She had known she had very little time to do anything to help herself, but had managed to reply to his last text to her with just four little letters, *HELP*.

She had switched the phone off and placed it in the bottom of her bag before Doctor Chris had returned from the bar. The last thing she wanted was a message alert while Doctor Chris was standing beside her. She had completed her mission in just enough time to welcome Chris back to where she had been told to wait for him. He returned with a celebratory bottle of champagne and two glasses.

She watched Chris pour the sparkling liquid into the two long-stemmed crystal glasses and return the bottle to the chilled bucket for safekeeping. He reached his arm out, silently placing the delicate glassware into her palm. Clicking the glasses together, he almost sang out his toast to her.

"To us, my dear!"

Kasie had no choice but to quietly accept the well wishes and take a refreshing sip of the chilled beverage. At that exact moment Kasie felt a different set of eyes on her. Not just any set of eyes. She felt him. She tilted her head and made eye contact with him. Her knight in shining armour or so she had very much hoped.

There he was, standing just steps from the entrance to the elevator with Marco planted firmly beside him. She noticed Marco reading something from a mobile. She couldn't tell whose phone it was, until she saw Marco's face, fused red with rage.

She only hoped that it had been her message he was reading. She had to believe it. They would have been waiting to hear from her. She felt sure that they had received her message and that both of them had now read it and both of them were there to help her. Instant relief washed over her body. *Everything will be ok,* she promised herself.

* * *

He couldn't believe what he was seeing. Kasie was there with Doctor Chris. Having watched the Doctor leave the bar, his curiosity was peaked as he waited to see where he walked to and who was about to receive the champagne on offer.

If by chance Doctor Chris had a business meeting, as he really couldn't imagine any other form of social interaction Chris could be engaged in, he wondered who it could be with. He watched the short, wiry scientist walk the length of the room. He looked so very out of place but somehow very confident, almost arrogant in his movements through the busy crowd.

He hadn't been aware that he had progressed toward Doctor Chris's position in the room, almost as if a magnetic pull had forced his body to drag it toward the scientist. It grew instantly stronger the moment he saw her, Chris's companion for the night. It was his Kase. He watched as she accepted the long-stemmed glass from him. He stared, seething at what was in front of him, almost burning a hole through the crowd with the intensity of his steely glare.

He couldn't understand why Kasie would be having a drink with Doctor Chris. Why she didn't arrive in time to meet as arranged. But he felt fairly sure that Kasie wouldn't make him wait two hours for the sake of the colleague that she loathed.

And the message, what had that meant? His initial reaction was that Kasie was in some kind of trouble. That she needed him with her immediately, but here she was in the club as planned. He became aware that she didn't look her normal easy-going self. Was it her stance, her uncomfortableness she normally had when she was around Chris or was it her dress?

For the first time he noticed her attire, a royal blue frumpy looking dress, the type of design one would have deemed fashionable only in the preceding decade. He was never one to care that much about women's clothing, but he knew Kasie and he knew this was nothing he had ever seen her in before. The clothing, the message, all of it, only added to the confusion he was feeling.

"What's going on?" he asked Marco.

Marco stepped in front of him and stopped him from walking any further. "I don't know but I need to find out more," he replied.

"Wait!" Marco said. "Let's just stop for a minute and try to work out what is going on here. I can see her too, and she looks perfectly ok to me, visibly uncomfortable, but perfectly safe. Let's just work this out before you go over there. You look like you are about to kill someone and I don't need three chances to guess at who that might be."

"You're right," he agreed as he let Marco continue.

"Let's step over to the corner and have a chat where it is a bit quieter, you can still see her from there. We won't let her out of our sight. I promise you," Marco directed his friend.

With a resignation that Marco was indeed correct and they needed more of a plan than just storming over to Chris and throwing him to the ground, the two men walked toward the far corner of the club. Marco's eyes never left Kasie's as they walked away.

* * *

Doctor Chris let out a little smirk. A sly turn of the mouth, nearly resembling a smile emerged on his face. Well that was easier than I thought it would be. Chris said to himself as he watched the two men walk away from him and Kasie and into the heaving crowd. Typical of these big men," he said. "They act all tough and think they rule the world until they are proven to be outsmarted. No brains, all brawn. And may the best man win!" Chris smiled as he turned to Kasie, his glass raised to hers in the act of toasting himself again.

"You make me sick, Chris!" Kasie fumed. "Is this just some ridiculous game to you? Are you truly threatening my life just to get one over him? You can't be that selfish and stupid surely?"

"Shh! Lower your voice. That is no way to speak to your future husband in public, my darling Kasie," Chris responded.

"No! No…this is not happening! I am leaving!" Kasie slammed the crystal glass on the nearest table and turned in the direction she last saw her two friends. She had barely taken two steps before Chris had grabbed her arm and jerked her to an abrupt halt.

"I have my finger on the button inside my jacket pocket. If you take another step, I will push the button. When I do, you will have enough poison enter your body you won't survive the hour, no matter how fast anyone can come to your rescue. Do you understand me?"

It took her every ounce of strength to stop herself from moving. She had heard what Chris had said. She didn't doubt that this maniac would be capable of pushing the button that would end her life but all she could think about was being somewhere safe. And she knew safety was with those two men that she only hoped were still somewhere in the club.

She had never felt as alone as when she had just watched the two of them walk away from her. She had felt certain they had read her message. She felt for sure that they were coming to check on her. She just knew that they would be able to help. Within a second her hopes were dashed as she watched them walk in the opposite direction from her and into the noisy crowd. They couldn't have left her surely but she didn't know what to think anymore.

She had seen him walking toward her and had read his face, an unsettling mixture of concern and anger. Not so strange she thought really considering the view he was taking in. She had thought he would bound over, comfort her, and confront Chris, but instead Marco had stopped him. Maybe concerned for his friend's wellbeing, maybe to stop him doing something that he would later regret.

Maybe Marco thought that she needed some space. Surely not, surely, he would not think that she would willingly stand up their boss for this disgusting specimen of a man standing beside her right now. Feeling absolutely deflated and barely unable to hold back her tears, Kasie resigned herself quickly to the fact that help wasn't coming. She turned to once again face Chris.

"That's better," he said, returning the glass back to her hand. "Now let's have that toast!" Chris's smug, arrogant tone was almost too much for Kasie to bear.

* * *

Across the room a similar struggle of consciousness was looming. Marco was barely able to contain his boss at the sight of Doctor Chris restraining Kasie. Both men were unable to look away from the scene, trying desperately to read their body language and make sense of what was going on. One thing they both recognised was that Kasie did not want to be in Chris's company.

They saw her try to leave, to walk toward where she thought they would be. They both saw Doctor Chris grab her arm and whisper something close to her ear. They could both recognise the signs of her tears welling up behind her eyes and then her surrender and retreat back to the pasty looking Doctor.

He was barely able to contain himself. It took every bit of strength he had to stay still. He allowed Marco to stop him in his place. He just wanted to walk over to her, to hold her, to ask her what was wrong and tell her that she was safe. Marco, the voice of reason, insisted they wait.

All of Marco's previous training told him that something was seriously wrong with the scenario playing out before them, but he didn't know what and until he had more information, he couldn't plan his next action. Marco recalled his previous search and rescue training. Having spent ten years specialising in search and rescue missions in dangerous communities abroad he was well versed in the skill of mission preparation and planning.

Marco knew that to be effective and efficient he needed all the information at hand and at present he had nothing more than a one-word text message and the unfolding visual of Kasie seemingly held against her will. He watched on to see what else he could learn from the interaction between his gorgeous friend, Kasie and her very unusual and therefore potentially dangerous colleague.

* * *

Kasie attempted to stop the flow of tears that were collecting behind her eyes. She looked at Chris and said. "I'm sorry, I really am. This is all just a lot for me to process. I won't do that again. I didn't mean to upset you."

"Oh, that's alright my darling Kasie. I imagine you will need some time to adjust to my rules, I just hope that you remember who is in charge here and don't do anything stupid to hurt yourself," Chris reminded her.

"I won't Chris, I promise," Kasie responded with real meaning. She was being honest with him. She really didn't want to get hurt and she knew it was through her actions alone that she could keep herself safe. "Chris, I just need to go to the bathroom for a minute. I really need a moment to fix my face and pull myself together. I promise I won't do anything else," Kasie pleaded with him.

"Of course, my darling, I want you looking your best when we are out together. Please take your time. I will be right here," Chris agreed almost too easily. The Doctor leaned in and gently kissed her lips. "Come straight back my darling, I will miss you!"

Kasie's stomach did a flip, coming from any other man in the room, that would have been a compliment, but she saw it for the hidden threat that it was. She couldn't get to the bathroom quickly enough and with regret knew she couldn't look back, look to see if her two friends were anywhere nearby.

* * *

And they were. The two men were standing behind a crowd of people, unable to be seen by Doctor Chris and Kasie but able to watch their every move. A glimmer of hope rose when they watched her leave the table to walk across the busy club. Without a word, they both knew this was their chance.

"I assume she is going to the bathroom," Marco was the first to speak.

His boss was quick to reply. "And we both know how to get there. Do you have your access?" he asked.

"Always come prepared!" Marco smiled as he held out the credit card shaped security swipe that allowed them access to all areas of the club.

Another benefit of owning most of the town was that they could access most of the buildings if they needed. And as luck would have it, this old building, previously an old colonial gaol, had just enough passages and doorways for them to know that they could get to anywhere they needed with no one else noticing. Without hesitation they headed for the area behind the bar.

Never losing sight of Chris for a moment, both men guessed they had to act with haste. They believed they didn't have much time to reach Kasie and find out what was going on before Chris came looking for her.

"I will stay here and keep an eye on him," Marco instructed. "You go find her and bring her out. We need to talk to her away from him, hurry!" Marco ordered.

His boss didn't need a second instruction. He was through the back door of the bar and into the cellar in an instant. Having played in these hallways as a child, he knew the layout well. Even the lack of lighting in the dark and gloomy corridors didn't prevent him from reaching the area where the bathrooms were in record time. As if luck was with him, he reached the area just as Kasie emerged through the bathroom door. A second later and he would have missed her.

* * *

Kasie having touched up her face and allowing herself some time to take a few deep breaths, began to feel much better. Not because she had a way out of this mess, but because she was starting to realise that she needed to take control and losing herself to end up a teary curled up ball on the floor was not going to help her in any way.

It was with this newfound determination that she readied herself to exit the bathroom to face Chris again. A plan slowly started to formulate on how she would rescue herself. Her resolve, her determination and her own inner strength lasted all of ten seconds when as she opened the door, there he was. Her very own knight in shining armour had come to rescue her at last.

Without enough strength left for anything more, she staggered the few steps toward him and collapsed into his arms, tears rolling down her cheeks.

"I thought you had left me here. Here with him! Where did you go? Didn't you get my message?" Her questions intertwined with heaving sobs went unanswered.

"We don't have much time Kase," he responded with urgency. "What is happening here?"

145

ELEVEN

THE DETONATION

She tried to pull herself together long enough to answer but struggled to get out all but a few words. "There is a tracking device in my back," she stammered. "He said he would kill me. It's filled with toxins." The relief at being back in his arms again overwhelmed her.

His face went as white as a sheet. His expression was stone-like, as he attempted to make sense of her explanation. Very gently, he lifted the neck of the back of her dress and pulled it away from her body to see the sight he could barely believe.

Kasie had a shark-tracking device firmly implanted into her shoulder. The skin around the area, red and raw as it was desperately trying to reject the foreign object.

"Kase, we need to get you out of here now. Come with me!" he demanded.

Kasie struggled to find her feet under herself and began to walk toward the narrow corridor and away from the main entry to the bathroom area. Stopping suddenly, she remembered one more important factor she had failed to mention. She turned to him and said. "He can detonate the tracker."

As he looked at her now blotchy, red, swollen face, he realised he needed to act quickly.

Just then a voice at the door appeared and if right on cue, there he was, the villain of the piece. Doctor Chris raised his hands in the air as he screamed that he would do it. Within what felt to be a second of his appearance Marco appeared at the door, grabbing Chris's hand in an attempt to dislodge the small black remote that he had firmly clasped.

But it was all too late. Doctor Chris had detonated the remote. It only took a few seconds for Kasie's unconscious body to slump completely into her employer's arms.

"Marco!" his boss yelled, "We need to get her out of here. Leave him, we need to get her help now!"

Without hesitation Marco was beside his two friends. Doctor Chris feeling the release of Marco's hold of him took this as a sign and a result of his great planning and quickly fled the club. He knew that he had to get himself out of there.

Kasie was vaguely aware of the conversation happening around her. She could hear the two male voices. She could feel their strong, firm arms around her weakened body. She knew that they were moving and with some speed. She couldn't raise her head. She couldn't speak. She couldn't walk. She couldn't move her body at all.

Instead her entire concentration was around the intense pain radiating from the device in her back. She felt a flood of warmth first circle the area near the device and then spread through her back, her chest, down her torso and slowly creep down into her legs and arms.

Along with the searing pain came the heat, the scorching heat that made her feel as if her body was on fire. Kasie wasn't aware of the noises, the shouting nor the screaming from her friends around her as her slumped unconscious body was carried through the now gathering and concerned crowd back to the waiting black sedan.

"Marco. Ring Dr Harris, get her on speaker!" he shouted as they were now seated in the car readying for a quick exit from the car park.

"Already on it!" Marco responded.

Marco had always been one step ahead. That was what had made him a great planner and the perfect person to advise his best friend. He had started dialling the number the minute he had entered the car.

"Hello Marco, is everything ok?" A female voice answering his urgent call echoed through the car.

"Doctor Harris, it's me," his boss responded to the Doctor from the back seat. "We have a serious situation. My friend has been poisoned. We don't know how much or what, but she has lost consciousness. I think we are losing her. We are on the way to the hospital now."

"I am here on shift. I will meet you. We need to get her an ambulance, where are you now?" Doctor Harris enquired.

"Don't bother, we will be there faster than the ambulance can reach us. Can you meet us at the emergency door, she needs your help, fast!" Hearing the conversation, the calm in his voice, you would have thought he was a trained professional.

He was coordinated and direct, but Marco in the front seat could hear the strain in his voice. He was keeping it together but Marco knew that just underneath the surface this was a man fearing he was about to lose the one woman he loved. Marco dreaded what would happen if she didn't make it.

"Doctor Harris. She is barely breathing. I can hardly feel her pulse, you have to help her!" His boss begged her again.

"Did she ingest the poison?" The Doctor responded to him.

"No, the poison was injected into her back through a device. A tracking device used for sharks."

"How?" the Doctor began to ask, but quickly realised it wasn't important for now. "Would you be able to remove the device?" the Doctor asked. "Or at the very least, stop the device from releasing any further toxins?"

"There was a remote, but it was only for detonation, Doctor," Marco quickly interjected. "I will remove it," Marco added without hesitation. "If that is what you think is best."

The Doctor confirmed her initial thoughts, "Without seeing it, it is hard for me to be sure. But I think the best option we have right now is to remove it if we can."

"I will pull over and take it out," Marco instructed his boss, his voice calm, expertly hiding his real sense of horror.

"No, keep driving, we need to get her to the hospital," his boss ordered him. "Her breathing is slowing. Hurry Marco, speed up!"

In the back seat of the racing car, his hands gently placed Kasie's head on his lap. He turned her unconscious body on its side to locate once more the small black box inserted near her shoulder. He pulled the unsightly blue material of her dress away from her body and held the box between his fingers.

He bent down and kissed the top of her head, "I'm sorry if you can feel this Kase," he whispered to her softly.

With careful precision, he tugged gently at the device until it began to come away from the skin. Seeing that the device was still excreting a clear liquid, he tugged harder until the silver needles that were attached to her skin were released and the box was now dislodged entirely from her back. He threw the offending piece of plastic onto the floor of the car and pressed firmly on the now bleeding skin where the box was inserted.

He lent forward again to whisper to his unconscious friend. "Please hang in there, Kase. I love you. Please don't leave me now."

In record time, Marco had made it to the hospital and as promised Doctor Harris was standing by at the entrance to the emergency department, surrounded by what looked like a team of doctors, nurses and emergency staff waiting for their arrival. Another benefit of owning most of the town was that on the odd occasion that he needed help, everyone was more than willing to give of their time and skills.

He had proven time and time again to every individual in Coral Cove that he was there to improve the quality of their lives, rebuild their town and their local ecology. Never once had he strayed from his word or faltered on his promise. He wanted to make his parents proud and not a person who knew him would doubt that indeed his parents would have been immensely proud of the man he had become. That was the reason Doctor Harris answered the call so promptly. The reason she would do anything to help this passionate young man who had done so much already for everyone in their little coastal piece of heaven.

With exact precision, Marco stopped the car just short of the emergency room door. A team of medical staff raced to the car and without a word, and with the practiced experience of a team who had done this hundreds of times before, they lifted Kasie from the car and onto the waiting gurney.

The two men shared a quick knowing glimpse before both going about what they had to do next. Marco sped off again knowing he had to locate Doctor Chris, while his boss ran alongside the gurney, promising Kasie, he would not leave her. Neither friend had wanted to make any demands of the other; instead they got on with what they both knew they needed to do.

As Kasie was rushed into the waiting emergency cubicle, a kindly nurse attempted to usher her very concerned friend away. "Please come with me," the nurse attempted. "She is in good hands. Now we need to make sure you are ok, please come and sit with me over here."

"I'm sorry," he responded with a kindness and consideration only a man of his value would be able to muster given the circumstances. "I'm sorry but I just can't leave her. I promised I would stay with her. She would want me to stay beside her. I can't go anywhere. Please understand."

Looking into his desperate eyes, the nurse knew there would be no convincing this man. She gave him a gentle pat on the back and said "I will get you a cold drink then. I will be back." With that she exited, leaving him alone to look on as the team of staff hurriedly worked around Kasie. One staff member taking what appeared to be samples of blood, the other applying oxygen through a mask, and another nurse preparing a cannula and an intravenous drip.

Doctor Harris was talking, barking instructions to staff, checking Kasie's pulse and rattling off statistics and numbers for the assigned nurse to record on her chart. He wanted to get close, to hold her hand, to tell her he was there, but he couldn't get anywhere near the bed and he knew he needed to let the staff do what they were trained to do. He would stay and wait.

It seemed no time at all before the business settled and there was only Doctor Harris and two nurses left at the bedside.

Feeling certain that she could now leave Kasie in the hands of the nursing staff, the Doctor walked toward the young man she had known his whole life. She could see how worried he was and she wanted to offer some form of reassurance. "She is stable. That is a really good thing. The best we can expect right now."

He sighed and for the first time realised that he had actually been holding his breath. That moment in time when the situation is so stressful, so intense that you can't even breathe. He didn't realise he was doing it. He only knew that it felt good to get a deep breath back into his lungs.

"Thank you, Doctor. I don't know how I will ever repay you. Thank you with all of my heart." He gently grabbed the doctor by the hands and raised them to his mouth. With the most-simple of caresses, he kissed the doctor's hands before returning them to her side.

"Please, I don't want you to misunderstand, she is stable for now, but we have a long way to go to work out what has happened here and how we can treat her. I am going to do everything I can, I promise you, but please don't thank me," the Doctor begged him for understanding. Trying to reassure him but at the same time not wanting him to have false hope that she was out of danger just yet.

"How is she?" A concerned male voice enquired upon entering the room.

"Marco," the Doctor answered him as she addressed the young man's companion. "She is stable and we will know more soon, I hope, when the blood tests come back. You should know that you two probably saved her life. If she hadn't arrived here when she did, I am not sure how long it would have been before she stopped breathing altogether. Can you tell me who she is? I thought I knew everyone is this town, but I can't seem to place her face."

As if unable to speak the words, his boss remained silent. "Her name is Kasie McCarthy," Marco responded. She is from Australia and has been working here for a few years on contract in the Conservation Society. She is a marine conservation specialist here to repair the reef and damage to the foreshore."

"Oh yes!" The Doctor responded. "I have read about some of the amazing work her team has been doing here. She is one very smart woman. How did you find her like this? What happened?"

"Doctor Chris, from the Society." His boss mouthed the words as if the disgust at saying his name was almost too much for him to survive. "He did this to her, he poisoned her."

"Where is he now?" Doctor Harris asked with a real concern that was evident in her tone.

"We don't know. He got away but we will have the entire police team on the search for him soon. He won't get far before we catch him," Marco informed her.

"And the sooner you catch him, the sooner we can find out what the poison was, the blood tests may take a while to single out the particular chemicals in her body," Dr Harris explained. "We will work as fast as we can but any clues as to what it was will be exceptionally helpful."

Unable to concentrate any further on anything other than being with her, her boss stepped away from the conversation and toward her bed. He had not taken his eyes off Kasie for a second the entire time he had been at the hospital. He now just needed to touch her, hold her hand and tell her that he loved her once more.

With a knowing glance, Marco and Doctor Harris moved away from the bed to continue their conversation out of earshot.

"Doctor Harris," Marco began. "I think it best that we chat about our security measures here. I have contacted our team and expect the first shift of staff to arrive here within minutes. I think it would be helpful if we could move her to a private room. Would that be possible?"

Doctor Harris shook her head in disbelief, finally beginning to grasp the enormity of the threat to the life of her young patient. "Yes, I can move her now. I will arrange for as much privacy as possible. Luckily the hospital is quiet at the moment, so it shouldn't be a problem. Do you think this Doctor Chris will return?"

"It is impossible to say," Marco continued. "Until tonight no one would have thought that he could attempt to murder someone and I am not prepared to take any risks with Kasie. I will do anything to keep her safe."

"I am sensing that this is a very special woman. Is she a friend of yours?" Doctor Harris enquired.

"I would say she is one of my most special people I have ever met. She is the sweetest, most caring person I know," Marco expanded. "My friend on the other hand here," Marco continued, tilting his head to indicate his boss, "I think he has just had the realisation that he is in love. I think this girl is the one and my best guess is that he was planning on telling her tonight. I'm afraid he didn't get the chance to."

Marco looked toward his boss with a knowing sadness that only a true friend could feel for another. "He will be devastated if he loses her, after everything he has been through, to finally find her to lose her too, I don't know if he could cope with it," Marco added.

"We will do everything we can, firstly starting with moving her to a safer location. I will have my staff begin that now. Are you able to stay with him until we get things settled? He looks like he could use you right now" Doctor Harris suggested.

"You know me, Doctor, there is nowhere else I would be."

After settling Kasie into her private room, Doctor Harris gave the two men the reassurance that she was still stable and test results would be coming as soon as possible to tell them more.

Marco watched as his friend settled into the comfy looking lounger positioned right next to the bed. He looked on and couldn't help to think back to the terrible memories of being in this exact hospital. It was only a few years ago he watched his best friend in this same location. Sitting alongside his mother's bed watching and listening to the sounds coming from the mountains of electrical monitoring devices hooked up to her still and lifeless body.

Marco knew then that he was watching a broken man, unwilling to give up on his mother, holding her, willing her to open her eyes. The end for his mother was slow, although never gaining consciousness from the horrific car accident her body didn't want to give up.

She had always been a strong woman and her fight to survive was only testament to that, but in the end her poor body had suffered too much damage from the accident to go on. She finally stopped breathing, her heart stopped beating and the medical staff knew that they couldn't attempt to bring her back again. The mechanical sounds of the machines stopped and loved ones said their final goodbyes.

As if the town and his friend hadn't been through enough with the devastation the tsunami caused, the loss of his mother had added unbearably to their collective heartache. The waters had barely had time to reside when the news came through that on a rescue mission to the most remote part of the island both his parents had been in a horrific crash. Rescuers on hand to assist any tsunami survivors worked immediately to save his parents but only his mother could be stabilised and transported to hospital. His father, the driver of the vehicle at the time had died on impact.

Marco remembered his best friend's parents fondly. He had spent as much time in their home, the mansion as he had his own house. They had become a second set of parents to him. Much loved and respected by the town, just as their son had now become. Being the elders of the town meant they held enormous responsibility for the land and the people that called the island their home.

And when the tsunami hit, his friend's parents had wasted no time in coordinating a rescue mission to find those most at need. The people in the outlying communities who chose to live off the land and call the shoreline of this beautiful piece of the planet their own. They had headed straight to help when their car veered off the road after hitting a massive sinkhole caused by the huge waves that had devastated the coastline.

There was no doubt the father had tried to regain control of the vehicle, in a desperate effort to protect his much-loved bride. But in the end no one could save them and the small island lost two of their most loved residents in just days. Their deaths were among the few suffered as a result of the natural disaster. Fortunately, the loss of lives of others on the island was minimal. Having learned to live with the ocean, the cyclones and tsunamis in this part of the world, people were well prepared and took no time to take the necessary steps to get their families to safety as soon as the warnings began.

It was, in the end, the town itself, the old historic buildings and the beach and reef that bore the brunt of the damage. It was this rebuilding that became the focus for the small community led now by the elders' only son. He had suffered so much and taken on responsibility he had never imagined would become his so early in life.

He had lost the two people most important to him and yet remained focused to continue to do their work on his own.

For Marco to see his friend here again holding Kasie and hoping for a miracle was almost too much for him to bear. "I am going to get some coffee. Do you want some?" he asked.

"Yes, thank you." His friend turned to him for what seemed like the first time to actually acknowledge he was there. "I'm sorry Marco, I am sorry for dragging you into all of this."

"Hey, she's my friend too, you know. I love her as well. And you might want to consider giving me some bedside time too. You never know, she might want to hear the sounds of my voice and not just yours." The light-hearted response was enough to bring a short space of relief and a slight grin to the face of the two men who hadn't had much to be jovial about that night.

"Ok, so bring me a coffee and you can have some time with her. Just not too much time. I want to be here beside her when she wakes."

"Well thank you, kind sir," Marco laughed. "I'll be right back with your beverage."

Trying purposely to take a little longer away to give his friend some time alone, Marco decided to do a security check of the hospital. His team had arrived and were stationed at the entrance to the private hospital room. Only a small and dedicated group of specialists would be assigned to work with Kasie, with Doctor Harris overseeing every detail of her treatment. No one other than the staff on the pre-approved list were allowed anywhere near her room.

They were not taking any chances. Marco quietly wondered to himself if they had done the right thing, if somehow they should have attempted to secure Doctor Chris Bartlett at the same time as rushing Kasie to the hospital. He was always doing this, second-guessing himself and his actions.

It came from his time in the search and rescue and the critical analysis after every operation. He had been trained to ask himself what they could have done better? What needed to improve? Also, what did they do well? That was the part, he knew he needed to concentrate on now, the fact that they had just minutes to get Kasie to the hospital and they did it.

They managed to keep her breathing and get her stable before the Doctor said too much damage was done to her body. He tried to remind himself there would be plenty of time to deal with Doctor Chris after Kasie had recovered.

Filing his way through the hospital corridors and down the various levels until he reached the coffee shop on the ground floor, Marco realised for the first time that it was daylight outside. This meant that he and his friend hadn't had any sleep, but he hadn't even noticed and even the realisation didn't in the least bit make him feel tired.

He wondered what it would take to drag his friend away to get some rest. He laughed to himself. He could have bet an even million dollars that he couldn't get him away from that bed, he thought to himself. That didn't mean he wasn't going to try anyway.

He finally returned to the eighth-floor room that housed his two best friends, piping hot coffee in hand. As the security staff opened the door to the room, the answer to his imaginary million-dollar bet was answered.

There next to the bed asleep in his lounger was his best friend, his boss. Asleep next to him, looking more as if she was enjoying a peaceful slumber than battling a near-death experience was the love of his life, Kasie.

In between both were their two hands, his entwined in hers, holding on so tightly as if the mere act of unjoining them would awaken her from her coma. True to his word, he hadn't left her side, not now and Marco expected not ever.

TWELVE

THE BREACH

"Are you awake?" Doctor Harris gently enquired as she placed her hand on his upper arm. "I am sorry to disturb you but thought you would like some good news." On hearing those magic words, he was instantly alert. "She seems to be improving," the Doctor continued.

"We have still been unable to identify the toxins. The lab is even suggesting that it may have been something we have never seen before. We are seeking specialist consults to continue to work on this but despite this, her condition is improving. Her vitals are getting stronger. She hasn't woken yet but we hope it will be anytime now and she is breathing unassisted, which is excellent progress."

"Doctor, I cannot thank you enough, you are a miracle worker!" he replied as he jumped to his feet.

"Enough already, I told you before, you and Marco are the reason she is alive. If you hadn't bought her in so quickly she wouldn't be here. We also suspect from the device that Marco bought into the lab, that the full amount of poison hadn't been injected into her system. At a guess, either something stopped the detonation of the device or the device faulted and didn't inject the full amount. Either way, it is great news, there was enough liquid in the tracking device to.… "

"To kill a great white shark?" he finished the sentence for her.

"Well, I haven't exactly worked with sharks, but at a guess, I would think so," she agreed.

"I have been trying to piece all of this together," he continued. "The tracking device we removed from her back was a project Doctor Chris had been working on. Kasie and I hadn't liked the plan and hadn't seen the need for tracking the Great Whites for the conservation we were doing but Chris insisted that for the re-population of the sharks, we would need to know more about their movements. Where they go to breed and to feed."

"This tracking device was the same model he had shown us as a sample, but never did he mention anything about a poison to be implanted into the sharks. I have people searching the labs now but so far they haven't found anything, but I wonder if Kasie found it. I wonder if she found out what he had planned and confronted him?"

He put his head in his hands to let out a deep sigh. "Why didn't she tell me first, why go to him directly without me? This shouldn't have happened."

Doctor Harris wanted to stop his self-doubt. "From what you said she messaged you, so she knew you could help her and you did. You really can't be so hard on yourself. You and Marco, you are like two peas in a pod, more like brothers than friends. He has been doing exactly the same. What if this? What if? You can't think like that. You have to focus on what you did to save her and what you will continue to do to help her get better."

"Are you telling me she will recover, Doctor? That she will be ok?" His face, the expression of a little boy who wanted to believe but dared to get his hopes up.

"All I can say is that she is getting better. It has only been forty-eight hours, so it is still early, but all initial signs are very good," the doctor reassured him.

"I want to tell you Doctor Harris and I haven't told anyone yet, not even Marco, although I think he has guessed. But Kase, this woman here…she is the one. She is the woman I want to marry. I want her to wake up to tell her that. I tried and I didn't get the chance. I can't think of anything else other than her being ok. I don't want to. I can't imagine any other possible alternative I could live through."

Almost begging for her to understand, he looked at the Doctor with a desperate plea to make things right again.

"Sweetheart, you know what, you do just that, think of her being ok. Imagine that and only that. Talk to her and tell her you love her. I see you haven't let go of that hand," she smirked.

"You must think I am the most ridiculous person," he responded, ever so slightly embarrassed.

"I see all sorts of men in here, men meeting their babies for the very first time, men just like you scared that they will lose the partner they love and I can tell you, they act tough in the outside world, but when they enter the hospital, men will cry more than the most vulnerable of the little children I see come through here. It is nice actually, it helps to restore my faith in mankind, especially when I see the other side, and the hurt and suffering all the time."

"And am I also to understand that I am the only person in Coral Cove that now knows the answer to the billion-dollar question that has ravished this town for the last decade? Can it be that you have just told me that Kasie and you are getting married? Have you truly decided? I thought the dating component of your plan only started with your birthday. How is it that you have made a decision already?" The Doctor teased him.

"Well Doctor, when you know you know and I believe I have known for years. I just couldn't do anything about it before now," he responded with a smile.

"Well, let's get your fiancé well again then, so you can start planning the wedding of the decade. Something wonderful for this town to celebrate after all the hardship we have lived through." The Doctor paused in thoughtfulness. "Your parents would be so happy for you right now," she added, a single tear forming in the corner of her eye at the memory of her close friends, lost too early in life to watch their only son marry. Never would they get to meet their grandchildren, never enjoy their future generations of children around the table to celebrate the special holidays together. The Doctor paused imagining how pleased they would be at this news.

"The moment she opens her eyes I want her to know. I want to ask her to marry me," the young man continued to explain to his confidant.

The Doctor looked a little concerned. "Maybe you could wait a day or two, I suspect after this Kasie is going to need a long recovery and a lot of looking after. Her body is fighting hard to expel this chemical and repair itself, so she won't quite be herself for a little while. Not to plan too far ahead just yet, but is there someone who can look after her when she gets out? Nearby family or close friends? I understand she comes from Australia, so I wondered if she had any family here?"

"There is not a chance this woman is getting out of my sight. I plan to take her to my house. I have the security and staff to care for her there. I hope that will work. Can you discharge her to my care?"

The Doctor couldn't help but laugh a little. "You know what? I can't imagine anyone else she would be better looked after by. So how about you? How about you take yourself home and get some rest and care for yourself so you can be ready to take her home when she is better. You know I am here. Marco refuses the leave the building. She will be safe here with us, I promise."

"Thanks Doctor, but I can't leave her, I promised her I would stay."

Knowing there was no point in continuing her losing argument, the doctor added, "Ok, well I am going to send you up some more food. This time make sure you eat it and try to get some rest."

"Thanks again, Susan. Thanks for everything yet again."

Doctor Harris left the room and couldn't help but smile to herself at what a lovely young man he had become. Knowing his parents for as long as she did and seeing his suffering at their early deaths, she was so pleased that he had found someone to share his life with.

Her heart felt lighter for him, that after the endless tragedies he and the rest of the town had suffered, finally some good had come into his life. Now, she thought to herself, to just ensure his young love makes a full recovery. With a renewed determination she headed back to the lab for an update on the test results.

More than three days had now passed and as promised Marco had even managed to catch a few hours sleep in the Doctors quarters. Both men had been fed and were in good spirits as they waited together by Kasie's bed. The good news was that Kasie's vitals were getting stronger by the hour and the Doctor had predicted she would continue to thrive once she was awake.

"I am going to insist that you go home and get some rest, you look like shit and I don't want to be responsible for Kasie telling you to go shower because she can't stand the smell of you," Marco joked with his friend sitting together by the hospital bed.

"I am not leaving, not you nor your small army stationed outside the door will move me. Do I need to remind you that I pay your wage?" His boss replied with a sly smile.

"Oh, please do! It has been days since you reminded me that I should owe you everything," Marco laughed in return. This had been the basis of their teasing for some time. Marco worked faithfully for his friend for the offerings of a meagre salary. A salary he did not want nor need. His boss's parents had been very generous to him in their will and had left him enough money to never need to work again. Both men knew this and the joke about holding down a paid position in the mansion was just a reminder at how fortunate financially at least both of the friends were.

"Well you do, and it appears I must keep reminding you until you completely understand that you owe me. I pay your way remember?" The joking between them was never taken seriously. Marco's employer thought of him more as the brother he never had than a paid employee. The light-hearted fun was simply their way of releasing some of the previous days' tension.

"Well lucky you have me, because poor little rich boy doesn't have a whole lot of other good friends around here unless he buys them boys' toys and throws them wild parties."

"Jealousy doesn't suit you, Marco!" His friend laughed at the ridiculous content of the light-hearted debate.

A soft, weak female voice broke through the men's lively banter, "Really?" She paused, "Is this how you two behave on my death bed?" the quiet voice spoke out.

"Kase!" "Kasie!" Both men yelled out in almost perfect unison, rushing to be closer to her, to give her a kiss and hug. She smiled a huge smile at both of them, knowing that the only explanation to any of this would be that these two friends had somehow saved her life.

"How are you feeling? Don't get up! Marco, call Dr Harris!" her friend was commanding. She recognised the voice even though her eyesight was still slightly blurry. He was sounding a little nervous, anxious even, but then she probably couldn't have expected anything different given the current situation.

"I'm ok…I think. My head hurts…and my hand too. My hand is kind of numb."

A rambunctious laughter left Marco's mouth as he realised why Kasie's hand might be feeling a little painful. "He hasn't let go of your hand for three days, it is probably numb from loss of blood. You might have to sue!" He doubled over laughing at this own humour.

Kasie tried to focus her eyes on the man sitting next to her bed, his hand entwined in hers. "Yes, that hand," she giggled quietly. Have you really not let it go for three days? I can't feel it."

She paused to catch her breath. She was tired but quickly gained energy and lucidity. She giggled softly. "Do I dare ask how you have managed to use the bathroom while holding my hand? No, actually please don't tell me I really don't want to know."

"Ha-ha… hilarious. This is a story for your grandkids!" Marco roared with laughter once more.

"Marco!" His friends yelled at him, both of their hands at that moment slipping apart for the first time.

"Oops, sorry boss. Sorry Kasie, I didn't mean to scare you or anything. I let him hold your hand but I drew the line at him impregnating you while you were asleep," Marco laughed again. The relief for him that Kasie was awake well overjoyed him to the point that he couldn't contain his excitement.

"I am so glad my sickness has offered you both so much entertainment. Could one of you start explaining to me what happened and how I got here?" Kasie questioned them.

"Before that Kase, I really need to speak to you," her boss interrupted her.

Marco was quick to stop his best friend. "No, don't. Please just give the girl a minute or two would you?" Marco protested. He wasn't sure what his boss wanted to say exactly but imagined from the look on his face that it might not be the best time to overwhelm Kasie too much yet.

His protests were not met with argument by his friend who understood that he really needed to give her some more time.

Kasie's face went a very pale shade of grey. "Oh my god guys, what are you talking about? Am I dying? What is happening? Please tell me," Kasie pleaded with them.

"See what you have done now?" Marco beamed at his boss, slightly angry at his lack of patience and need for constant control over every last situation.

"Oh Marco, please tell me what is wrong?" Kasie begged her friend for an explanation.

Seeing this as an opportunity to lighten the mood, Marco leaned in to whisper in her ear. "It is just you never told me you had a hidden tattoo," he smirked as he lifted his head away. So happy that Kasie was well, Marco felt energised and playful.

Feeling just so slightly embarrassed, her face going red at the thought of the two men in her room seeing her naked. She had hoped it wasn't the case, that surely the hospital had protocols around this kind of thing. Surely, they would have made the men leave to room to undress her.

Suddenly she had two concurrent thoughts. The first was that she was wearing a hospital gown with no underwear and the second was that her boss himself admitted he hadn't let go of her hand in three days. Embarrassment set in for Kasie. She suddenly felt very shy around her two best friends.

"Again, so glad I could provide you with so much entertainment. Hey who do you have to talk to, to get some good drugs around here? My head feels like it is splitting open," Kasie asked of the two men.

"Marco, didn't I tell you to call Doctor Harris?" His boss was suddenly extremely serious and directive again. Kasie wondered what was going on between her two closest friends.

"You did boss, but I had to stay here and protect our sweet Kasie from you and your leachy hand grabbing behaviours," Marco joked back at him seemingly unaffected by his boss's demanding tone.

With that, as if on cue, Doctor Harris entered the private quarters. "I assumed from the laughter coming from the room that we had some positive progress. She turned her attention to her young patient. "Hello Kasie, I am Doctor Susan Harris. How are you feeling?"

"Tired," Kasie began, but becoming thoughtful paused and changed her answer, suddenly feeling overwhelmingly grateful to be alive, "Amazing, thankful to be here. Although trying to get any details from either of these two fools has been nearly impossible. My head is throbbing and I wondered if I could get some drugs please? I don't think I know how the rest of my body feels just yet."

"I would be happy to organise some pain relief." With that Doctor Harris pressed the alert on the remote on the bed and within seconds a friendly nurse enquired as to how she could help. "Could you get Miss McCarthy some pain relief please?"

Turning her attention back to Kasie once again the Doctor continued. "I think if we give you some time to get your bearings again, we could then explain your treatment and further recovery options."

"I thought we had sorted that, Doctor Harris. She is coming home with me as soon as possible."

Her boss had suddenly become very authoritarian again, even with the Doctor. Kasie had never seen him this directive. She had a quick flashback and remembered she had in fact seen him like this once before and it was on the night of his birthday party.

She remembered the night vividly, him refusing to take her name off The List. Him insisting that she stay the night with him, then making her promise to have drinks with him to discuss The List. All of which seemed a lifetime ago now. Again, now she found herself the focus of his assertiveness. What exactly did he say to the Doctor about her coming home with him? Kasie was feeling a bit hazy and wasn't exactly making sense of everything she was hearing.

"I would like an explanation please, but I think I need more sleep first," Kasie explained, feeling very frustrated at the lack of control she had over her current situation but also an overwhelming need to close her eyes again.

Everyone in the room including the Doctor suddenly looked very sheepish.

Doctor Harris was the first to respond. "Kasie, how about we get your pain under control first, fill in some gaps for you and worry about your discharge details after that. How does that sound?"

Kasie simply nodded. She was suddenly feeling too tired to argue with anyone anymore.

Doctor Harris continued, "Ok men, I insist that you leave the room, while my patient rests."

Interrupting the doctor before she had time to finish her instructions, her boss spoke first. "I don't want to leave her."

Doctor Harris responded, "You won't be far away, I will be the only person in here and the two of you can wait by the door."

The two men reluctantly obeyed and walked to the entrance, but not without first turning their attention to their friend, now resting peacefully, her eyes closed.

As the door closed behind the two men Doctor Harris looked at her sleeping patient, relieved that her treatment seemed to be progressing well. With a sense of relief, she lowered her head and let out a small sigh. It had been a long, tiring few days and she feared it wasn't about to quieten down any time soon. Not until the perpetrator of this vicious attack on her young patient was found.

As Marco and his best friend exited the hospital room, the two impressive guards turned their heads to greet their employers. Just as James, the larger of the two men locked hands with Marco in greeting, James's attention was diverted to his ringing mobile in his pocket. "Excuse me boss…" he said as he reached for the phone. "This could be Alex."

The men on the security detail at the hospital were numerous and spread far. Alex, an older and much trusted employee was on a mission to speak to hospital staff, finding flaws and possible access routes into the hospital. He was determined to ensure the building was on full lockdown for their special patient who needed to recover.

Marco nodded and paused to listen to await the update from Alex. Few words were exchanged, they didn't need to be for Marco could see from the look on James's face that the news wasn't good. As James ended the call and returned the phone to his pocket, he locked eyes with Marco, "I think you might need to see this."

"What is it?" their boss demanded.

"I've got it," Marco replied. "You stay here for a minute with her. I will be right back."

His boss nodded in agreement and walked back through the hospital door. If anything was wrong, he knew the one place he needed to be was right there beside his precious Kasie.

Marco and James headed toward the lift, leaving the younger of the two-man security detail, Anthony to keep watch.

"Marco…" James began as they stepped into the elevator and pushed the button for the ground floor. "There appears to have been a security breach. A pharmacist has reported a stolen security swipe." They are now assessing if anything has been stolen or…" he hesitated before adding, "…tampered with."

* * *

Back in the hospital room Doctor Harris looked up as the young lover re-entered. "I thought I was clear, that you need to let her have some rest... alone!" Doctor Harris ordered him.

"Something has happened," he replied. Marco is checking it out now. I thought it best if I stay with her for protection."

She looked into his desperate, sad, tired eyes and couldn't imagine how she could say no to his pleading. "Just please, let her rest. When she wakes, you need to let me know immediately. I will wait for the pain relief to arrive and then I will leave so the two of you can get some more sleep."

A knock on the door followed and the nurse entered with the medication. Doctor Harris, swiftly and without speaking, lifted the medication from the nurse's tray, injected the needle into the bottle and turned to inject the pain relief directly into Kasie's cannula, a procedure she had successfully performed thousands of times before in her long career.

* * *

"Tampered with?" Marco questioned from the descending elevator. His immediate thought was with Kasie and her request for drugs to assist with the pain. "No, we need to get back up to the room!"

Without delay, James was pushing elevator buttons as Marco was retrieving his phone. He promptly tapped a few numbers and placed the phone to his ear. The elevator still on its descent to the ground floor had refused to stop. The doors opened as Marco was hearing the ringing of his boss's phone but no answer. James pushed the eighth-floor button, taking the elevator on a direct route to the hospital room, much to the dismay of waiting patients and families who were hoping to enter the lift on the ground level.

As the doors closed, Marco began to feel a sense of panic and was yelling into the phone, "Answer, goddamn it! Answer your phone!"

The ringing of the phone in the quiet of the hospital room was nearly enough to push Doctor Harris over the edge. She turned her attention to the young man with enough of a sneer to let him know that she wasn't happy. The last of the pain relief entered the cannula, passing directly through to Kasie's bloodstream.

As if also disturbed by the ringing of the phone, Kasie let out a small groan. Her weak, weary body shuffled in the bed slightly until she finally settled and fell asleep again.

"Shh!" Doctor Harris demanded of him.

"Sorry," he whispered. "It's Marco. I will go outside."

"Yes, you will," the Doctor agreed with him.

As he accepted the call on his phone, he didn't immediately answer, but instead walked back outside the door so as to not disturb the sleeping patient.

Once outside, he hadn't needed to place the phone to his ear to know something was wrong.

"Boss… boss… are you there?" Marco's frantic voice rang in his ears.

"Yes, what is it?" He demanded to know immediately.

"The medication, it might have been tampered with! Has the nurse arrived back with the pain relief yet?" Marco rushed to explain his concern, his voice now echoing through the phone and down the hall as he exited the elevator and ran back toward the hospital room.

Marco arrived at the door to the room to see his boss's face turn from its normal healthy glow to a sullen, sickly shade of pale grey again. He didn't need to wait for a reply. He knew the nurse had arrived and the pain relief had been administered.

Marco ran past the security and with his boss into the hospital room. "Doctor!" he yelled. "The medication may have been tampered with."

"Oh my god." The Doctor dropped her hand to her side and faced her patient.

"How?" she demanded.

"Security was breached, we don't know for sure," Marco responded.

Doctor Harris walked toward her sleeping patient, raised her hand and felt for her pulse. The nurse who was still present began pressing buttons on the beeping machine. All looked well so far.

The Doctor remained calm but increasingly concerned as she checked her patient's breathing and spoke softly, "Kasie?"

There was no reply. "Kasie, how are you feeling?" Her tone rose as her concern for her unresponsive patient grew. "Kasie, can you hear me, can you wake up?"

Kasie was vaguely aware of someone talking to her. For the third time in the space of days, she felt that now familiar feeling of darkness creep over her. Her head was feeling fuzzy, she could hear voices but couldn't quite work out what they were saying. Her headache was intense and her head was hot, hot like it had been placed inside an open fireplace.

Her body felt heavy and faint. She could hear the voices but she couldn't reply. She wanted to say that she felt weak, hot, sick, and she wanted to vomit but her body couldn't respond…not to answer, not to move…not to do anything but fall into a deep, dark, silent sleep once more.

THIRTEEN

THE MANSION

Kasie's eyes fluttered open ever so slightly. Her head was heavy. Her body felt unyielding and painful. She tried to move her feet then her legs but nothing more than a small flex of the muscle was possible. She didn't attempt to raise her head from the pillow. The throbbing at the top of her spine and neck was unbearable. She imagined this was how it felt to be hit by a bus. Every muscle in her body was hurting.

She tried to work out where she was as she struggled to open her eyes. The room around her was bright which helped. It felt like daytime, the sun's warm rays filtered through the room. It also felt as if she wasn't alone. Her hand, she remembered her brief conversation with her two friends. Her hand, she couldn't feel her hand again. Was it him?

She struggled to open her eyes wider. She tried to turn her head toward the blurry image next to her. Who was it? Was it him? She certainly hoped so.

The image next to her wasn't moving. Was he asleep? Her companion was extremely still. Her eyes were adjusting to the light and to the room around her. She noticed colours, bright colours and furniture unfamiliar to her. She turned her head ever so slowly, trying desperately to take in her new surroundings.

She couldn't work out where she was and it didn't feel at all similar to the hospital room. She felt a slight tug on her hand. She turned her head back to the chair beside her bed. The image that began to clear in front of her was thankfully a familiar one, a very familiar one.

"Kasie," Dee said, ever so quietly. "Oh, thank God you are awake. I was so worried about you."

"Dee!" Kasie felt the tears pool in her eyes and knew she couldn't hold back this growing sense of relief as she recognised her best friend from Australia.

"Where are we?" Kasie managed to stumble the words from her dry, parched mouth.

"Shh," Dee responded. "Just rest, try not to ask too many questions. I will explain all later. Everything will be ok!"

"Oh Dee," Kasie's tears couldn't be stopped. She didn't know where she was. She didn't know what had happened to her, but she did know her lifelong friend was with her and that was all she needed.

Dee, after rising from the chair perched herself firmly on the side of her friend's bed. She wrapped her arms around her friend's slim, weak body. She stroked Kasie's hair as her tears flowed. "It's ok. It's all going to be ok," she repeated.

"I love you Dee," Kasie sputtered.

"I know Kasie, I love you too. I'm so glad you are ok. I thought I had lost you."

Kasie allowed herself to slowly fall back to sleep feeling safe and secure wrapped in the arms of her friend.

***

The next time Kasie's eyes began to open was two days later. Feeling as if she was trapped in a terrifying, repetitive nightmare Kasie tried to adjust her eyes to the room and the people around her. Unlike last time when the room around her was silent, this room was filled with chatter. "Where am I?" she began to question the people around her, still slightly out of focus.

It was a male voice that answered her this time. "Kase, you are home now," the confident voice replied.

Her head was still fuzzy as she tried to make sense of what she thought she heard. The voice she recognised but the words were confusing to her. Her head was doing a strange, slow process of formulating a response without fully understanding what she was hearing.

The words came from her mouth, quietly and with a hint of an emotion, not yet easy for her to place. "Am I at the mansion?"

The male voice and several others responded with a quiet and knowing laughter. "Yes Kase," the male voice continued, "You are home with me and you are safe here."

A rush of feelings began to emerge. Her head, her body still weak and tired were unable to process all the emotions at once. She felt the familiar tears swell behind her eyes. Had she just imagined Dee beside her? Had she dreamt of being in the hospital, a lovely older female doctor treating her pain? What was her name, she thought to herself? If only she could remember her name, she might begin to distinguish her dreams from reality.

Dee, where was Dee? Was she here in the room? She struggled to raise her head, feeling a hand behind her assisting her to try to sit up. She willed her eyes to focus, to give her some clarity and some answers to her questions.

"Kasie, try to move slowly, your body has been through hell. Don't rush it," the caring familiar female voice beside her cautioned her to take things carefully.

"Dee, is that you?" She directed all her attention to the figure beside her. Her eyes finally clearing as she took in the gorgeous image of her best friend sitting alongside her once again on the bed. "I didn't just dream you. You are here?"

"Of course, I came as soon as I heard. The private jet helped to get me here quickly of course," she added with a giggle.

"Thank you" was all Kasie could manage before the flood of tears began streaming down her face once more. Feeling increasingly mad at herself for not managing anything more than a few words and buckets of tears each time she woke, Kasie was happy to just be held again.

The comfort of her best friend gave her a renewed sense of energy and resolve. She needed answers. She wanted to know how she came to be at the mansion and what had happened to her since that horrible memory of the night at The Gaol.

She heard the familiar male voice from the corner of the room ushering people out, "Let them catch up. Please come back in a few minutes," he was instructing the attending medical staff.

Exiting out of the door, Kasie thought she recognised the faces. The other faces from her dream. "Is that the Doctor from the hospital?" Kasie asked him.

"Yes, that's Doctor Susan Harris. Do you remember meeting her? You were pretty out of it at the time," he responded.

"What happened? How did I get here?" Kasie asked.

Dee responded this time. "Lets' take some time, just rest and go slowly, everything will be explained. Ok?"

"Just tell me please, why I am here and not at the hospital?" Kasie pleaded with her friends for answers to her many questions.

Her boss addressed her question. "It was Doctor Chris, Kase. He hasn't been caught yet. He got into the hospital and tampered with the pain relief the Doctor gave you. I had no choice but to bring you here. It was the only place I could truly keep you safe."

She could never have imagined that one small statement could illicit such opposing emotions in her…fear at the thought that Doctor Chris was actually trying to kill her, and at the same time feeling safe that she knew she was in the best place possible for now.

"Thank you!" she replied.

"And Kase, there is one more thing I need to tell you," he continued.

"No!" Dee interrupted. "Not now, she just woke up."

He bowed his head, almost as if ashamed of his actions. But what could he have done to ever feel guilty of, Kasie wondered? This man had saved her life, and not just once but by the sounds of it, multiple times. She owed this man her life. She wanted to let him speak to say whatever he felt was needed to be said.

"It's ok, please continue," Kasie prompted him. How could she deny this man anything he wanted after all he had done for her?

His face lit up as his eyes met hers. Although feeling weak and without any energy, her body still managed to respond with that nervous feeling in the pit of her stomach and the rush of heat to her face as she was beginning to notice lately whenever he was this close to her. He smiled at her. His wide, beautiful, sexy smile beamed with radiance glowing through his eyes.

People say that you can smile with your eyes and this is what she had seen him do to her so often in the last three years she had known him. More so lately, she thought to herself. His smile lit up his deep, gorgeous green eyes. His face so perfect, so inviting. His lips so irresistible, bringing back to her such vivid memories.

As she looked at his lips waiting for his mouth to move as he continued to speak, she remembered their kiss. From her memory she replayed their kiss in his office then later in his bedroom. Her mind started to wander back to the taste of his mouth on hers, his body against hers. She might have been mere days recovering from a near death experience but that didn't stop her body responding to this gorgeous man in front of her.

She didn't even realise she was beginning to smile as Dee's voice broke through her fantasy thoughts. "No, I insist, you will let the Doctor back in and we will talk… alone…outside." The last three words paused for added effect obviously held some hidden meaning, meant just for the two of them.

Kasie had never heard Dee so forceful in her life. This was her best friend, the girl who had partied with her through the later years of high school. Never caring as much about grades as she did about watching the guys play basketball at lunchtime or planning the next big party when her parents went away for the weekend. Kasie wondered why Dee was all of a sudden ordering the man she called Prince Charming out of the room, out of his room in his very own home.

Kasie feared that her two friends were maybe not getting along. Strange, she thought. She had actually held the belief that Dee had a bit of a crush on their friend. What woman didn't really? When Dee had come to visit her previously, she was amazingly eager to meet the man Kasie had been talking about in her long phone calls back home.

She saw the minute that Dee met him, that she was just as affected as every other woman in Coral Cove with this gorgeous specimen of a man. She almost thought Dee might find some reason to stay, try her luck against the hundreds of other women who wanted to make this bachelor their very own.

Kasie wondered why there was now this tension between them and what in the world they would have to talk about alone. Her mind was racing with possibilities. What if he had fallen in love with Dee? What if during this time she had been unconscious her two friends had, through their combined concern for her, found the support and comfort in each other and fallen in love. Stranger things had happened. And it would be just like Dee to fall in love with such romance movie style. She was never one for convention.

Kasie caught herself in her thoughts and felt incredibly selfish for begrudging either of these wonderful people anything but happiness. They are both amazingly generous people with a lot of love to share. Good on them if they had found each other. Kasie's head was telling her one thing. She wasn't sure why her heart was feeling something so very different.

"She's right. We can talk later," her boss's voice interrupted her thoughts. He leant down and placed a soft and delicate kiss in the middle of her forehead. He placed his mouth beside her ear and whispered, "I'm so glad you are ok, I've missed you, we will talk soon."

Her heart sunk. He had all but confirmed her thoughts. A kiss on the forehead wasn't really what she was expecting. Not what she had been fantasying about as she had looked at his smiling face and his seductive lips. She felt so stupid, how could she be fantasising about this man who had clearly fallen for her best friend. She felt ashamed of herself.

"It's all ok, whatever you want to say, it's all ok with me," she replied, hoping that her words came out more sincerely than they sounded in her head.

"Good," he replied with a cheeky grin. "That is good to hear. Rest up. I will let Doctor Harris in." He stood up and headed for the door.

Kasie turned her attention to Dee who appeared to actually have steam coming out of her ears, reminiscent of the cartoons from her childhood. Dee didn't look happy. She hoped she hadn't done something to upset her. She didn't know what to say.

Dee faced Kasie and placed her hand ever so gently on top of hers. "You just rest. I will take care of your friend."

That's what I'm worried about. Kasie thought to herself, but didn't dare to utter the words out loud. With that, Dee stood up and headed toward the door, quickly catching up to her generous host.

What came next was like a bolt of lightning striking straight through the door to the bedroom and onto her still tired body. A mad rush of sounds, yelling and activity followed. The mad rush of hype and activity had a name. Its name was Marco.

Like a small kid who had just been released from school for the start of his summer holidays, Marco ran through the door, past his boss and her best friend and straight toward the bed. "Kasie! I can't believe you are awake!" he screamed as he ran toward the bed.

"You thought I would remain in this bed in a comatose state forever?" Was all Kasie could manage to reply. "You gave up on me pretty quickly didn't you then?"

Marco had made it to her bedside in record time, leaving behind two scornful faces looking at him with a strange mix of distaste and humour. One of which appeared to be the Doctor, obviously waiting outside and expecting to be the next person to approach Kasie's bedside.

The Doctor now standing at the entrance to the bedroom, hands on her hips with the face of an annoyed headmistress about to scorn her favourite student. "Marco," she demanded, "I told you she needed rest and you could see her later!"

"No Doc, sorry," he argued. "I had to see my girl!" Marco assumed the position on the edge of the bed recently vacated by his boss, who was now standing in the doorway looking just a hint annoyed by the unscheduled intrusion. "How are you, Kasie?" Marco asked with genuine concern.

"I am feeling surprisingly good, I think," she replied with some hesitation.

"I missed you so much. I was worried about you. I thought we had lost you," Marco continued.

"Well, you should have had more faith Marco, a little poison isn't going to stop me."

"That's what I wanted to hear, Kase. So, when are you going to be ready to join me for a cocktail and a dip in the pool? I have earned some time off recently," he smirked, looking directly at his boss in a way that was asking but at the same time telling him this request was a non-negotiable.

"Um, well let's just wait and see what the Doctor says," Kasie answered.

"Yes indeed, and if the Doctor could get to her patient that would also help her progress I should think," Doctor Harris was humorous but directive in her response to the unfolding situation she found before her. She couldn't in anyway begrudge the warm embraces these friends shared. She had seen a lot of situations unfold in her years of work in the emergency department but not often had she witnessed this much love and concern in one room. She smiled knowing that the future for these friends whatever it held was one of support and unconditional love for each other.

"Yeah, ok," Marco gave up in defeat. "Just know, that I missed you and I love you and I won't let anything happen to you again. Understand?" Marco added.

Kasie felt the tears well up again, but needed to answer before the waterfall of her emotions began streaming down her face once more. "Yes, Marco, I love you too! And thank you for everything. I don't know how I can thank you enough."

Marco smirked and gave Kasie a wink before he replied. Always one to add the humour to a serious situation he couldn't help but want to lighten the intense mood in the room. "Well maybe we can work something out baby?"

"That's enough Marco!" His boss yelled at him. "Let her get some rest!"

His sudden outburst witnessed by everyone in his presence. His tone and the instant anger behind them a surprise to both Kasie and Dee. It was obvious to everyone that the last few days and the near loss of his friend had caused a great deal of strain on him.

"Ah don't worry about him. He's just jealous," Marco continued seemingly without a care in the world about his boss's sudden jealous turn. "You, me baby and a cool cocktail." Marco was intent on having his fun and in turn brighten up the recovering Kasie's day. He didn't need to worry about the orders barked at him by his best friend. There was never any malice in them. There had never been nor would be, he imagined, any real reason for them to disagree. He had utter confidence that he could continue this foreplay with Kasie and provoke his boss without a single consequence other than emotional release for them all.

"Marco!" Dee yelled at him, suddenly assuming her turn to bark orders at their lively and energetic companion. She had witnessed enough and although she had learnt much more about the friendship the three of her friends shared, she was still somewhat unclear as to the extent of the banter that they would each endure from the others.

"That sounds like fun," Kasie replied, suddenly feeling like she wanted to be part of the antagonistic enjoyment Marco was having with the others. She embraced the moment and was relieved to be having a little bit of fun at her boss's expense.

It was the Doctor's turn to speak her mind. She had waited patiently and really just wanted to check on her patient and allow her to get back to her life as quickly as possible. "I am all for a nice cocktail after what we have all been through, but let's just wait until our patient has had her vitals checked should we?" Doctor Harris interjected.

"Bye Marco, love you too baby," Kasie couldn't resist to add, flirting just a little for her friends' benefit. She let Marco lean down and kiss her forehead then watched as he took to his feet and walked toward his boss and Dee.

As all three friends exited the bedroom and closed the door, Doctor Harris was finally able to make her way to the bed to check on her patient. "You do look surprisingly well, considering what you have been through Kasie. How are you feeling?"

"Actually, good Doctor Harris. I am starting to feel much better. I think having those three around me has helped me more than anything. I know that seems hard to believe."

The doctor continued her line of questioning while at the same time taking Kasie's vitals, pulse, blood pressure, temperature and checking the readings on the endlessly beeping machines around her. "You know what Kasie," the Doctor continued. "You are actually doing really well. You are recovering much better than I could ever have hoped for."

"Ok, so maybe it is time for you to tell me what the hell happened to me," Kasie requested.

"That I will do. Where should I start?" the willing Doctor replied.

"Start at the moment he phoned you to ask you to help me. I can only imagine that is where it all began."

"Correct, I was already at the hospital when I got the call. You know him well then?" the Doctor questioned.

"I know him well enough to know that he was the only person who could save me."

The Doctor couldn't agree more. "Well your good judgement saved your life. Him and Marco both, you know that those two men, they would have done anything to get you better. You really must have made quite an impression on both of them."

Kasie didn't know how to answer, not now, not when she had realised that she wasn't the only one who had managed to make an impression on the town's most eligible bachelor. A tinge of something rose in her chest. It wasn't jealousy, she thought to herself but more a sense of loss. But how could that be? How could she feel a sense of loss over someone who wasn't even hers to begin with?

After all, she had chosen to take her name off The List. Leaving herself unable to date him, ineligible to ever actually have a relationship with him let alone become his wife. How stupid she suddenly felt at the realisation that she was feeling sad about losing the man she never even had in the first place.

She felt more than a little guilty to feel bad that she had lost him to her best friend. The woman she loved most in the world, the woman who she would most want in the world to have her happily ever after, her fairytale ending.

She needed to distract herself from these selfish thoughts. "Sorry Doctor, I wasn't listening, would you please continue, what happened after you got the phone call?" Kasie focused all her attention to take in the details of the emergency room dash and treatment, including the very harsh reality that Doctor Chris had taken even further steps to try to end her life.

* * *

In the large open hallway outside the bedroom stood Kasie's three friends. The tall, dark-haired boss looking angrily at Marco as if expecting some explanation for his erratic and out of character behaviour. Marco staring back at him, without a care in the world now that Kasie was alive and well. And finally, ready to confront the men for the truth, the newest member of the foursome, Dee.

Dee stood staring angrily at both of the two men. Barely able to contain her frustration at their testosterone driven teenage angst type behaviour, Dee was the first to speak. "Well I hope you are both pleased with yourself. The Doctor asked you both to take it easy on her and here you are acting like jealous adolescents."

"Do you want to explain what that was, Marco?" His boss was quick to add. He wanted to get clear with Marco that he expected things to run exactly as he instructed. No deviation and no impromptu recovery plans that involved Kasie.

"Hold on here boys!" Dee interrupted him with more than just a tone of sarcasm. "You both need to explain to me what is going on here and convince me why I shouldn't just put Kasie on the first flight home as soon as she is possibly well enough to catch a plane?"

Sensing defeat unless he admitted the truth, the mansion owner was the first to respond. He didn't want to be misunderstood. He wanted Dee to understand completely and fully his feelings for Kasie. He couldn't bear the thought of Kasie leaving him, not now, not ever.

He took a moment to consider the right words. He had only admitted his true feelings to two people. Doctor Phoenix, who had known for some time the extent of his feelings for Kasie and now Doctor Harris. He swallowed before beginning to speak.

"I am in love with her. I am going to ask her to marry me. That is why you can't take her away from me."

Dee had figured out as much. She had seen how he looked at her. She guessed it from her last visit here. She had guessed that although Kasie saw the two men as great friends that at least one of them had feelings for her that went far beyond a traditional friendship.

She recalled that every time she got a call home, Dee half expected to hear Kasie tell her she was staying in Coral Cove for good. She had waited to hear that Kasie and the gorgeous boss had started dating and that she realised she loved him more than just a friend.

But each conversation was about the latest party she had been to at the Mansion, or how she had stayed and watched sports with the two men, or beat them in games of pool, taking their money or whatever dare they had chosen to gamble on that night.

She had questioned Kasie's feelings towards both men and had no doubt that Kasie would be honest with her if she felt something for either of them. Dee guessed this was the thing he needed to talk to Kasie so desperately about. She had guessed since she had been back, that this man was feeling more than just mere friendship for Kasie.

This was a man who despite his growing empire, his town to manage, the reef to restore and the endless social commitments he had scheduled had not left Kasie's side. This was a man who sat by the side of the bed of the woman he loved, not letting go of her hand, hardly sleeping, not eating, not leaving her safety and wellbeing to anyone else. This was a man who loved a woman deeply and forever. Dee had so many questions she hardly knew where to begin.

"Does Kasie feel the same?" Dee questioned him.

Marco could sense how difficult this was for his boss to discuss. He wasn't someone who was all that comfortable with disclosing his feelings. Without giving his boss the chance to answer and hoping secretly to get him off the hook from what he imagined was going to be a detailed interrogation from Dee, Marco responded with his normal wit and humour.

"Well Dee, it's like this. If she doesn't want him… she can always have me!"

Dee was taken aback by the confession of love by Marco. "Wow, some girls have all the luck, don't they?" She giggled in reply. She knew Marco was joking. She guessed that he was trying again to lighten a serious situation with humour, but at the same time she imagined there was some truth behind the words that he spoke. She saw his confession of love as a kind of cathartic release.

Marco suddenly saw the hurt in Dee's eyes. He knew well enough lately what it felt like to be a third wheel. Around two people who although they might not be able to admit it, were falling deeply and madly in love. He didn't mean at all to place Dee in any discomfort.

"Now, now, don't be like that," Marco added, raising his arm and placing it gently on Dee's shoulder as he turned her around and began to walk her down the hallway. He figured it would be best to give his boss some time alone with Kasie. He thought he would do the appropriate thing as a host and entertain Dee to give the others some time alone.

And if he was going to be honest with himself, he wouldn't mind at all spending a bit of alone time getting to know this smart mouthed, strong willed Aussie.

"You know what Dee? I know I am no Prince Charming, but I am a pretty good cook. I do make delicious cannelloni or would you prefer a prawn linguini, being from Australia and all?" He turned to glance at his boss. He had hoped the reference to the nickname he hated so much had stirred him up just a little. He waited for a response that didn't come from his stubborn friend.

Feeling flattered by the sudden attention, Dee laughed. "The cannelloni sounds good to me." She didn't know why Marco had all of a sudden taken an interest, but to be honest she was more than willing to get some time away from this madhouse to get some rest with maybe a drink or two to help her unwind.

"Great, dinner at my place then. Are you ready now? Or would you like some time to grab some clothes? I have a great hot tub so don't forget your swimwear... or not!" he teased her gently.

His boss was grateful for the impromptu intervention. He knew exactly what Marco was doing and planned to thank him personally for it later. "Who have you turned into Marco?" his boss demanded to know, "The Hugh Hefner of Coral Cove?"

"No mate, I leave that to you," Marco laughed. "And we will also leave you to spend some time with your girl. We will be back tomorrow." He looked at Dee, "Only if that is ok with you?"

Dee smiled at the thought of some alone time with Marco. He was proving to be most entertaining and the thought of some down time after everything they had been through was very attractive to her. "I could use a cocktail and a spa after all of this. Sounds great to me," Dee replied.

Marco was secretly pleased. He was looking forward to returning to his home even just for a few hours. "See you, boss, take good care of our girl!" Marco added with a smirk as he led Dee down the hallway.

Suddenly alone, he turned his attention back to the bedroom door and the woman he loved. He knew he had a desperate urge to tell her everything and to let her know that she was the only woman for him. That, in fact, she always had been. That he had known for a long time, even since the day he met her that she was the one for him. But Dee had asked him the pertinent question - how did Kasie feel about him?

His greatest fear through all of this wasn't that he would lose her. He never let that thought become a reality in his head. Instead he just focused on her getting better. And once better, as soon as she was able to talk to him again, he needed to tell her. He desperately needed to let her know that she was the only woman for him. That he wanted her to become his wife.

A sudden terror crept into his consciousness. What if she said no? What if she didn't feel the same way about him? He knew she loved him as a friend, she had told him that often enough, just as she had told Marco and Dee.

Kasie was a loving, caring person and a person capable of making deep connections with others. A person, he thought you could describe as having a good heart. She had taught him that not long after she first met him. Something she had learnt from her travels, the concept of good heart, bad heart.

Kasie had told the story of sitting in a bar in Thailand and chatting to the working girls, of them telling stories of the men who had paid for their company. Some of their stories were horrific; of tourists they described as scarily creepy, others who were kind to them. Taking them out for meals and sightseeing and helping them and their families out financially. Some men even coming back year after year to visit their favourite worker, each time bringing with them some money or clothes or presents for the women and their families.

These women, Kasie had told him knew men better than anyone else. These were women whose very lives depended on making smart decisions. On making decisions to work out which men might be kind to them and which may hurt them. So, when Kasie heard them talk about the concept of good heart, bad heart she fully believed that they had formulated a philosophy that she could believe in.

It was on one of their quiet nights playing pool with her friends that Kasie shared her travel story and shared her belief in the philosophy of good heart, bad heart. He knew straight away, even if Kasie herself didn't that when she described a good heart, she was describing herself. He knew that this was a woman who could love with all her heart, her family, her friends, maybe even one day him, if he was fortunate enough.

He needed to talk to her, he couldn't wait a second longer to tell her how he felt. He headed back towards the bedroom door.

FOURTEEN

THE DAYBED

He knocked twice and waited for the Doctor's reply. "Come in."

He turned the handle on the door suddenly feeling quite terrified at what was about to happen. What if she didn't feel the same way? He couldn't get the thought out of his head. He tried to squash the fear to the deep recesses of his brain as he turned the handle.

He pushed the door open and entered the bedroom. To his surprise, the bed was empty. The Doctor was sitting in the far corner of the room writing in what appeared to be a medical file. Apart from the Doctor, the room was empty.

"Where is she?" he asked, concerned about the very sudden vacancy in the bed.

"Actually, you may not believe this, but she is taking a shower," the Doctor replied.

What felt like the stresses of days of worry that had formed a permanent frown on his face turned into a smile and an overwhelming sense of relief at the recovery of their precious patient.

"So, she really is ok then?" His question was more of a plea for good news than a legitimate question needing a response.

The Doctor nodded. "I believe so. I have taken more blood and will have that analysed but from what I can see her vitals are good, she is feeling well, although obviously very tired and weak still. She is well on the way to making what seems to be a full recovery.

"How Doctor? How is this possible? No long-term side effects? No permanent damage from the toxins?" he begged to know more detail.

"It is simply too early to tell any of that. All I can say for now is that she is feeling good, she looks well and she wants to go outside for some fresh air. Do you think you could help her with that?" the Doctor asked with what appeared to be a bit of a playful smirk on her face.

"I believe I can!" he replied and with that marched toward Susan, reached down and pulled her out of her chair and gave her the longest, strongest and most enjoyable hug she'd had in years.

"Thank you, Doctor. Thank you for everything. I don't know how I can repay you. Anything you want I will provide. Anything the hospital needs, I will do everything I can to make it happen. I will never be able to thank you enough!"

The Doctor tore herself away from her gracious host. "You already give us everything we need. You and your family have always been incredibly generous. I am just glad I could do something for you in return. I am relieved she is feeling well. I trust that you will continue to keep her safe and cared for?"

"I have security here around the clock, she is safer here than anywhere else in the world and I will endeavour to keep her here for as long as Chris is out there."

"Good to hear. I am going to leave her for the night, but the nursing staff are staying on a round the clock roster until we decide otherwise, just in case there is anything she needs.

They will also need to check her vitals and they have enough safe pain relief, should she want anything. I am on call and you know how to reach me. Call me if her condition deteriorates in any way. Let her rest… please…I can't emphasise that enough. She needs to rest to fully recover," the doctor pleaded with him for understanding and compliance to her instructions.

"I will," he replied, his head bowed. He knew he needed to help her recover but also didn't want to waste another minute before he told her how he felt for her.

"But?" the Doctor enquired. "I sense a but coming at the end of that statement."

"I want to tell her that I have made my decision. I need to tell her that The List doesn't matter anymore and that I want her to be my wife."

The Doctor paused for a moment reflecting on her response to his plea for support. "You know what I think?" The Doctor replied. "Only you can make the decision about when is the right time to tell her that. I wish I could say don't do it, but after everything the two of you have been through, I don't feel like I should be advising you against it. Just do what feels right but give her time to think about it. It might come as a bit of a shock to her, especially after all of this."

He imagined the Doctor knew more than she was letting on, "What has she said to you doctor?"

"You know I can't say anything to you about our conversations and really we didn't talk about you. I just get a sense that she cares very deeply about you and that she knows you care about her as well."

He took the advice. He knew that it made sense. "Take care, Susan and good night. Thank you again for everything."

"Sleep tight sweet boy. Rest up yourself. I will see you in the morning." He watched as the Doctor gathered her things and closed the door quietly behind herself.

He settled himself into the chair the Doctor had just vacated and waited for Kasie to emerge from the bathroom. He didn't have to wait long. The bathroom door opened and there she was, the woman who he hoped would someday soon become his wife. She looked beautiful. Her long blonde hair was still slightly damp from her shower. Her bare face looked fresh and youthful again for the first time in days. The colour had returned to her cheeks. His Kasie had returned to him.

She was dressed in her favourite pair of loose grey Sea Shepherd pants and a white t-shirt. This woman looked sexy in anything she wore. As if reading his mind, she interrupted. "I'm sorry but I dressed for comfort rather than glamour tonight."

He smiled as he took her in. "You look beautiful, you look so well. How are you feeling?" He enquired.

"Actually, really good, I feel tired but actually well and maybe even a little bit hungry I think."

"I can fix that," he replied eagerly. He had confidence that his house staff would be more than happy to make something for the woman they knew was recovering in the bedroom upstairs. Should I ask Helen to make something for you? She has been asking every hour if you are ok and if she can make something to assist with your recovery.

"Only if she is still working. I don't want to disturb her if she has finished for the day."

"You know what Kase? If I don't ask her to make something, I will fear every bite I taste for the next year may have been tainted as if to punish me for my negligence. And it is still early enough. She hasn't finished for the day just yet. Let me call her now. But can I ask you something?"

"Sure, ask anything." There was nothing Kasie wouldn't do for the man who saved for life.

"You don't seem surprised to see me here. Were you not expecting the doctor?"

"Not at all. I told the doctor to go home and get some rest and I asked her to invite you in. You know, just in case I needed some help. Plus, she hesitated for just a second. I need to talk to you alone."

He couldn't help but smile, a wide grin from ear to ear at the thought that she too felt something and wanted to speak to him as well.

"But you can stop with all that grinning! I said talk! Nothing more. Nothing less. I just wanted some time alone with you."

"Well I am sorry if my grin offends you Kase," he said as he rose from his seat and moved closer to her. "But those were the most magical words I have ever heard and there is no wiping this smile from my face. I will call Helen, while you finish getting ready."

It was her turn to grin. "Sorry to disappoint you, but for tonight this is as good as it gets, no make-up, no heels, my nails desperately need a manicure and I imagine no amount of tinted moisturiser can make this skin look any less pale or translucent right now."

"Maybe you look like a woman who was nearly dead only a few days ago."

"Gee thanks Prince Charming, but that's not exactly how a woman likes to be described," she laughed.

"Please don't tell me you are calling me that too. It is the most humiliating nickname a man could ever receive. You know I'm not a fan of it."

"Well, what would you like me to call you?" Kasie enquired.

"Um, my name," he responded immediately as if it was the most obvious of answers.

Kasie smiled. "I think I am liking Prince Charming more right now," she giggled a little as she teased him. "So, what do you think I need to do to prepare for dinner with a real-life Prince? A change of clothes? A little lip-gloss? A bit of tan wouldn't go astray right now either I imagine," she added.

He stepped close again, close enough to touch her hands and hold them in his own. Close enough to look her in the eyes, to have that same effect on her stomach. He made her skin feel absolutely electric to his touch.

As his eyes met hers, he spoke softly and slowly. "You will always be perfect to me just the way you are."

She snatched her hands away surprising both of them with the abruptness of her response.

"Did I say something wrong?" he looked worried.

"I'm sorry, I just…I'm not sure. I just feel tired I guess." She wasn't ready to begin the conversation just yet. She needed some fresh air. She would continue this difficult discussion with him when they were outside.

"How about I have some food bought up to us then? We can talk here."

"No," she responded without hesitation. "It looks like we might just catch the sun setting and you know me, I always prefer the outdoors, I need some air. Can we eat by the pool and chat there?"

"Perfect!" he said in a way that made her wonder about what he might be referring to.

"Is that your favourite word for tonight then?" She teased him.

"I should think so," he responded with a wry smile. He couldn't imagine a more perfect outcome to the days that had preceded them. The woman he loved was alive and well. She seemed to be recovering at an incredible pace and hadn't expressed any discomfort with being moved into the mansion. He was now for the first time in a long time alone with Kasie and preparing to confess his profound love for her. She took his hand and began to make their way to the ground level pool area.

No sooner had they settled on the largest daybed by the pool then Helen arrived with their meal. "Since when do you do poolside deliveries, Helen? Was there no one to help you?" he asked his loyal staff member.

"Please. I needed to check on my girl. How are you sweetie? You look really well," Helen asked as she turned her attention toward Kasie.

"Much better thank you Helen." And Kasie honestly knew she wasn't lying. She hadn't felt this normal in more than a week. "Hey," Kasie suddenly remembered, "Shouldn't you be on a holiday in Tahiti right now?"

"Plenty of time for that," Helen answered quickly in what seemed like a poor attempt to avert the attention away from herself.

Kasie looked at Helen's boss for further explanation and he was quick to oblige. "When Helen heard you would be coming back to the house to stay, she refused to go on her holiday, saying instead that she needed to be here to help look after you," he explained to Kasie.

Kasie felt like crying. "That is so sweet," she said. "But I feel terrible, for being the reason you have missed your holiday."

"She hasn't missed it. I will ensure that she takes her holiday and this time I am sending her away for a month." Their boss was most direct in his decision and planning for leave for one of his most valued staff members.

"I will come back like some real housewife looking woman, all tanned up and dressed up in the latest fashions," Helen giggled. "He is giving me spending money as well you know."

Kasie smiled. "Well you deserve every bit of it," she added, feeling relieved that she hadn't been the cause of Helen missing her much-deserved luxury break.

Staring back down at the food, Helen continued, "We did some research and found out that the best food for your recovery is simply cooked organic vegetables, so I went out today to the organic market and have made you some sautéed asparagus, some grilled field mushrooms stuffed with spinach and fetta, some of my own home-grown tomatoes and some freshly baked sourdough with garlic and olives. Oh, and some lemon infused water and green tea. Some of your favourites I think."

"You are amazing, Helen! And you have made me even hungrier. Thank you so much!" Kasie was overwhelmed with the thoughtfulness from her companion's much-loved staffer. Helen had been running the catering and housekeeping functions of the expansive mansion for years. Over this time, learning exactly how he enjoyed his meals and learning quickly how to cater for his numerous celebrations. In doing so Helen had become quite the entertainer and the ever-present young company around her had given her a new excitement for entertaining again.

"It is my pleasure dear. I am just so relieved that you are well and happy to hear you are staying with us. When you are feeling better, we can have a bit of a menu planning session, so I can make sure I have all of your favourite meals here for you."

Helen appeared genuinely pleased at the prospect of a new full-time houseguest and a female one at that. It wasn't that she didn't enjoy the company of her employer and Marco. She did of course love the energy and playful banter that they exuded, but she did rather relish the thought of having a woman around the house once again on a more permanent basis.

Kasie politely replied, "Thanks again Helen. We can chat more tomorrow maybe." Feeling a little confused at the planning going into her apparent extended stay, she was determined to find out for herself what others seem to know that she somehow didn't about her residency at the mansion.

"Good night to the both of you. Take good care of her, boss," Helen added before she left them alone again and made her way back into the now dark and quiet dwelling.

"Well?" Kasie began as soon as Helen had walked from earshot. "Do you want to explain what she meant by staying with us?"

"Ok, before you start yelling at me, please let me explain," her friend replied.

"Please do," Kasie crossed her arms as a show of seriousness and waited for the words that would explain the obvious miscommunication.

"I just let Helen know that you needed some time to recover and that I had hoped you would stay here to get well again. Here where you have people to look after you and care for you," he tried desperately to explain.

"I would imagine I could also recover in the comfort of my own home, wouldn't you?" Kasie challenged him.

"What about Doctor Chris? He knows where you live?" Her companion quickly reminded her of the very serious danger waiting for her outside the walls of the secured estate.

The reminder of Doctor Chris and his very real attempts to take her life jolted her back to reality for a moment. "Point taken, but only for tonight," she replied despairingly. The thought of Doctor Chris lurking around her house was too much to think about. "As soon as it is safe, I will return home, but for now, I can't thank you enough for everything you have done for me. I don't think I will ever be able to repay you for absolutely everything I have put you through."

"Kase, can we talk about you staying here? And by that, I mean staying here permanently?"

Kasie was taken aback by the bold and seemingly out of context suggestion. She had no idea why there would be any need for her to stay at the mansion beyond a few days. "I think we have other things to talk about, don't' you?" Kasie replied.

"That we do," he agreed with her. "May I start please? There is something important I have been needing to say to you."

"Please," she interrupted him. "You don't need to, I already know."

He was more than a little surprised to think that Kasie might already know about his plan to propose. He was outraged at the thought that someone had told her his plans before he had a chance to do so himself. His immediate attention went to whom that could have been. He first thought was Doctor Harris. He had told Doctor Harris his plans. Doctor Harris also had time with Kasie alone, but it didn't make sense. She wouldn't say anything to Kasie surely. She was a professional and a loyal friend of his family. He doubted she would have said anything out of context.

Marco was also a suspect, although he couldn't imagine his best friend betraying him like that. He wouldn't say anything to her, plus he hadn't had a moment alone with her since all of this had happened.

His mind lapsed back to the conversation in the hallway only a short time ago. He wondered how serious Marco was when he told Dee that he would be interested in a relationship with Kasie if she would have him, but he couldn't believe that was possible. His jealousy was getting worse by the day. He recognised that for himself. He needed to keep it in check.

His mind then turned to Dee. He hadn't told Dee that he was planning to ask Kasie to marry him but yet she wasn't at all surprised when he did disclose. They had spent many hours by Kasie's bedside. He guessed it wouldn't have taken a psychic to work out that he had some very strong, very real feelings for her friend.

"I imagine Dee has told you already then?" he asked his friend, still waiting not so patiently for a response from her.

Kasie swallowed hard. He had just confirmed himself, her worst fears. She tried to stop her stomach from doing somersaults. Don't be ridiculous, she instructed herself silently. She shouldn't be resentful or upset that her best friend had potentially fallen for the adorable bachelor. She needed to get her head clear on this, she should be happy for them both.

She felt nothing but love and respect that he had decided to take this time alone to tell her the truth. To be the first to tell her the truth that he had fallen in love with her best friend, Dee.

The vague but not so distant memory of their own intimate encounters from just days earlier came streaming back into her mind. She felt guilty at the thought of what they had done. It was innocent really, just two friends blurring the boundaries a little. She had never intended for it to happen but now she felt remorse and wondered if Dee knew about their behaviour at the party.

Kasie began to put the pieces together. The storyboard she had begun to build in her head was that her boss in the last few days had fallen in love with her best friend. She really was immensely pleased for both of them. Or at least she was trying to be.

"She didn't need to tell me, it was obvious. I know you have tried to tell me already and I truly thank you for that. You really don't owe me an explanation and I really am overjoyed for you."

"Overjoyed for me?" He questioned her. "Or do you mean overjoyed for us?"

"Yes, you are right I am sorry. I am happy for both of you."

It was now his turn to feel totally confused. "Kase, I am not sure we are having the same conversation here."

"I don't think we really need to discuss this any further," Kasie was quick to shut him down. "I understand how you feel, I am happy for you both. I love you both. I really am pleased that you have found the woman that you want to share your life with."

He felt his frustration reach boiling point. What the hell was she talking about and why wouldn't she let him just say what he wanted to say? It was hard enough to speak the words that had been ruminating in his head for months, years even, but now he wasn't even being given the opportunity to tell her how he felt in his own words.

He was feeling frustrated beyond belief. He couldn't wait another second. He reached out his hand to the side of her face and gently placed his hand on her cheek. Connecting with her, his eyes looking directly into hers and without a word he bent down, closed his eyes and kissed her.

Kasie was shocked beyond words. What was he doing? What the hell was he doing…to Dee?

"Stop!" Kasie insisted as she pulled her mouth away from his. "What are you doing?"

"Kissing you, or at least trying to." His answer was serious yet playful.

"But you can't kiss me, I can't do that to Dee. You shouldn't do that to Dee. Where is Dee anyway? Why isn't she here?"

His head had started to hurt. She was making his head spin with her ramblings. He wondered if the others had been correct. He wondered if it was indeed too soon to tell her. Maybe she just needed more rest as the Doctor had instructed.

"Kase, Dee is fine. She is with Marco right now, in his hot tub, probably enjoying a cocktail."

"What? Why? Why would she be with Marco?" Kasie felt confused beyond words. She had started to feel as if she didn't understand a thing that was going on in her mind. The constant confusion was exhausting her.

"Why not? He is actually a pretty good catch you know. Not as good as me in case you have any ideas of course, but still a decent guy. She could do a lot worse," her friend offered by way of explanation.

"Stop!" Kasie yelled with frustration. "Back up a bit. Are you telling me that you and Dee aren't in love? That she is with Marco?"

It was all he could do not to laugh. "Dee and I? Kase what are you talking about? There is no Dee and I."

"But you said that you needed to tell me something and she stopped you and she said that she needed to talk to you, and you… you? I don't know any more what's going on." Kasie paused, obviously overwhelmed with confusion. "And why the hell is she spending the night with Marco?"

"Kase, please tell me that last question was not you being jealous about Marco? That would be just too much for me to handle tonight?"

"No, of course not! I love Marco and I love you," she tried to reassure him. "I just feel confused and tired. It's overwhelming."

Kasie thought for a moment longer, trying to piece together the events that had unfolded before her. "What were you and Dee disagreeing about? What was it you wanted to tell me that Dee wouldn't let you? I just don't understand anything at the moment."

"Understand this!" And with that he again raised his hand gently to her face, lowered his mouth onto hers and kissed her. His kiss was a sweet combination of frustration, desperation and passion. He kissed her as if he wouldn't last another second without kissing her.

And this time, she didn't stop him. This time she allowed herself to fully embrace every tantalising touch of his warm, sweet lips against hers. She enjoyed his tongue finding hers in her mouth and flirting delicately with it.

She relished his strong hands on her, one now making its way down her body and stopping at the curb of her back, the other moving from her cheek, brushing through her hair on its way to the back of her neck where it supported her head. She gave in to her body as it slowly collapsed onto the sunbed. She didn't want this kiss to end, she didn't want to think about Dee or Marco or Doctor Chris or even Miss Helen who she was vaguely aware may be witnessing the event from her position in the kitchen. She just wanted this man to kiss her and never let her go.

"I love you," he whispered to her.

"I love you too," she responded. She looked into his deep green eyes and knew that whatever else was happening around her, this was the truth, that she loved this man deeply and uncontrollably.

She looked up at his gorgeous face. She was now lying flat on the daybed, his warm, hard body directly over her. Unaware of the weight of his body during the kiss, she imagined he had not wanted to hurt her and was holding himself up with his elbow. He moved her frame slightly to the left, allowing enough space for him to lay flat on the bed. He turned her body onto its side so that her head was now laying comfortably on his chest.

His strong arm was enveloping her from behind, drawing her close to him. She found a soft spot to place her head and as she laid her cheek against his chest, he bent his head down and kissed her on the top of the head. "I do love you Kase and I don't want you to go anywhere."

She thought for a minute, wanting to protest, but she couldn't because she felt exactly the same way. Laying on the chest of the man she loved, she felt safe and well. She had never experienced this feeling before. It was at the same time and in equal parts both amazingly comforting and absolutely terrifying.

This feeling she didn't know how to describe. It was like floating on a cloud; it was as if nothing else in the world mattered. It was as if nothing could hurt her. It was as if she could stay this way forever. Peaceful and at home with the man she loved. That was exactly what this felt like. This felt like home.

FIFTEEN

THE UNINVITED GUESTS

The lovers had most likely known, at least subconsciously that there was potential for onlookers to their kiss on the daybed. Consciously, they probably hadn't even given it a thought, even with the amount of people milling around the estate. Staff, security, friends and medical personnel alike, there was most likely over a dozen people who could have easily witnessed their romantic scene for two. It would have been understandable to be seen, if only by pure coincidence. They weren't mindful of their very public display of affection. They had no one else in their thoughts but each other.

They could have never imagined that the onlookers to their very public kiss were more than just innocent bystanders. That two people had witnessed at least part of the intimate encounter between the marine scientist and the town's most cherished bachelor.

* * *

Only moments before the kiss the two women had been allowed in the front door by Anthony, the newest and youngest of the security staff at the mansion. Anthony was still learning the ropes from the more experienced staff but as everyone had been on constant roster, most of the more senior staff were enjoying a well-deserved night off, leaving Anthony to work the front gate safety for the night.

He had been at several of the parties already, including the big thirty-five party, awaiting like so many others the big announcement. He had also been hand-picked to perform security at the hospital with James and up until now had always worked alongside one of the older, more experienced personnel.

He had the responsibility of the front door security on his own and had answered the gate intercom and as directed only entertained people who were on the list.

This may have been his undoing because little did he know but there were two lists.

The List he had become familiar with was the long list of gorgeous eligible women all wanting to become his employer's wife. Wanting to be the one lucky woman to marry the wealthy landowner. He had initially thought the idea insane, but as he had come to know some on the women better, he could only imagine how unruly and crazy life would have become without The List.

This List consisted of the women who had nominated themselves as those willing to date and potentially marry the town's most eligible bachelor. The List was long, but also very beautiful or at least in Anthony's opinion anyway. The List made his security detail at the house ever so enjoyable and entertaining if not more than a little eventful at times.

Some of the women would go to great lengths to get his employer's attention, accidently losing their bikini tops in a wrestle in the pool or stripping down to the smallest of small string bikini. He knew that he was under strict instructions that only the women on The List and known friends to his employer were allowed entry into the house on party nights or dinner events.

That part he knew and understood. The key component of his role that he didn't understand is why no one had told him of tonight's dinner party and why there were two women waiting at the entrance of the mansion without Marco there to show them through to the festivities.

He hadn't quite known what to do, so he suggested the women go out to the balcony area to wait for the others while Anthony set out to find Helen or Marco or someone else to explain to him where to direct the arriving guests.

* * *

It was the last thing in the world Tiffany and Alice had expected to see. Their potential husband, their single friend, writhing around on a daybed with some woman, but it had happened, right before their eyes.

Anyone could understand their confusion, after all Tiffany was agreed the hot favourite amongst the women to marry him given the recent departure of Kasie from The List. She felt that given her future status of wife it was only expected that she would make the journey to the mansion to check in on her future husband.

Everyone around town had been talking about him. No one had seen or heard from him in days. They knew that his private jet had taken a quick trip but was currently at the airport. And his yacht was safely moored up so he hadn't taken any unexpected sailing trips.

They also knew that he was last seen at The Gaol on the night after his big thirty-five-year birthday bash. There were some strange rumours circulating about him taking a drunken girl to the hospital but Tiffany had doubted the validity of this particular piece of gossip.

Tiffany knew that he had enough staff and security to take care of any medical emergencies so they had ruled that rumour out as a vengeful, resentful individual who wasn't in the inner circle, as they liked to refer to themselves, trying to spread gossip about the town's bachelor.

The women stood in shock, having made their way through the gate thanking their lucky stars that the new guy had been on security detail and with enough flirting and confusion they had convinced him that they were invited to a dinner party. They assured him that they had arrived early, which would have been very unlikely for Tiffany.

The women were thankful to be shown to the entertaining area, traditionally used for dinner parties while Anthony searched for their host. Making their way to the dining area the women helped themselves to a cocktail from the bar and progressed to the balcony to wait for their friend's impending arrival.

As they looked out over the pool area and the ocean beyond, they remarked at how dark the area was, normally used to attending parties the women hadn't often seen the surrounding grounds in such dim lighting. Lit only by a few candles the area looked strangely romantically staged. It was then that they noticed the couple on the daybed.

Wondering who the very affectionate couple might be, they came up with a few suggestions between them. A naughty security personnel and one of their very own friends they had guessed at first. Or a couple of members of house staff who reside and work on the premises.

It wasn't until further inspection that Tiffany injected into the dark, quiet night. "Hell no, that isn't, is it? And oh my god, who is that woman with him?"

Alice immediately noticed what Tiffany was referring to. They watched the couple kissing passionately on the daybed, oblivious to anyone around them. The man perched on top of the woman as he kissed her and allowed her body to slide further down the daybed. Finally stopping after what seemed like forever, they appeared to exchange a few words and he manipulated her onto his chest, placing his arm around her. They watched in shock as the image before them formed a little more. There was no denying who the man on the sunbed was.

Both girls watched in horror as they witnessed what they imagined could never have happened, not as long as The List and the promises around it were followed. The promise that their friend would not have any woman alone in his home until after he had made the announcement that he would start dating. The announcement that was supposed to happen at his thirty-fifth birthday party but didn't. Then only after he had announced to the party that he would date would he entertain a woman alone in his house.

Thinking this was a fair and honest way for each woman to have a chance to get to know their bachelor and possibly make him fall in love with them, everyone agreed. And yet here they were, standing in his house, watching him passionately kiss and then finally fall into a familiar embrace with this unknown woman.

Neither Tiffany nor Alice could make out who she was in the darkness. It wasn't just the lighting making it difficult for them to see. It was the fact that he seemed to be covering her. He was sheltering and protecting her from the chilly night air.

They could easily make out his form in the darkness. No one else in Coral Cove had his stature, his body, his physique. And after all it was his house, he was the one person they were expecting to find here. But this woman, they couldn't make out who she was. She must have been someone form The List. But whom?

For the duration of the kiss she wasn't within their line of vision, instead she was underneath their friend and now… now it seemed he was hiding her, placing her in the corner against the edge of the daybed, wrapping his arms around her and now pulling a blanket over her as she lay perfectly still wrapped carefully in his strong arms.

Was he purposefully hiding her from their view? What was going on and who was this mystery woman? Tiffany pulled her phone out of her purse and frantically started dialing.

"You will never guess where we are and what we have just seen. You need to come now!" she instructed the female voice at the end of the phone.

* * *

Tiffany and Alice were not the only onlookers to the candlelight dinner by the pool. Also in the house unbeknown to Kasie and her boss were Marco and Dee. Having agreed to take some time out in Marco's hot tub, they decided to hang around for a short while and have a game of pool, just in case either of them were needed.

They both knew that their friends desired some time alone but also wanted to be there in case either of them wanted or needed some support. They hadn't figured they would play so many games, but one thing led to another. Firstly, Marco winning and Dee requesting double or nothing, before Dee winning the next game and then Marco requesting best of three, the winner.

After several games and several beers, they decided no one had come looking for their assistance so they should head back to Marco's for dinner and a soothing hot tub and cocktail.

Just as Dee had finished throwing some clothes in a bag, Marco called her to the window. "Hey Dee, I know it's wrong to watch but you might be interested to see this."

Dee headed to the window not sure what she was about to witness, but having a good guess that it might involve her best friend and her boss. Dee was right, and there in the darkness lit only by a few solitary candles were their two friends, snuggled up under a cover, lost in each other's arms.

Dee couldn't be happier for them both and it took every inch of control and a few harsh words from Marco to convince her not to run down there, throw herself on top of both of them and tell them how happy she was that they were finally together.

"Let's not assume he has told her everything just yet… ok? We will know more in the morning. For now, let's just be happy that they are together and safe. We should go and enjoy a cocktail. We have both earned that much at least."

"Let's go Marco!" Dee yelled. "Ha-ha, that rhymes."

"Ha. Hey have I told you, you are one cool woman and I am enjoying your company?"

"Sure, I get that, but don't go falling in love with me or anything. I am flying home in a few days. Now where are those drinks?" Dee was thoroughly enjoying her time with the charming Marco. She was beginning to understand why it had been so hard for Kasie to return home as she had planned.

Marco grabbed Dee's bag and the two of them made their way to the front door.

As they descended the first staircase a noise startled them both and as they looked toward the outside entertaining area from the middle of the hallway, they could barely make out the hushed voices.

"Stay here!" Marco directed Dee as he headed down the stairs. Aware that no one should be in the entertaining area, Marco's thoughts immediately raced to Doctor Chris and the unlikely scenario that he had managed to break into the mansion.

As Marco cautiously entered the dining area, he was relieved to hear a female voice, relieved even more to recognise the voice as Tiffany.

Tiffany had always been the smartest, prettiest and most popular of their female friends growing up in Coral Cove. Loved by all and brimming with confidence, this also meant that she became the most likely woman to marry the heir to Coral Cove, until that was, Kasie arrived.

Kasie had effortlessly fitted into the social circles of the coastal town, having the qualifications and skills to mix with scientists and researchers during the day and having the social grace, beauty and elegance to transform for a glamorous night at The Gaol or at the mansion parties. Kasie was respected not only for her friendship but also for her work she was tirelessly performing to rebuild Coral Cove's reef and marine ecology.

Although all of the girls loved Kasie and included her in social events, none of them really saw her as a threat to stealing their local bachelor. After all, they all agreed that he would most likely choose a Coral Cove born woman to marry.

He would choose someone he had known and trusted, someone who had known his parents and whose parents were also part of this town's historical fabric. Kasie was a welcome visitor but just that. She was someone who had committed to work there but was always talking about returning home to her beloved family and gorgeous life in Tropical North Queensland in Australia.

All of the women loved Kasie, because she wasn't a threat. Even when she continued to top the tally board of hours logged with their bachelor, all of the women put it down to talk about work and work together on the reef. Some even suggesting that Kasie and Marco had a bit of a romance brewing and that was why she was always at the mansion.

Taking Kasie out of the tally equation, Tiffany was far and beyond a clear leader on the tally board. Having known the bachelor and his family since they were both kids, most of the women, even if they secretly hoped they would be the one, assumed that the future wife of the Coral Cove heir would be Tiffany.

"What the hell, Tiffany?" Marco erupted. "What are you doing here?" He walked toward her and Alice, demanding an immediate answer from them.

"We just wanted to drop in and check on him, we have been worried, everyone has been worried about him." Tiffany was unforgiving in her deception to enter the house.

"And how did you get in? Where is Anthony?" Marco continued his interrogation. His fury was rising as his concern grew for the increased threat to their patient in the house.

"Marco, don't be mad. If it was you, we would have done the same thing, we just told Anthony we were here for a dinner. We just wanted to make sure you and he were all right. No one has seen either of you for days. We were worried," Tiffany continued, trying hard to convince Marco of her deception with some mild flirting.

Marco walked toward the balcony toward the scene he knew was unfolding in front of the two women. He looked down at the pool area to see his best friend and the woman who would become his wife. He felt a sudden and very fierce protectiveness over both of them.

"Tiffany! Alice! You know you can't be here uninvited. I will have to tell him what you have done. I just hope he doesn't take this betrayal as cause to remove you from The List," Marco threatened the two women.

"Betrayal?" Tiffany screamed back at him. "And what do you call that? She raised her finely manicured finger and pointed towards the pool daybed? Who the hell is she and why is he here alone with her?"

"Enough Tiffany! You don't understand any of this. You can't. So please just leave before this gets any worse," Marco begged her for compliance.

"What's getting worse?" Dee asked as she joined them from the hallway. She had heard raised voices and guessed from the tones that no real security threat had been found.

"And who the hell is she?" Tiffany screamed as she watched Dee enter the room and stand protectively behind Marco.

"Enough Tiffany! You are not doing yourself any favours here. You need to leave."

Anthony appeared at the entrance to the dining area. "I am sorry Marco, I thought there was a dinner. I wouldn't have let them in otherwise."

"That's fine Anthony, you didn't know and Tiffany and Alice shouldn't have lied to you. They both need to leave now."

"Yes boss," Anthony replied, walking immediately toward the two women to escort them to the front door.

"And Anthony, absolutely no more visitors, understand! I expect there won't be any parties or dinners for some time, so we shouldn't be expecting any more visitors to the house for a while," Marco carefully explained the instructions once more to the young man.

"Yes boss." Anthony bowed his head in shame at the small indiscretion that was turning into a major incident. "Come on, Tiffany, Alice, let's go," Anthony ordered the girls.

"I am going to tell the others about this, Marco. This isn't right!" Tiffany yelled at him. "And, who is she anyway?"

"Ten times the woman you will ever be!" Dee responded, "Now play along with the nice security and do as he politely asked you to and… leave."

Everyone took a pause. It was Alice who was the next to speak. "I know you! You are Kasie's best friend. I met you when you came to visit her. We had drinks at The Gaol. Do you remember?"

"That's great!" Tiffany responded to her friend with a thick layer of sarcasm draping every word that came out of her mouth. "Well maybe the two of you would like to go grab some drinks while I sort this out then?" She added.

Dee swallowed and stood in silence, realising it was only just a minute or two before the girls were able to piece two and two together.

"Wait!" Tiffany's voice rose with a tone of anger. "If you are Kasie's best friend visiting from Australia?" Everyone else remained silent, waiting for the inevitable to happen. "That means…" Tiffany continued, "That must be Kasie down there with him."

Nobody confirmed the accusation, but nobody denied it either.

Anthony spoke again, "It's not like that, Tiffany. Kasie has been very unwell, she is just staying here to recover." Knowing he had to do something to sort out the mess he had allowed to occur, Anthony tried desperately to help the girls understand the innocent nature of the situation.

Marco turned to Anthony and yelled, "That's enough! Get them out of here and keep your mouth shut Anthony!"

"Oh my god," Tiffany began again, "How could you all betray us like this. So, has she moved in? How dare she! How dare he! Is this why no one has seen him? He has shacked up with that little Australian slut?"

Marco couldn't move fast enough. His feet were somehow momentarily stuck to the floor. He watched as if everything around him was happening in slow motion and as if he was unable to stop the next horrible scene from playing out in front of his eyes. He watched as Dee, without hesitation, stepped toward Tiffany. She lifted her open palm to her eye level and waved her hand back as if being pulled by an imaginary rubber band.

Marco watched helplessly as Dee then ferociously ricocheted her hand through the air, making contact with a slapping sound straight to Tiffany's right cheek. Without pausing she screamed at Tiffany, "Nobody calls my friend that!"

Not one to condone physical violence unless absolutely necessary, Marco couldn't help but smirk a little and be somewhat proud of his feisty Australian friend. Watching Tiffany grab her face, now red with the shape of Dee's palm, he finally spoke. "Tiff, you kind of deserved that."

"Well thanks Marco. Thanks for nothing!" Tiffany fought back. "You have known this skanky little bitch for what, a few days? You have known me your whole life. How could you let her do that to me?"

Marco launched himself forward in just enough time to grab Dee's hand propelled once again with perfect precision toward Tiffany's cheek."

Not game to let go of Dee, he held her hand and started toward the stairs.

"Anthony, get the girls home now. No delays, no stops, just straight home."

Alice joined Tiffany and helped her toward the stairs and the waiting car.

As soon as they were out of earshot Marco couldn't help but let out a small chuckle. "Remind me never to upset you," he smiled as he turned to Dee. If he had to admit it, it was a bit of a turn on for him to see a woman act with so much passion.

"I'm sorry Marco, she just made me so mad. She wasn't even prepared to hear us out. How could she call Kasie that, after everything those two people have been through these last few days? I'm sorry, I guess I just lost it."

Marco placed a protective arm around Dee. "It's ok, we will deal with it tomorrow. Let's go babe."

SIXTEEN

THE MORNING AFTER

The following morning, Kasie was awoken by a light knock on her bedroom door. "Come in," she instructed her visitor.

Holding a breakfast tray and wearing the widest grin she had ever seen he entered the guest room. "I thought breakfast in bed was in order. I brought up double, so I hope I can join you?" He looked at her, silently praying for an answer in the affirmative.

"Don't you have a town to rebuild or something?" Kasie smirked.

"I have nothing else to do today but wait on you Kase. Consider me your humble servant at your beck and call," he teased her.

She wondered to herself if this man had any flaws at all. How could someone be so charming this early in the morning and so incredibly sexy? She guessed one day she might start to see the inevitable annoying habits in him that eventually come to the surface when you spend large amounts of time with another person but until that day he remained in her eyes at least, perfect.

Wearing a simple white t-shirt that hugged his bulging biceps she enjoyed seeing him regularly in more casual attire than she had been used to. It didn't really matter what clothes the man wore, he looked like a god in everything he put on his back and even more so when he wore nothing at all. She smiled at the memory of his naked body in his shower on the night of his birthday.

"It's great to see you smiling," he laughed a little, interrupting her very guilty and sensual daydream of him.

"Was I? I didn't realise." Her cheeks flushed at the thought of being caught fantasising about him again. This was becoming a regular pastime for her. She was so caught up in her memories that she hadn't even realised he had placed the breakfast tray next to her and crawled into her bed beside her, pulling the covers over himself.

Her cautious glance at him brought a smile to his face.

"Am I a little overdressed? Should I take my shirt off too?"

"Oh?" she squirmed under the covers not even realising that she was only wearing her underwear. Like many people, she felt most comfortable wearing very little to bed.

So very caught up in her own thoughts about his naked body again that it hadn't even occurred to her that she was nearly naked herself. She hadn't time to answer before he had ripped his shirt over his head and she felt his strong, warm hand on her stomach, his face moving closer to hers, his breath against her neck sending shivers down her spine.

"Um, maybe we should eat," she said as she raised herself to a sitting position on the bed, the sheets held firmly against her naked breasts. She glanced down at him now lying on his side, his head resting on the palm of this hand. His smile could melt hearts. The scene felt surreal.

"I guess you need to eat to get your strength back". He smirked. "So how are you feeling today?"

"You could probably answer that yourself considering how quickly you seem to always manage to be feeling me in one way or another." She smiled at him, a flirtatious grin erupting over her face.

"Well if I had to answer, I would say you feel absolutely gorgeous."

"Are you always this charming first thing in the morning?" she challenged him.

"How can I not be when I am sitting here in bed with the woman of my dreams?"

"Ok, so charming is bordering on just plain cheesy now." She laughed at the thought of her being anyone's dream girl. She was flattered by his compliment but had never thought of herself as anything more than just plain Kasie.

"Plus, mornings are my favourite time of the day," he added, interrupting her thoughts again.

"For what… or shouldn't I dare ask?"

"I can show you if you like?" he hinted suggestively.

Typical man, Kasie thought to herself, sex wasn't ever too far from the mind. "Mmm…" Kasie couldn't find the words to reply. She felt a sense of relief within herself that at least the medical treatments hadn't affected her sex drive. She needed to draw on every ounce of her self-control to stop herself from reaching over and kissing those gorgeous lips of his.

The scene turned serious for a moment. "Kase. I am just so happy that you are well and that you have agreed to stay here."

"I have agreed to stay for the time being," she corrected him. "This is only temporary remember. As soon as it is safe to leave, I need to go back home."

He was quick to reply, "Kase, I need to talk to you about that."

Worried about what it was that he wanted to say, Kasie wanted to delay any further conversations for now. "How about we eat first, I'm starving."

"Me too!" He smiled at her with a smile that she imagined said, "Yes, I'm hungry too, and not just for food."

With another knock on the door, this time not so light and not waiting for a response, in bounded Dee. Seemingly not surprised to find the two of them in bed together, Dee waltzed over the bed, folded her legs under her and made herself comfortable at the foot of the bed facing the both of them.

"So, what's the plan for today?" Dee enquired while plucking a strawberry from the bowl in front of Kasie and popping it directly into her mouth.

"The more relevant question might be, what happened last night?" Kasie replied. "I understand you spent the night with Marco."

"I don't think I want to hear the answer to that," he chimed in. "I think I might leave you two to your girlie chat." He began to make his way out of the bed. "But remember it isn't polite to kiss and tell, Dee."

"How very old fashioned of you," Dee laughed before she added, "Women tell each other everything or didn't you already know?"

He was standing at the edge of the bed pulling his t-shirt back over his head. "Nothing like added pressure to perform well in the bedroom then," he laughed with them.

"I can't imagine you've had any complaints in that department?" Dee flirted back at him.

He turned his attention back to Kasie, his eyes catching hers. "I do aim to please." He tilted his head back and laughed as if laughing at his own cheesiness this time. "Good morning, I will see you two lovely people after breakfast."

Both sets of eyes watched his every step as he headed for the door and closed it gently behind himself, stopping for just a second to again glance back into Kasie's eyes.

The door was barely closed before Dee let out a huge sigh. "Is it possible for that man to get more gorgeous by the day?"

"Oh yes," Kasie agreed. "For him I think it is."

"You are one lucky girl Kasie" Dee added. Prince Charming, he is indeed, gorgeous, smart, the body of a god and funny. I never realised he was so funny."

"And sexy," Kasie added.

"And…" Dee continued, "Totally, absolutely smitten with my best friend."

"Yeah well, we will see," Kasie responded.

"What do you mean, you will see?" Dee questioned. "You two got to talk, didn't you?"

"We talked a little last night, but we were both so tired we ended up falling asleep." Kasie suspected there was more to her friend's question than she initially responded to. She wondered what

Dee might know that she wasn't letting on. "What do you mean talk, Dee? What do you know that you are not saying?"

Dee looked concerned, "Kasie, look, forget I said anything, please. I think I need to go and do something." Dee looked increasingly nervous as she stood up ready to leave as if attempting to flee the scene of a crime.

Kasie wasn't letting it end there. "Girl, you sit back down now and tell me everything you know."

"Kasie, I can't. He'd kill me if I say anything."

"Dee!" Kasie spoke sternly in her most threatening voice. "I will kill you if you don't!"

Quickly admitting to total surrender, Dee flopped back down on the bed. Letting out another weary sigh, she paused and tried to think of a way to stall Kasie. She realised she had said too much already but also that her friend would be persistent until she finally gave up the pertinent information.

She took a deep breath in before finally speaking. "Kasie… your Prince Charming," Dee paused again. She really didn't want to be the one to tell her friend this important information but she knew she was pushed into a corner. "He is planning on asking you to marry him."

Kasie sat frozen, unable to speak. Feeling her body tense, her throat restrict and her mind explode with unanswered questions. "But he can't!" Was all the she was able to utter. "I'm not on The List. I took my name off The List."

"Well, I don't think The List matters to him anymore. Not after nearly losing you Kasie. This man isn't about to let those snobby town women dictate who he is going to marry."

"You don't understand, Dee. It isn't like that at all. They are not like that. He came up with the plan to create The List to be honest and transparent with everyone."

"I know he is a prize catch but do you really think the island will be in uproar if he doesn't date according to some crazy list?" Dee challenged her seemingly naïve friend.

"It's not just about who he is going to date. The woman that he marries has to make a commitment to continue his family's work. To develop the town, repair the ecosystem, to live here forever. To raise children here and for them to continue the work. This is his family's burden. Not his to choose nor to turn his back on."

"So, what's the big deal with you doing all of that? You already are here repairing the reef, so aren't you already working towards his greater plan?" Dee searched for a reasonable explanation from her friend as to why his plan wasn't feasible for her in the long term.

"I am, but I am still an outsider. I always will be. The woman he will marry has to be someone who was raised here, someone whose family was also committed to building the town. It is the island's tradition."

"That's ridiculous Kasie! People will fall in love with whom they fall in love with. You can't manufacture love and direct people to marry out of a sense of generational responsibility. And besides, I have met this Tiffany girl that everyone thought he was going to marry and she hasn't got a thing on you Kasie," Dee explained further.

"Tiffany? How did you meet Tiffany?" Kasie questioned, feeling anxious to hear the answer.

"Last night. Look I wasn't going to tell you but Tiffany and Alice broke in last night."

"Broke in?" Kasie asked in alarm. "What, here at the mansion?"

"Well, not really broke in, they were let in and um…to tell you the truth, I think they saw your little candlelight romance by the pool last night. To say they were happy for you both would be a huge lie," Dee continued to fill Kasie in on all the details.

"Oh no, this is bad!" Kasie frowned as she removed the covers and got up from the bed."

"Umm, Kasie, I think you forgot your shirt," Dee laughed.
Looking down at her nakedness, Kasie replied, "Yeah I seem to keep forgetting that."

"Ha!" laughed Dee, "I'm sure most women would forget to wear clothes if they had Prince Charming bringing them breakfast in bed too."

Kasie couldn't find the humour in the moment. Instead she threw on the nearest dress, grabbed her bag and started collecting her assorted clothing, products and phone accessories from around the room. "How did I end up with so much stuff here anyway? It looks like I've moved in," Kasie mumbled to herself as she collected her belongings in her oversized bag.

"He asked me to bring your things for you. I figured you would be here for a while. Hey what are you doing?" Dee asked with concern.

"I have to leave! I can't do this to him. I can't let him break his promises. He is not that man. He wouldn't have done this to anyone if it hadn't been for my accident."

"Kasie, firstly, if you know anything about this man at all, you would know that he will do what he has to do to make things right. He loves you and he isn't going to just let you walk out of his house like this, not after everything you have been through." Dee paused for a moment before revealing the other and much more serious reason for their extended stay at the mansion.

"And secondly, are you forgetting Doctor Chris is still out there somewhere and this accident that you are referring to wasn't accidental at all. It was a mad man attempting to take your life, and not once but twice. Kasie, you can't leave like this. Stop packing the bag and come and sit back down on the bed."

"No, Dee. I cannot wait! I am leaving and as my best friend you are going to help me. No questions asked."

Dee knew her friend well enough to know that she wasn't going to talk her out of this. She only hoped that someone else would have better luck.

The two women finished their packing and headed down the wide formal staircase for the front door. As if on cue and with perfect precision timing as always, her boss exited his office and met Kasie face to face in the vast mansion entrance.

"What's happening Kase?" His gorgeous face was fraught with concern.

Kasie turned to her friend, handed her the bag she was holding and asked in a quiet but firm voice. "Can you please wait outside for me and see if you can find us some transport."

With regret, Dee took the bag and walked past Kasie, stopping only momentarily in front of their host to simply whisper. "Sorry"

He turned to watch Dee walk through the front door and then turned his attention back to Kasie. "Can you tell me what is going on here?" He demanded of her.

"Can we talk in your office?" Kasie asked, also fearing this wasn't going to be as easy a task as she had first imagined.

"There are people in there. Let's go to my room," he suggested.

"Um, I don't think that is a good idea," Kasie responded.

"Come on Kase, you are safe with me, please just come and talk to me," he begged once more.

Kasie surrendered and allowed him to take her hand and gently lead her up the huge staircase to his master bedroom. As he opened the large wooden door of his room, Kasie felt a tinge of nervousness growing inside her. She hadn't the first clue what she was about to say to this man. He continued to hold her hand as he led her to his bed. Sitting on the edge of the bed himself, he motioned for her to take a seat next to him.

"I don't think I should sit," Kasie cautioned.

"Please Kase, I am not going to jump on you if that is what you are thinking. As much as I would like to, mind you."

His humour eased her mind and she sat next to him on the edge of the bed. He was patient as he sat silent waiting for her to speak. His concerned eyes searching her face for any clue as to what was about to be revealed.

"I don't know where to start," she began. "But I think I need to go home."

"I thought you agreed to stay here until you have recovered Kase? What has changed your mind?"

"I think I need to go home, home!" she elaborated further.

"What does that mean?" The obvious concern in his voice was rising.

Kasie paused and glanced down at her hands, entwined in his on her lap. "I think I need to go home to Australia." She felt the familiar sense of tears welling. She could hardly believe the words falling from her mouth. She couldn't bear to look into his eyes. She couldn't let him see her moment of weakness. She hadn't planned this and hardly knew where the words were coming from before they had fallen mysteriously from her mouth.

As if knowing he had to do something, to glance into her eyes to be able to connect with her again, he slowly moved from the edge of the bed to the floor beneath her. He wanted to allow her to share all of her fears with him.

Positioning himself in her direct line of vision, his eyes searched for hers desperate to make contact. His hands tightened just ever so slightly around hers as if to strengthen his weakening hold on her.

"Kase, I won't try to stop you from going home. I won't even try to talk you out of it. But I need to tell you something before you do that. There is something I need to let you know before you go," he continued, his voice timid but sure.

"Stop!" Kasie demanded. "I don't want you to say what you are going to say."

He stopped. "Well that wasn't exactly the response I was hoping for." He dropped his head in despair.

He couldn't leave it there. He couldn't risk the chance of losing the woman he loved without confessing his desire for their shared future together. "But I need to tell you Kase, that I have been planning a way to ask you to marry me. This isn't exactly what I had in mind for a proposal, but I need you to know."

Kasie didn't know how to respond, she didn't want to hurt the man she loved in this way. She didn't want to cause him any more pain in his life.

"I know… I made Dee tell me."

"Oh," he replied. The realisation of the situation suddenly hitting him as he added, "Well that definitely wasn't the way I wanted you to find out."

"I'm sorry. She kind of let something slip and I threatened her if she didn't tell me."

"That's ok, it's not like I have the ring or anything yet, so this isn't the real proposal or anything." He was desperate to keep the conversation light and not too overwhelming for Kasie.

"But you are on your knees," Kasie giggled, feeling relief that they could share a moment of humour together.

"So, you would like the old-fashioned proposal then? Me on bended knee presenting you with the largest diamond on the planet?"

Kasie smiled. "That sounds lovely, but…" She began before she realised she didn't know what to say next.

"But?" He begged her to continue her thought. When she couldn't he tried to find the words for her. "But you already knew I was going to ask and you had made the decision to move back to Australia anyway?"

She paused before responding. "It wasn't so much a well thought through plan as my need to just escape all of this for a while."

"Escape from me?" The hurt in his eyes and in his tone were undeniable.

"Not from you, from this. I can't be part of all of this. I can't be the woman you marry. You know that as much as I do," Kasie pleaded for understanding from her friend.

He struggled for just a moment to consider her words. He tried to imagine why Kasie didn't think she was the woman he should marry. She seemed so convinced. "If you had of asked me three years ago, who I would marry, I would say most definitely it wouldn't have been someone from outside of this town, you are correct. But a hell of a lot has changed in those three years. A lot has changed even in the last three days. It's not that I can't marry you Kase."

He paused to make sure she was truly listening. He needed her to hear his next few words very clearly.

"It's that I can't marry anyone but you, Kase."

He stopped again and collected his thoughts, trying desperately for her to understand once and for all, the depth and desire of his love for her, "I love you Kase. I have loved you for a very long time and I have known for a very long time that you would be the woman I would ask to marry."

At hearing the words, Kasie could feel her heart almost burst with love for this man kneeling in front of her. "I love you too!" Tears began to spill down her cheeks as she released her grip on his hands and dropped to the floor to hold the man she loved.

The two of them sat for what felt a lifetime, her sobbing quietly into his strong arms. His lips perched on the top of her head, his arms drawing her close to him and pulling her face to be placed right next to his heart.

"Please don't leave me," he begged her once more.

"I just don't know," is all she could sob in reply.

SEVENTEEN

THE GENTLEMAN

Contrary to Kasie's very clear instruction to her, Dee had failed to locate transport for her absconding friend, instead choosing to find Marco inside the enormous mansion to update him on the current drama unfolding between the love-struck duo.

"She can't go back to her house and neither can you. It simply isn't safe there until Chris has been found," Marco instructed her. His manner was professional and to the point. Dee could see the trained professional in front of her and understood that he was skilled at recognising danger. She looked further past the professional and saw her new friend, looking anxious about the safety of the people he cared about.

"I know. I tried to convince Kasie of that, but she is one stubborn woman. I am just hoping that your boss has more persuasion than me with her now."

"Well, if anyone can charm a woman into staying, I'd say it would be him."

"Come on, let's go and grab a coffee and leave them to work this one out."

"Lead me to the kitchen, Marco" Dee playfully flirted back in return.

* * *

Back in the master bedroom, the two friends were silent and still. "Kase?" he whispered softly into her ear. "Kase, I think we need to get you into bed."

Kasie slowly opened her eyes to find herself still wrapped in his arms, his embrace holding her as she drifted back from her light slumber. The emotion of the morning had drained her of all energy and she had resisted to the overwhelming temptation to close her eyes for just a short while. She had fallen asleep almost instantly and there he sat with her, holding her. Hoping she could find peace in his arms.

"You are persistent," she smirked at him.

"I am glad you have realised that," he agreed. "Now, let's get you into bed so you can get some rest." He lifted her up in his strong arms, carrying her from the floor and onto his mattress. He masterfully pulled the covers back to reveal the crisp white linen.

"I'm only letting you put me in your bed because I am too tired to walk to my own room."

"Of course," he said with a wry smile.

"And I am not going to let you take advantage of me," she smiled in return.

"I am a gentleman Kase, I wouldn't take advantage of a woman in your weakened state." His wide smile grew.

The two friends paused as he stared into her face glowing with emotion. She looked exhausted but a hint of a glimmer shone through her wicked eyes which made him smile.

"I might let you join me for a cuddle though," she flirted innocently, eager to continue to enjoy the warm embrace of his strong arms.

"Well, thank you. I might just take you up on that offer." He flirted back as he walked to the other side of the bed and lifted the covers to climb in next to her. Placing a protective arm around her, they positioned themselves. Their bodies perfectly entwined as if they now both understood they were made to fit together.

She closed her eyes then opened them immediately as she smiled a cheeky grin, "I might even let you kiss me just once before I go back to sleep," she flirted with him eagerly.

Not needing any more encouragement, he lifted his head. He placed his forehead against hers, his green eyes drilling into hers, "I might just accept your kind offer of one kiss then." And with that his mouth met hers once more, his luscious lips pressing gently against her open mouth.

She responded as if her body was made to be this close to his. Her mouth meeting him while her tongue found his in his warm, sweet mouth. Her body responded instinctively as she moved closer to him, her hands feeling his hard chest and his tight abdomen through his thin cotton shirt.

She felt his strong hand move down her back, pass the small of her spine and onto the cheek of her bottom. His hand parked there to give her plump flesh a playful squeeze. His hand took a firm hold on her and pushed her body into his. She felt a rush of heat seep through her core and explode through her skin as if to heighten her desperate need to be near him. His lips pushed firmly onto hers, frantic to taste every inch of her mouth.

The heat was becoming unbearable, her hands reached beneath his thin shirt pushing the material up past his chest and over his head.

As he assisted her to lift his shirt over his head he paused and with an attempt at seriousness asked, "Are you sure I am not taking advantage of your weakened state?" He repeated his teasing words back to her.

"No, I am not entirely sure of that," she smiled as she replied.

"We can stop?" The half question, half suggestion didn't come out of his mouth as genuinely as the words might warrant.

"We could." She smiled at him as she pulled him close again, her lips finding his. His hands moved skilfully over her body as if to outline every trace of each curve. His hands stopped at the base of her neck, at the top of the zipper on the back of her dress. With ease he found the zipper and slid it slowly and seductively down her back as he placed his two large hands on her shoulder blades. With slow intent, his masterful palms slid gently over her shoulders bringing with them her now opened dress.

His hands continued slowly across her bare breasts and down her torso and then her legs until the dress was peeled from her body and placed gently on the floor beside the bed.

"You did that with ease," she smiled into his eyes.

"Still not taking advantage I hope?" He smiled back.

"Oh no, you definitely are taking advantage now," she replied.

"Should I stop?" he asked, his boyish, innocent eyes pleading with her to say no.

She paused for effect. "Don't you dare stop!" she cautioned him. Her eyes dropped to motion towards the zipper of his jeans, her hands coming together to begin to slowly unzip. "Should these come off too?" she questioned.

"They most definitely should," was his instant reply. He had wanted this moment to happen for years. He had held back his feelings, his intense passion for her long enough. He needed desperately to be close to her.

She slowly and teasingly unzipped his jeans and began to peel the denim from his warm body.

His hand gently cupped her face to bring her eyes to his once more, "Remember, I did warn you…" He paused wanting to make sure she fully understood the seriousness behind his words. "I once warned you, that when I got you back into my bed, I was never going to let you leave again?"

She swallowed hard as she remembered the promise he had made to her the last time they were together in this room. She felt a flush of embarrassment and a fleeting moment of hesitation that she forced herself to push away. "I was warned," she finally managed to reply.

"Should I stop?" She teased as she momentarily paused while pulling the final leg of his jeans from his body.

"Don't you dare stop!" he mimicked and smiled the most gorgeous smile she had ever seen. He rolled onto his back and placed his arms either side of her chest and lifted her near naked body of top of his. He took a moment to enjoy the view of her against him before bringing her mouth down to his face once again to meet his.

"Is this to stop you from forcing yourself onto me?" She cheekily asked.

"No, this is for you to control how far this goes," he replied.

"Ever the gentleman." she giggled.

"It is taking every ounce of my self-control to not rip those panties off you and make love to you right now," he said with the perfect amount of desperation and hunger for her.

His words made her feel so powerful, so in control and more desired than she had ever felt in her entire life. She smiled a giant grin as an idea formulated in her head. She rose to her feet, one leg balancing either side of his gorgeous torso.

His eyes darted desperately back and forth over every inch of her naked skin as he tried to etch every single image onto his memory. He slowly and purposefully as if to indicate a form of surrender lifted both of his hands, clasped them together and placed them underneath his head.

She smiled down at him. Her eyes locked to his as she ran her hand down the line of her body, stopping at the lace edge to her tiny white panties. As her grin widened her hand peeled the underwear from her skin. She skilfully balanced as she lifted first one leg and then the next as she removed her last item of clothing from her body.

Now standing legs astride him, her underwear on the tip of her finger, she gave the material a playful little twirl and giggled as she launched them into the air, landing them expertly onto his bare chest.

His eyes still fixated on hers. Unable to tear himself away from her seductive glare, he unconsciously licked his lips, as if thinking of a decadent meal he was about to consume.

With one swift and abrupt movement, he reached up towards her and threw her body playfully down on the bed, moving quickly on top of her naked body. He moved his mouth next to her ear and whispered the sexiest five words she had ever heard, "You've asked for it now."

Her back arched in ecstasy as he moved his hard, hot body against her.

Bang, Bang, Bang, came the noise that shattered through the now electric air.

"Kasie, are you in there?" There was hardly a moment's pause before a second and this time more forceful interruption. "Kasie, I know you are in there, open up," Dee's voice filled the room.

Unable to believe what they were hearing the two lovers froze in silence. "Don't answer!" he whispered in her ear. "She might just go away."

"Kasie, I know you are in there, open up," Dee ordered.

As if sensing no retreat from Dee, he lowered his head and whispered softly again. "Do you know who I really want to send back to Australia right now?"

Kasie nodded and whispered back, "I can guess."

"Dee I will be there in a minute," Kasie yelled at the closed door.

"Ok," Dee replied, seemingly oblivious to the moment that she had just intruded on.

They locked eyes once more. He let out a sigh. "Are you ok?" he asked.

"I'm fine… you?" She answered, concerned more for his wellbeing than her own.

"I think I need a cold shower," he sighed as he replied. "You have escaped my evil clutches for now," he continued "but believe me, this is not over."

If his words were meant to sound like a threat, it was the sexiest, most seductive threat she had ever heard. He lifted himself from her body and sat upright in his bed. She mirrored his movements until the two of them were sitting facing each other.

He placed his hand against her cheek and kissed her lips gently. "Tonight?"

Her stomach did a massive backflip at the thought of continuing their foreplay again in just a few short hours. "We'll see," she replied without offering a firm commitment.

His head bowed in defeat. "You are killing me, you know that, don't you?"

"Ha-ha," she giggled. "You are the strongest man I have ever known. I think you will survive."

"I love you Kase."

"I love you too, my perfect gentleman."

Kasie waited a moment to watch her lover rise from the bed and walk the length of the bedroom and into the shower. She could barely control her thirst for him as she stared at his delectable backside making its way to the cold shower.

She found her feet and Kasie opened the door to Dee's concerned but knowing stare. "Doctor Harris is here to see you," her friend informed her.

"Ok thanks," Kasie replied, opening the door further to join her friend.

Dee couldn't resist a glance past Kasie to the shirtless Adonis standing just a few metres behind them. Towel wrapped around him and ready to jump into the soothing cool water. "What is it with you and him? You only have to be in a room together for a few minutes before your clothes start falling off?"

"Really?" Kasie smirked as she traced her friend's line of vision to glance back at the god-like creature standing behind her. "Do you really have to ask me that question?"

"No," Dee admitted, "I would be exactly the same if I were in your shoes. Probably worse," she laughed.

He moved toward the two women in his doorway. "You know Dee, as much as I love you, you are very quickly becoming one of my least favourite people living in this house." His face lit up as a giant smile ran from ear to ear.

"Yeah," she replied, "I guess I deserve that. But I am just looking after my girl."

His face met hers as he stepped towards her, "Our girl." He placed a protective arm around Kasie's shoulder, leant toward her and placed a gentle kiss on her cheek.

It took all of Dee's strength not to melt into a puddle right there in his doorway. How could a man be so perfect? Sexy with an absolutely perfect body, incredibly intelligent, funny and the most caring man she had ever met. And a billionaire as well.

How she envied her best friend but at the same time was so happy that this amazing man loved her and cared for her just as much as he did. They shared a silent but knowing glance as if to say to each other. *Agreed.*

"Ok, you two," Kasie interpreted their unspoken conversation. "Enough of this competitiveness, it is impossible to know from one moment to the next whether you two are going to make out or kill each other."

"Ha-ha!" Dee added with great sarcasm. "We are good, I am happy to share you. After all this drama lately, you really have become too much work for one person alone."

"Well thanks for that Dee. Love you too," Kasie joked. "So, let's go, I don't want to keep the lovely Doctor Harris waiting any longer than she has already."

EIGHTEEN

THE RECOVERY

After receiving a good health report from Doctor Harris with instructions for more rest, lots of good food and less stress, Kasie decided to head to the pool area for some fresh air. Lying stretched out in her white bikini, a present from her host and relaxing next to her best friend, Kasie felt for the first time in days a feeling of stillness. It was the most honest feeling of quiet contentment and wellbeing she had felt in a long while.

Embracing the sun as it kissed her skin, bringing with it the most delicate sensation of warmth, Kasie allowed herself to drift slowly into a comfortable and peaceful sleep.

"Oh my god!" Dee gasped. Her words stirring her friend from her light slumber. Kasie opened her eyes just in time to see him launch himself from the side on the pool, through the air and into the clear blue water beneath him in one of the most technically perfect and graceful dives she had witnessed.

"He just can't leave you alone, can he?" Dee complained in the form of a question that she really didn't need the answer to.

"I guess he is just worried," Kasie replied in his defense. Hearing her words of protection for him made her realise just how close she had become to their handsome host.

"You don't need to explain that to me Kasie. I'm not blind you know," was Dee's slightly irritated reaction to her friend's unnecessary justification. She was a first-hand witness to the epic love story unfolding in front of her eyes.

The two women watched as the blurred outline swam under the water directly toward them. His head breached the surface of the clear liquid just as he made his way to the sandy coloured pool tiles nearest them. His perfect face broke through the water, his dark brown hair sticking to his olive skin. His deep green eyes opening to take in the two women.

His wide smile beamed at them. He raised his strong muscular arms, placing them on the edge of the pool one after the other until finally resting his chin gently on top of them. His full attention was on the two beautiful friends enjoying the luxurious sunbeds.

Dee was the first to speak, "Do you know that you haven't stopped smiling since Kasie woke up?" She questioned her host not really expecting an answer but simply sharing her very positive observation.

"Any guy would be smiling if he was looking at what I'm looking at, the two most gorgeous women in Coral Cove laying seductively on my sunbeds. One of which, I expect to be lying in my bed in just a few hours. You know who you are," he teased them.

"Is that all you ever think about?" Dee challenged him, "Sex?"

"Well, lately it is." He shot Kasie a knowing glance. "Want to join me?" he hissed sexily at her. "The water is divine."

Kasie parted her lips to answer, but shouldn't have bothered as Dee bounced from the sunbed and ran toward the pool yelling. "I will!" She raced to the edge of the tiles and without missing a step jumped into the water, legs tucked under her assuming the bomb dive position. She landed in the pool just inches from her host, drenching him with the refreshing clear, cool water.

Kasie smiled as she watched her two friends begin to wrestle. She was truly relieved that they got along so well, especially given that Dee had no hesitation in sharing her displeasure that Kasie had stayed in her new home for what she described as far too long. Dee had on more than one occasion suggested that he was to blame. She questioned whether Kasie had become more than just an employee to him and had started to form a life there as a result of her growing attraction to him.

She watched as they playfully splashed each other and laughed out loud like two teenagers. Here before her, were two of the most important people in her life. Why she agonised, did they have to live an ocean apart from each other?

Kasie felt that bitter sense of being torn again at the thought. She was reminded of the conversation from earlier in the day, the man she loved telling her he wanted to marry her. She looked at his face glowing with joy as he grabbed Dee and dunked her under the water.

It would have been the perfect image, if only… her thoughts trailed off… if only she didn't have to choose. She loved this man. She knew she truly did. She had never felt this way before. Of course, she had been in relationships, she'd gone on many dates, but each time the guy felt more like a potential friend to her rather than a potential partner.

She had always been able to enjoy close friendships with the opposite sex. Being a lover of the outdoors, spending her teenage years at the beach, surfing with the guys, she often found herself the only girl on a board. It wasn't as if she didn't have the opportunity to fall in love. The opposite was actually true. She had more than just a couple of guys tell her they were in love with her, but each time she never felt like she could honestly say it back and really feel the meaning of those words in her heart.

She truly felt like she loved their friendship, enjoyed their company, but never had she felt what she imagined to be that stomach churning, yearning love she had seen in the movies. Not, that is, until now.

It appeared it was now Dee's turn to hold him under the water. Their impromptu game became more and more energetic by the minute. Dee had her two hands placed firmly on the top of his head, pushing down to keep him without breath. The full weight of her small frame forcing his body to remain trapped without air beneath the surface.

"Don't hurt him!" Kasie yelled to her friend.

"Oh, he's a big boy. He can look after himself," Dee yelled back, brushing off her friend's concerns. "And did you see what he did to me?"

I wonder… Kasie continued to think to herself… I wonder what it would take for Dee to stay too? She paused for a moment, a smile forming on her face… Marco… she had to remember to quiz her friend again later when they were alone. And this time she wasn't going to let her brush off her interrogation. She needed to find out more about what was actually going on between the two of them.

Her smile melted somewhat as she remembered her promise to her parents, to her family and the rest of her friends. She knew that although having Dee with her would make the decision to stay easier, she still had her friends, family and work back home to return to.

Home… she thought to herself. Funny how that word could have so many meanings. Right then, right in that moment in time she felt as if she was home. Just as the moment she remembered back, the moment when she placed her head on his chest on the daybed. She glanced across the pool and to the area where the daybed sat vacant and welcoming.

Her face beamed as she remembered again their first real kiss. Not that the kiss in the office or in the bedroom didn't count, but their first knowing kiss. The first time that she allowed herself to admit that she had real feelings for this man.

She remembered the kiss of the night before and then laying in his arms, her head gently resting on his warm chest. That she thought to herself, that was the feeling of home. She smirked at the realisation that for the very first time she realised what the old saying meant, home is where the heart is.

"Kasie come in," her friend yelled at her.

"No thanks Dee, I'm happy to just rest here," she replied. She noticed once more that her eyes felt heavy. She dropped her head back down onto the soft cushion and allowed herself to drift off into a peaceful slumber.

The play in the pool continued while Kasie slept. Never once taking his eyes off his lover, he relished the opportunity to spend some time alone with Dee. Through Dee he was able to learn more about what made Kasie tick. He particularly wanted to understand this intense drive she had to return back to Australia.

Dee tried her best to explain with the limited understanding she had. Kasie hadn't really mentioned much to her except that she missed her parents and worried about them as they got older. She wanted to be able to spend the important occasions with them, Christmas, birthdays, anniversaries and she felt terribly guilty about all those times she had missed in the last three years.

He of all people could understand Kasie's desire to be close to her parents. He missed his parents every day of his life and would give anything to have them back even for an hour. He suddenly felt guilty at asking Kasie to stay, to give up that closeness, that bond she obviously shared with her family. He knew that if he wanted to make this work, he had to come with up a solution to Kasie's homesickness and a way for her to remain connected to her parents and extended family back home.

He suddenly felt very certain that a trip to meet her parents in the not too distant future was in order. It would be exactly what Kasie would need after everything she had been through. And on top of that, his own old-fashioned values told him that he should meet her parents before going any further with their impending plans for marriage.

He made a note to plan some time off to take the trip back to Australia with Kasie. Visiting her hometown of Port Douglas for the very first time was something he had been looking forward to. Seeing the place where she grew up, visiting the special unique beaches like Oaks Beach that she reminisced about would only bring them closer together, he was certain of that.

He walked over to Kasie asleep on the sunbed. The sight of her peacefully snoozing knowing that each day she would get stronger and stronger made him smile. He couldn't resist but to touch her once again.

Kasie didn't know if she had been dreaming as she felt herself slowly drift from her sleep to re-join her idyllic surroundings. She wondered if she had imagined his warm gentle touch on her as she purposefully lingered in a place of half sleep, half consciousness, not wanting to wake herself if this was indeed a dream she was enjoying.

She listened for clues from the sounds around her, but all was silent. Her body felt warm, both she thought from the heat of the sun's rays and the touch of his fingers. She smiled to herself, not yet ready to open her eyes. She let herself soak in the feel of his strong but gentle hands on her sensitive skin.

"You two really are starting to make me feel sick. Is there any chance you can spare the rest of us and save that for the bedroom?" Dee joked.

Her host looked at her with serious intent. His mouth a wry smile and his eyes alight. The only clue he gave her of his sarcasm was his slightly upturned left eyebrow. "Well, I had tried that, but someone interrupted us, if you remember correctly."

Kasie heard his deep masculine voice reply to her friend in jest. She wondered how long they had been at it. Joking, playing with each other, spurring each other on. Finally, being able to enjoy the laughter and lightness of a day in the sun.

"Yeah, yeah. I'm going to make us some drinks." Dee's voice faded into the distance as she walked from the sunbeds and back into the grand mansion.

Kasie slowly opened her eyelids finally to drink in the sight of her gorgeous lover sitting beside her. She glanced down at her body to see his hands on her, layering cream on her long, toned legs. She glanced once more back to the man beside her and into his eyes, unwilling but without control under his power she smiled at him. She tried her best to appear displeased but her sparkling eyes were unable to betray her heart as she continued to stare into his deep green seductive eyes longingly.

He finally spoke, "I didn't want you to get sunburnt." He smiled at her as by way of explanation for his actions.

She looked skyward toward the retreating sun, guessing she had been asleep for some time. She estimated that it was probably late afternoon. "Do you think that maybe the sun is going down?" She tilted her head to the side in a knowing smirk.

He laughed, realising his plan had been foiled. He raised his hands to her, his palms turned toward her in the sign of surrender, "I'm sorry, just trying to be a good host here." He paused, waiting for her response, "Always one to own up to my mistakes." He paused again for dramatic effect. "I would be happy to wash the cream off for you?" He smiled more widely, in a look that was hopeful but determined.

"Ever the generous host," she giggled back at him. Her skin was now burning to touch. Having him near her made her body react in ways she had only ever read about in fiction.

"Do you have this effect on every woman?" she asked him.

He threw his head back in laughter. "Ha," he replied before his expression became serious once more.

"Yes, I do," he laughed again at her before regaining his serious but flirtatious tone. "But now that I will only ever be with just the one woman for the rest of my life, my special super human powers of seduction will be concentrated. No longer needed to be able to stimulate and tantalise the hundreds of women in Coral Cove, my super powers will store and multiply and focus so that there will be enough energy in this one little fingertip…" He paused as he ran his strong index finger along the length of her calf, over her knee, up and along the soft skin of her thigh stopping only as he reached the small knot of her bikini string.

Placing his finger gently under the string and lifting it ever so slightly away from her body as if to remove her bikini bottoms altogether, he continued. "There is enough energy in this one little fingertip to pleasure you over and over again all night… every night."

Her body was on fire, her skin felt like electricity. Her body was his willing victim, begging him to remove her bikini right then and there. They were frozen in silence, her eyes unable to meet his which were now scanning the length of her body like a starving wild animal needing to devour her in order to stay alive.

She had to bring herself back to reality before this went any further. She felt her body giving in to the urge, yearning for him to be close to her again. Yearning for the touch of his skin to warm every inch of her hungry body. "So, I might need a shower now." She paused, embarrassed that he would see straight through her ploy to escape him. "To remove this cream of course, is what I meant."

"Or there is a very comfortable spa in our bathroom, if you would prefer me to run a bath for you?" His sentence ended in a very hopeful tone.

"Our bathroom?" Her eyebrows raised in surprise. She hadn't thought of any part of the mansion belonging to her, least of all the master ensuite.

He didn't hesitate to reply, "Yes Kase, our bathroom, it is connected to our bedroom." He leaned in to kiss her plump, rosy lips.

She raised her hand to his chest to playfully halt his progress. "As much as I love the sound of the words, "our" and "bedroom" put together, it also scares me to death right now."

"Really?" he scoffed at her. "Because it just makes me horny as hell." He pushed past the pressure of her hand on his chest and placed a generous kiss on her lips.

Kasie felt her stomach tighten, her face flush as the rest of her body went limp with surrender under his touch.

NINETEEN

THE OUTING

Having managed to finally convince him that she needed another night of rest alone in the guest room, Kasie woke the next morning feeling more energetic than she had in days. She threw on some clothes and made her way to the kitchen in search of a hot, fresh coffee.

Laughter from the pool area echoed through the ground floor doors and into the kitchen. Kasie followed the joyous sounds to find Dee, Marco and their host laughing and joking away over hot coffee and a freshly cooked breakfast. All eyes turned to her as her lover stood up to greet her.

"We thought we would let you sleep in," he said as he ushered her to the table. "I was going to check on you soon and bring you breakfast in bed." He smirked at the thought of it.

"Maybe best that I join you down here then," she smiled back at him.

Good mornings were exchanged all around. As Kasie settled in the chair nearest her best friend, she focused her attention on Dee.

"Dee, I was thinking of heading to the office today to check on things and swing past my house to collect some more clothes, would you like to join me?" Kasie asked.

Marco and his boss shared a silent but meaningful exchange as Dee replied. "Sure, sounds good, what time do you want to go?"

"Probably straight after breakfast," Kasie responded in a very business-like fashion.

Her lover couldn't remain quiet and needed to voice his concerns. "Maybe it is best to wait for a few more days Kase," the strong, deep male voice of reason interjected. "You really should rest to get your strength back and then there is also the issue of Doctor Chris. He still hasn't been located. It really isn't safe for you to be out until the police find him."

Kasie wasn't accustomed to her freedom being questioned. "I am sure Chris has long left Coral Cove. He surely couldn't have evaded police for this long. The island isn't big enough for him to have anywhere left to hide."

"Especially when the boss here has had every staff member and anyone else he can, looking for Chris day and night since this happened," Marco added.

"So, where do you think he is?" Dee asked the trio of friends. The women had been left out of most of the details of the search for Doctor Chris but Dee was curious as to any theories they held as to his whereabouts.

Marco thought about his response for a moment. "We have had minimal leads to pass onto authorities to be honest. It is as if he simply disappeared from the face of the earth. But we will keep searching. Someone must know something."

Dee's expression suggested she had a theory brewing in her mind, "Maybe, he you know, killed himself or something."

"Dee," Kasie protested. "How did you come up with that idea?"

"It's not that I wish that for him. It just seems impossible for someone to just disappear and not be heard of again unless…"

"Please, Dee, no more. I can't think of that."

Marco was next with the questions, "Kasie, what are you saying? That you hope he is safe and well after everything he did to you?"

"No, it is not that I wish him well," Kasie tried to explain. "It is just he must be a very unwell man and he probably needs professional help."

Marco and Dee sat silent, confused looks painted on their stunned faces. Kasie's lover reached over and embraced her hand in his as he addressed his friends, "That is why I love this woman. She has a good heart. She wouldn't want to see anyone hurt. Not even someone like Chris who deserves everything he is going to get."

"Well you are a better person than me," Dee replied. "I would want him to suffer if he had done that to me." Dee paused as she thought more about the potential threat that still existed. "So, where do you think he might be Kasie?"

Kasie shook her head. She had no idea where the man who had tried to kill her not once but twice might be hiding. She had thought about him many times in the days since the attack. She had been replaying in her head the chilling speech uttered from this very unwell individual.

She had scanned the memories of her interactions with Chris, trying to recall if there was some way to have anticipated what had eventuated. She was normally one to trust her instinct, to pick up on situations or people who might make her feel unsafe, but with Chris there was nothing. There was no hint at the intense feelings he obviously carried for her. There was no clue as to the plan that he had hatched for the two of them to run away together. She felt disappointed in herself. Disappointed that she hadn't picked up on the potential danger and managed the situation better.

She was only grateful that it was she on that fateful day that approached Doctor Chris about the tracking device. She would never have forgiven herself if something had happened to Annie or Aretha. There were no limits to what Chris might have been capable of doing if either of the two young interns had admitted to him what they had found out.

Kasie began to formulate an answer to her friend's valid question. "I really have no idea where Chris may be hiding, but surely he can't be local still. This island isn't big enough for him to be hiding this whole time and for no one to have seen him. Isn't it more likely that he has run already? Escaped past the border controls and fled the country. He could be anywhere in the world by now."

"But Kasie…" Dee continued. "Do you really think he would leave the country without you? It sounds to me that he had a very clear plan of dragging you away with him. Do you think he would give up on you so easily?"

"He had no choice. He won't be getting close to Kasie again. That I can assure you," Marco added protectively. He was already feeling the pressure of not finding Doctor Chris before now. He had gone over and over in his mind the intricate details of the night of the abduction and questioned himself endlessly over what he might have done better. He was enraged to consider Doctor Chris ever finding Kasie again. He blamed himself for everything that had happened. He should have known better. He should have seen this coming.

Dee continued her line of thinking. "Did he tell you when or how he planned to run away with you? Or where he was taking you?"

Kasie tried to think back. "He said that I should tell people that I would happily follow him to whatever part of the world he wanted to go."

"Stop please," their host intervened. "I can't hear this. I can't bear to think of how close I came to losing you Kase." The mansion owner himself had been doing endless head miles, questioning how his sweet Kasie had ended up in the hands of this maniac. He had no idea at present how to find the mad man who nearly killed his future wife. The memory of that night was etched into his soul. He couldn't hear any more of it now, not until he had found and dealt with Doctor Chris with his very own hands.

Marco's mobile rang. He stepped away from the table and answered, "Hey." His casual, friendly tone was at one with his personality and in stark contrast to his very serious and determined best friend and employer.

Helen appeared with breakfast and hot coffee for Kasie. "I hope this was what you were feeling like," Helen said as she presented her offering.

"It looks amazing. Thank you, Helen. I am starving." Kasie was a gracious guest and so very appreciative of everything the people around her were doing to keep her safe and assist her recover.

Marco returned to the table with the determination of a man on a mission. "We have a lead on Doctor Chris," he told the group of friends.

His boss stood from the table. "Let's go to my office, excuse me." He offered his apologies to his breakfast companions as he rose from his chair and began to make his way toward the house.

"It sounds like it is safe for me to go out then." Kasie offered the statement to the two men in the form of a question just before they entered the house. She watched them both stop dead in their tracks before turning their attention back to the table and the two women who they were trying to protect.

Marco looked at his boss reassuringly. "If I am tailing Chris, then they should be safe to go." He focused on the two women. "You can take my car. Anthony can drive you. Don't leave his side, understood! I will let him know now."

Kasie and Dee knew it wasn't a battle they were going to win so didn't even attempt to argue with Marco's very direct instructions. "Ok, thanks Marco. I really appreciate that," Kasie replied.

Marco watched his boss return the few short steps to the table to kiss Kasie firmly on the lips. "Stay safe, I will see you soon when you return. Don't be gone long. You still need your rest."

Neither men were one hundred per cent comfortable with the current arrangements, preferring for the two women to stay safely in the mansion until the threat of danger was completely removed. But both men were well aware of the near departure from the house the day before and knew it would be pointless to argue with their two very independent, strong-willed friends.

Marco spoke to his boss as they walked back toward the mansion. "Anthony is proving to be a hardworking employee, despite his small error in judgement a few nights ago. He is more than capable of keeping an eye on the two of them for a few hours." Further sensing his boss's discomfort, he reassuringly added, "They will be fine, I will follow up on this lead on Chris and take a few of the guys with me. I will keep someone posted at the house as well. We are closing in on him, I can feel it."

His boss nodded his agreement in silence while Marco continued to attempt to reassure his friend. "And Kasie is right. He doesn't have many places to hide here on the island, so if he has chosen to stay around, we will find him. We will find him soon."

* * *

Aboard the anchored yacht *The Kingdom,* not far beyond Kasie's sacred reef sat Doctor Chris Bartlett. He looked down at the table below him to the ringing mobile. As if waiting on this call, he picked it up and answered it without saying a word. He listened intently to the caller on the other end. "How long?" he asked. He seemed satisfied with the caller's response. "Yes," he added, before he hung up the phone.

He was feeling relief to finally be getting off the floating torture of a boat he had to call home for the last week. He had felt nauseous the entire time he had been aboard. Sea life wasn't for him. He felt far more at home in the comfortable confines of his laboratory. The laboratory that his boss had now secured, ensuring he couldn't enter and take any more of the precious research he had worked so tirelessly for. The audacity of the man fired within him the hatred he had brewing for years. Watching him walk in and pretend to be in charge. Watching him making eyes at his darling Kasie.

Watching him strut around the building, the man about town shutting down one idea after the next that the good scientist had felt so kind as to share with him. It was then that Chris had decided to make contact with Eric Cobalt. He realised quickly that the way to real money and a opulent future was to partner with the businessman who had promised him riches beyond his wildest belief. If only his darling Kasie would realise all he had done for her - for them - for their future together as husband and wife.

He needed to see her again. To tell her once more that she had to join him. That he had been planning this for the two of them for a very long time and that with her he could make his millions, billions even. Enough he was sure to rival the wealthy town owner that held his Kasie prisoner. He clawed at his scalp. Clenching his fist around the cluster of hair, he yanked it hard. The pain as he pulled the strands from his scalp, a temporary relief to the anguish bubbling inside him.

Chris was quick to ready himself for the job he had planned to precision. He looked at the gun on the table. Still not sure whether he would be able to fire it if the need arose, he decided to take it with him anyway. He lifted the gun and secured in carefully into the pocket of his pants. He hadn't planned on using it but if it was a matter of his life or someone else's, he felt confident he could do what needed to be done.

And an extra insurance policy couldn't hurt. After all, his plans hadn't exactly worked out as he had hoped. First that ridiculous excuse for a man had stolen his Kasie away from him. He didn't think he would have the guts to try something so brazen, but than again he knew he wasn't the smartest of specimens.

Then taking her back to his pitiful excuse of a mansion. He hadn't expected he would go to such extremes for one woman. After all, he could have any woman in Coral Cove. For Chris on the other hand, there was only one. Only Kasie could make his plan complete. It was only Kasie for him. With her knowledge and talent for research they had formed the perfect partnership. And he knew she felt it too. She was just at times as weak as the rest of the women she spent time with. A man with a bit of money and women would do anything. They would forget their own passions, their own dreams to marry a man with a fortune.

Chris had hoped that Kasie was being taken care of. That she was at least well enough to fend off any unwanted attention from that rich, pretentious prick. Hadn't she shown him she wasn't interested in him by taking her name off that ridiculous list of potential future wives? That in itself was proof to Chris that she had tried to tell him, but he wasn't listening to her.

The rage at the thought of that man with his Kasie was making his head pulse. He put his hand into the pocket of his pants to feel the hard metal of the gun handle. If he had to kill anyone, he had hoped it would be him. And if he found out that he had hurt Kasie in any way, he didn't know how he could let him live.

With focus and speed Chris gathered the various bottles, needles and medical supplies he had collected on the table around him. He packed the items in a small bag and placed his phone in his jacket pocket as if expecting another call sometime soon. He made his way to the yacht's tender and without further delay, started the outboard motor and headed for shore.

* * *

Dee had enjoyed visiting the research facility again. It had been some time since her last visit and she was even more impressed at the progress Kasie and her team had made to the reef's conservation program. She was proud of her best friend. Of all the hard work she had been putting in and of her passion for what Dee herself agreed was such a critical area of work. Like Kasie, Dee was a firm believer in the conservation of the oceans, of all ecologies in fact.

She had always been an avid supporter of cruelty against all animals and conservation. Whenever possible she had raised funds, spread the message and even rallied when the opportunities arose to support her causes.

Dee had watched as Kasie greeted her concerned staff, gracefully answering questions about Doctor Chris and his attempts to harm her. She didn't have to explain much at all really, as in most small towns, word of her misfortune had spread quickly.

Dee could tell the staff were genuinely relieved to see Kasie back at work and none more so than the two young women she assumed were the two interns that told Kasie about Doctor Chris's work, Aretha and Annie. Both women approached Kasie with concern and remorse. Kasie wrapped her arms around them both.

"So sorry, we are so sorry," they both mumbled through their teary eyes.

"Shh," Kasie comforted them. "You have nothing to be sorry for. You raised the alarm. You both should feel so brave for speaking up. I am just so glad that nothing happened to either of you."

"Could we see the area where the device was?" Aretha asked shyly.

"It's actually healing really well," Kasie explained as she lowered the t-shirt to show the two young girls the red scarred area where the tracking device had been implanted.

Annie began to cry once more, "I am so sorry we did this to you."

"No, Annie, please don't say that. It is all fine. Look, I am ok and what's even better is that we can destroy all those tracking devices. They are never going to be used on the sharks on our reef."

"So, you ended up being the human test for them?" Aretha added, trying to find the humour in the moment.

"Yes," Kasie replied with a thoughtful pause. "Very unfortunately yes, I was."

"But tell me, how did you know about the tracking devices?"

The two interns looked sheepish. They exchanged knowing glances before turning their attention back to Kasie and the important question she needed answered.

Aretha spoke first. "I know it is wrong but we did a bit of snooping. He left his email account open one day when he went out and we had a look."

"But what made you suspicious enough to do that?" Kasie was hopeful to get to the bottom of the mystery.

"Just a hunch I guess," Annie confirmed. "Like you always say, trust your instincts."

Kasie smiled at the two young girls. She congratulated them for their bravery and for trusting their instincts. The relief she felt that no harm had come to either of the girls was immense. Kasie felt an overwhelming sense of good fortune that Chris hadn't clued on to their snooping.

The tour of the research facility continued uneventfully and Kasie and Dee bid their farewells for the time being and headed back to the waiting car.

"When do you think you will return to work?" Dee asked as they walked through the car park.

"Tomorrow, if I could," Kasie replied. "But Doctor Harris has forbidden me from working for another week or two yet. She wants me fully recovered before I go back. And then there's, well you know who… so that's a battle I am not going to win in a hurry. I will just lay by the pool, do a bit of reading there for a week and see how I am feeling after that."

"Smart girl," Dee added. "And interesting to see how quickly you have settled into the obedient wife role." She added the extra words with a giggle in an attempt to tease her best friend a little about her seemingly complete turnaround on her adamant stance to return home to Australia.

Kasie looked straight ahead, her face suddenly void of any colour. Her stomach once again began its routine of turning itself into knots.

"What?" Dee demanded, looking at the shock in her friend's face.

"Wife?" as the word came out of Kasie's mouth, her stomach tightened a little more.

"That's right, Kasie, you are soon to be wife to the adorable Prince Charming himself... What does that make you?" Dee toyed with her some more, "Princess Charming... ha-ha... no, that doesn't sound right... Princess Charm... ha-ha."

"Dee, you are not funny. Stop it or I am going to be sick. My stomach is a mess with anxiety at the mere thought of it. I am absolutely not ready to begin any conversations about being anyone's wife just yet."

"I'm sorry, I shouldn't be so mean to someone who is so unwell. You have been getting those stomach cramps a lot lately. Did Doctor Harris say that could be an expected part of your recovery after what you have been through?"

"I haven't thought to tell Doctor Harris to be honest," Kasie responded. "I didn't think it was anything, just nerves and stress maybe."

"Or?" Dee playfully winked at her best friend.

"Or what?" Kasie questioned her friend, feeling alarmed at any other possible explanation.

"Or you could be expecting a little baby Prince or Princess Charming," Dee laughed at her own joke.

Kasie's face went from pale to translucent. "Oh," she said, grabbing at her now cramping stomach. She doubled over as the pain became more intense.

"Kasie, are you ok?" Dee asked as she held out her arms to comfort her friend.

"I just can't handle any conversations about marriage or babies right now. It is just all too much to think of," Kasie replied. "And thankfully, pregnancy isn't even an option right now. Not when we haven't even had sex."

It was Dee's turn to be shocked. But the other morning, he was in your bed and then in his room. I just assumed that the two of you had been well you know, getting to know each other better."

"Dee, it isn't like that. Well not really. Well…" Kasie was struggling to find the words to describe what was happening. "Just trust me, we haven't."

"How have you resisted that gorgeous body? I want to jump him every time I see him. And he is constantly touching you. He always has his arms around you, or is kissing you or caressing you. It has been driving me crazy. How have you been able to hold out on him?"

"Well, I almost haven't. But that is all I am going to say about it. Let's get in the car," Kasie answered her friend.

The car ride was as smooth as a ride could be given that Marco had insisted Anthony drive the women in his own personal brand-new BMW. But somehow Kasie just couldn't get comfortable. She didn't need to scan her body for long to realise that the discomfort was again coming from her stomach.

She placed her hands on the middle of her lower abdomen. She thought back to Dee's absurd suggestion that she was pregnant. Thank god, she thought to herself. She had enough going on without having to worry about the idea of being pregnant as well.

Her stomach twisted again in pain. She winced slightly, then turned to her friend who was now staring back at her. A horrific thought entered Kasie's mind. "Oh my god Dee, what if?"

"What if what? I thought you said that you and he hadn't done anything."

"It wasn't him I was thinking of." Kasie's eyes began to water. The thought that had entered her head was unbearable. The pain that the thoughts brought with them were uncontrollable.

"Dee, I was unconscious for hours at the Lab." She could hardly bare to let the words escape her mouth. "Oh my god Dee, what if he?" Her words turned to muffled sounds unable to escape through her sobbing.

"Oh Kasie, you couldn't be, he couldn't have," her friend tried desperately to reassure her.

Kasie quickly did the calculations in her head. She added the days and weeks together and turned to her concerned friend once more. "But Dee… I am late." She hadn't thought about it until now. She had enough to concentrate on. She had barely been aware of what date it was, let alone when her last monthly cycle was.

Without saying a word, both girls knew what the other was dreading. "Oh, Dee, what if I am pregnant… with?"

Dee turned to Anthony, who was staring quietly ahead at the road. "Anthony," Dee said, gaining his immediate attention. "Can you please drive us to the hospital?"

Taking control of the situation while her friend sat next to her unable to speak, Dee reached over and grabbed Kasie's phone. I am calling Dr Harris to ask her to meet us at the hospital. Don't worry Kasie, we will take care of this."

It took only a short time for the girls to reach the hospital and meet with Dr Harris. She took yet another sample of blood, promising she would ring Kasie as soon as she had the results back.

"Please, just don't worry about anything until we have the results back," Dr Harris empathically explained to the girls. "The pain could be caused by a number of things, which I promise you we will investigate. How about going home now and getting some rest."

"I will take her straight home, Doctor," Dee promised.

"No, I want to still go by my house Dee. I need to get some things. I promise we won't take long."

"Ok," the Doctor relented. "But please be quick and get back to the mansion and to bed for a good rest. You really are rushing through your recovery and you need to take it easy."

* * *

Back at Kasie's house the two girls remained quiet while purposefully collecting the required items and packing them into two large overnight bags.

Dee was the first to break the silence. "Is there anything else Kasie?"

"I don't know." Kasie paused. "I can't think." Giving up the pretense that she was actually being productive, Kasie slumped onto the edge of her bed. Dee placed herself beside her friend. "I'm so sorry Kasie, I am so sorry for joking about all of this. I can't imagine what you must be going through."

Kasie stared directly into Dee's eyes as if pleading with her, "But what if? What if I am?" she begged her friend for an answer.

"Maybe you should try to not think about it yet. Not until you have to of course. Wait until we know either way. Dr Harris said she would ring as soon as the results are through."

"It's impossible to not think about it. I feel sick Dee," Kasie continued.

"I know Kasie." Dee felt like crying for her friend. She couldn't bear the thought that this was happening to her, not after everything she had been through. What sort of a sick man would drug a woman and then potentially violate her like this?

Dee knew she had to return Kasie to the mansion. She had to convince her to talk to him about the possibility of this pregnancy. Dee knew that he would take care of her. He would wrap her friend in his arms and make her pain disappear.

TWENTY

THE KINGDOM

Back at Kasie's house the girls had all but given up on packing. "Come on Kasie, we need to get you home," Dee demanded, standing up from the bed.

Kasie's swollen eyes met her own. "Home Dee? How can I go home to him? How can I go anywhere near him again if there is the slightest chance that I am pregnant with Chris's baby?"

"Kasie, I'm sorry but I insist. And I hate to do this but if you don't come with me now, I have no choice but to ring him and you know he will be here in minutes. I'm sorry, but we have to get you back. You know that between him and Marco they are ringing every thirty minutes asking where we are and when we will be back. I can't keep delaying them. They are worried about you and it sounds like their leads on Chris didn't go anywhere. It's not safe to be here any longer. We have to get back."

Kasie dropped her head in despair, her hands catching her face and covering her eyes as she wept. "I know," she mumbled through her fingers. "I know."

"It isn't safe for you to be away from the mansion. Please let's just go," Dee begged her friend again.

Kasie hesitated before speaking again. "I will. I just need a few minutes to myself. I need to think about how I am going to tell him."

Dee lent down and kissed her friend on the top of the head. "It's going to be ok," she said. "I will take the bags and wait for you in the car. Don't be too long. Ok?"

"Ok," Kasie agreed.

Kasie listened as she heard her front door close. She heard Dee's footsteps walk toward the car and the boot of the car close with she imagined her bags neatly packed inside.

Still holding her head in her hands, she allowed herself to truly let go. She sobbed into her palms. The sobs turned into wails as she released the pent-up emotions of the last few days.

With so many thoughts racing through her head and so many emotions charging through her now trembling body, Kasie was acutely unaware that at that very moment, a hand had reached out and grabbed the lock of her front door, silently twisted it and in doing so, locking her inside.

* * *

Doctor Chris could only make out every few words of the exchange between the two women. He had grown impatient with this Dee girl for insisting that his Kasie return to that excuse of a man. He was proud of his fiancé for standing up for herself. And all too relieved when that loud Australian left the room and left him and Kasie in peace alone together.

Just at that moment, his phone rang again. Absolutely outraged that someone would choose this precise moment to ring him he let out a quiet sigh of exasperation. He looked at the number, pressed answer and placed the phone against his ear. Without speaking, he listened intently to the voice on the other end. Chris's pasty white face morphed into one of disgust as he turned to face the bedroom from which he could hear her muffled cries.

Chris whispered only three words in the form of a question. "Pregnant to him?" He waited for the immediate reply and then hung up the phone. With renewed purpose he started for the bedroom, taking massive strides as if he couldn't reach her fast enough.

He was furious that this man had done this to his darling Kasie. How dare he touch her! How she must have fought him back, resisting his advances and yet he would have continued. Continued with his torment, oblivious to the growing distaste his darling Kasie must now have for this demanding billionaire. How dare he think he can just take whatever he wanted whenever he wanted because he happens to have money.

Sensing a presence in the room from behind her moist hands, Kasie didn't look up to respond, "I need just a few more minutes, please Dee," she begged.

"We don't have a few minutes to spare, my darling Kasie," Chris answered her. Kasie shot up from the bed, instinctively placing a protective hand on her stomach. Stretching her other hand out to indicate for Chris to stop, she pleaded with him, "Please Chris, stop… don't hurt me… you don't understand… I could be…" The words didn't want to leave her mouth. "I could be…" She hesitated again.

"Pregnant? I already know"! Dr Chris finished her sentence for her. And if you don't want you or your baby to be hurt, then you will do exactly as I say. Now let's go. We are leaving through the back door."

Her mind was racing. How did he know? How could he know? She felt faint, her legs felt like they would cave in beneath her. She took a deep breath in and sighed.

"Kasie. Now! I am not joking with you. You either move now or I will put you to sleep again and move you myself," he threatened her.

"But…" both hands now protectively placed on her stomach. "But you could hurt the baby."

Showing no signs of compassion for the highly distressed woman, Chris demanded her attention, "Then move now!"

Compliantly she began to walk to the bedroom door, seeing no way out other than to obey him she managed to take one small step after another. She stopped as she reached the hallway, turned to him and with the last ounce of energy she had to resist him, asked, "Is Dee ok?"

"Yes, for now. But if you don't leave this instance, I can't promise she will stay that way for long," Chris abruptly instructed her.

The thought of Dee suffering because of her was all the motivation Kasie needed to walk through the back door, down the stairs and toward the waiting car. Chris hopped behind the steering wheel and without a moment's hesitation he started the engine and headed to the wharf.

* * *

Waiting patiently for her friend in the silver BMW at the front of Kasie's house, Dee sat deep in thought. How this would all play out she had no idea, but she was sure of one thing. She needed to get Kasie home as soon as she could.

From there, she had hope that things would work themselves out. After all, Kasie didn't know for sure whether or not she was actually pregnant. Maybe this would all turn out to be a false alarm and things could quickly go back to normal. Well as normal as possible for Kasie and her future husband.

Dee looked at her watch and willed Kasie to come and join her in the car. She reached out for the handle to the door, grasping it momentarily before stopping herself. She was torn. She knew her friend needed some time alone to think through what she might want to say but she also knew that she had to get her home as soon as humanly possible.

* * *

Driving at dangerous speeds to avoid being followed Chris wasted no time in making for the wharf only a few moments drive from Kasie's house. Once arriving at the wharf in record time Doctor Chris pulled the car into the underground car park. He turned the engine off and looked over his shoulder as he spoke to Kasie. "I am trusting you to not do anything stupid, after all your life, the life of your baby and your stupid Australian friend are all at risk here."

"I know, I promise, please just don't hurt Dee, please," Kasie begged him.

Chris returned his attention to the front of the car. He carefully searched through some papers on the front seat, found a pen and again turned to her.

"You are to write a letter to that pretentious excuse for a boss saying that you are returning home to Australia and that he isn't to follow you. Tell him that it is over. Write it in your own handwriting. No attempts at anything." He handed her the paper and pen.

Kasie reluctantly took the paper and began to write;

I will…

Kasie paused with no idea what to write next.

"Do you want me to dictate something to you?" Chris smirked

"No, I can do it," Kasie sternly replied back.

She returned her attention to the page and began to write.

With a smug sense of satisfaction at a job well done, Chris picked up his phone and made a call. "Yes, all done, pick it up now and deliver it immediately."

Hearing the conversation from the back seat, Kasie felt the anger rise in her stomach. "So, who is your sneaky little delivery person then?"

She was furious to think that Chris wasn't working alone, that someone from this town must have been helping him. She knew he had inside information. He had information about the possible pregnancy, information that was only hours old. Who would possibly be working with Chris?

"Wouldn't you like to know," he answered with a satisfied little smirk.

It made sense, Kasie thought to herself. Someone had to be holding Dee, so he couldn't be working alone. She thought of Dee and wondered where they were holding her. Hoping, praying that she was ok and would be released without harm.

"Finished?" He ordered her.

"Yes, but you have to promise that Dee is ok and that you are going to let her go," Kasie bargained with him.

"Yes, yes, hand me the letter." Chris took the letter and read it quickly. "A bit overemotional, wouldn't you say?"

"Well, it had to be believable didn't it?" Kasie's stern words shocked him but also made sense to him.

"Yes, true. Ok let's go." Chris placed the letter into an envelope and turned to her as if nearly forgetting a crucial part of the plan. "Place his name here.

She obeyed and hastily scribbled his name on the envelope so as not to prolong the agony a minute longer. Chris dropped the envelope on the front seat, got out of the car and walked to the back of the car to open Kasie's door.

"Come, my darling. Let us board our luxury yacht and sail away together into the sunset." He let out a laugh that made her spine shiver.

"Where did you get a luxury yacht from?" Kasie enquired as she ascended from the car.

"You're not the only one with wealthy friends, my darling. I told you before it isn't the local old family money that is going to support us now. It is the big business dollar that will provide us with the luxury we deserve."

"Don't call me my darling anymore!" she angrily snarled at him.

"Fine, what should I call you then?" He smiled "My wife perhaps?"

* * *

Dee looked at her watch for the tenth time. What was Kasie doing in there? She had to get Kasie home. She was really beginning to worry about her. She quickly exited the car and headed for the front door. Turning at the door handle, Dee was surprised to see that it wouldn't budge.

Knowing she was the last person to leave the house, she immediately began to panic. She knew she hadn't locked it. She wondered why Kasie would have locked the door. Why would Kasie have locked her out when she knew she was waiting outside for her?

Dee proceeded to bang on the front door. "Kasie, open up, we need to go now!" she yelled through the glass.

Listening for the sounds of footsteps walking toward the door, Dee was silent.

"Kasie, come on now, you are really starting to worry me. Open the front door." Still nothing. Dee walked back down the few stairs and headed around the back of the house straight for the door.

She was pleased to find it opened straightaway and she let herself inside. "Kasie, where are you? Come on let's get going" She called out into the empty space. Dee's fear for her friend was rising by the second. With every unanswered plea, she became more and more panicked.

Finding the bedroom empty, Dee began to frantically search the rest of the house. Room after room of nothing was all she found. "Kasie, if you don't answer me, I swear I will…" Her voice trailed off. She would do anything to see her friend's face right now.

Dee unlocked the front door from the inside of the house and ran out to the waiting car. Anthony seemingly oblivious to everything was waiting in the front seat. Dee ripped opened the front car door and yelled to Anthony. "She's gone, she's not in there!"

Seemingly unnerved by the drama, Anthony calmly replied, "I will drive around and see if I can find her. She can't have gone far. You stay here in case she returns." He started the engine but turned once more to her before leaving.

"Hey Dee, maybe best not to tell the boss just yet. You don't want to worry him if it turns out to be nothing."

With that Dee slammed the door and watched the car pull out and head down the street and around the corner. She pulled her phone out of her pocket and called his number. She realised she had no idea of how or what she was going to tell him. But she knew she shouldn't delay a second longer ringing the man who would help her find her missing friend.

"Hello Dee," he answered on the second ring obviously expecting a call, "I thought you would have been back by now."

"Listen." she began, best just to get it out there straight away she thought. "She's missing, I can't find her." She let out a huge sigh, feeling some relief that she had brought another person into this nightmare.

"Where are you?" he demanded.

"At her house," Dee replied

"I'm coming, stay there."

* * *

Kasie headed down the wharf and toward the waiting tender. Being led by the hand by Chris, she was sensing an uneasy feeling of déjà vu. It was days since she had found herself in a similar setting, six days, eight days, she wondered. She had truly lost track of how long she had been unconscious for.

She vividly remembered the last time she was in his company, walking toward the elevator at The Gaol and feeling that same sense of pending doom. She remembered her thoughts about the seconds to disaster shows she watched with Dee. She tried to find clarity now as she was hoping that there was some way she could prevent him for forcing her into the small tender.

As they neared the edge of the wharf, the tender came into full view. "Wait, Chris." She stalled. "I am feeling unwell. I think I might be sick."

"Well that is what happens when you stupidly get yourself knocked up now isn't it? I will have something on board the boat you can take for that." He paused for only a moment. "Now move, we need to get going."

She looked around the empty wharf searching for somebody, anybody who might be able to help.

"He is not coming, your ridiculous bachelor. He should be receiving your note very shortly. He isn't coming for you." Chris smirked with a sense of evil satisfaction.

Seeing no other alternative, Kasie stepped inside the tender. She honestly did mean it this time when she informed him again. "I'm going to be sick. I really am!"

* * *

The search of Kasie's house and surrounding area provided no clues as to Kasie's whereabouts. In no time at all every available emergency service worker had been called to the spot and to no avail.

Darkness fell without word from her. Anthony's drive-by of the local streets provided nothing. His boss seething at the fact that he had let Kasie disappear demanded Anthony return to the mansion to wait further questioning from Marco.

Dee looked at her friend, searching for any words to say to lighten his pain but she had nothing. The exhaustion of the day had finally started to kick in and she felt empty, heavy with all sense of hope beginning to fade.

She turned to her friend and looked into his heavy eyes. Without speaking he grabbed her into his arms and held her tight. "Let's get you home, you look exhausted." For a moment, safe in his arms, she felt like everything was going to be ok again.

* * *

The tender had floated quickly and purposefully to the huge luxury yacht before them. "The Kingdom?" Kasie questioned him. "What the hell egotistical name is that for a boat?" She spat every word, not attempting in the slightest to hide her contempt for him.

"Quite relevant really, don't you think? You, me, our Kingdom," Chris replied. As they pulled up along the wooden stern of the yacht, Kasie placed one foot on the boat, one still in the tender. She stood still for a moment, a delicious idea rising in her mind. She gave the distant wharf a quick glance and readied her body for the dive into the deep dark water beneath her.

As if reading her thoughts, Chris grabbed her arm roughly. "Come on now, don't be stupid. I know you could swim back, but I would catch you well before you reached shore. Believe me, you are not getting away so easily this time." Chris paused, tightening his grip on her delicate arm. "I trusted you once. I won't make that mistake again."

Obediently, she placed her second foot on board the boat. She began to focus her attention on a new plan or at the very least as much information as she could gather from the scheming scientist. "There is only one person narcissistic enough to name their boat The Kingdom. I am pretty sure this is Eric Cobalt's yacht isn't it?"

"Like I said my dear, you are not the only one with wealthy friends." His face wrinkled into what Kasie imagined was his very unsavoury version of a smile.

Kasie stepped further onto the back deck and followed the luxury wooden detailing into the large interior galley. Chris was only a step behind her, obviously not trusting her enough to let her out of arm's length for fear of a repeat escape attempt.

"Your bedroom is down there towards the bow," Chris instructed her.

She froze in fear, unable to move in any direction.

As if again reading her mind, Chris spoke. "Don't worry. I'm not going to touch you."

She let out a small sigh of relief.

"Not until you have dealt with that!" He continued pointing toward her stomach. "I am not going to touch you while you are carrying his bastard of a child inside you."

TWENTY-ONE

THE NOTE

As the car pulled into the driveway of the Mansion, a small glimmer of hope rose in Dee. What if Kasie had just been for a walk and had made her way back here? The idea sounded plausible at first, but knowing her best friend as she did, highly unlikely. Kasie wouldn't for a moment put her friends through this crippling fear knowingly.

She would have rung and told them she needed some time. She would have insisted that they not worry, that she would be back as soon as she could. Knowing that Kasie hadn't contacted any of them, Dee was left with a hopeless feeling of dread. The two friends alighted the car and without speaking made their way up the stone stairs to the mansion's front door.

As the two companions reached the top of the mansion stairs the door opened and there. he stood face to face with Anthony. The saying, if looks could kill must have been written for this very moment, Dee imagined.

"You," he muttered more to himself than to Anthony.

Anthony looked like a little boy who had stolen money from his father's wallet and was about to pay dearly for it. "I am sorry boss. I don't know what happened. I searched for her straight away but she wasn't anywhere nearby."

"I can't hear this now," his boss replied. "Have you finished with Marco?"

"Yes," came the quiet and soulful voice from the hallway. All sets of eyes turned to look at Marco standing just metres behind Anthony. Marco met his friend's eyes and turned his head down in despair.

"You both better come in," Marco continued as he lifted up his right hand to show the reason why. "I have something." And there, held tightly between his fingers was Kasie's handwritten note encased in a crisp white envelope with just one word, a name written on it.

Anthony took the opportunity to walk past the two friends as they entered the mansion doors. He stood still and prepared to close the door behind himself. The curiosity was almost unbearable as he stopped momentarily to glance back and witness the three faces frozen, merge together and join in the middle of the great entry.

Anthony stayed just a moment longer, unable to walk away as he watched Marco hand the note to his boss. All three stood in silence. Anthony closed the door behind him and paused for a moment as he pressed his eyes closed and mumbled almost silently under his breath, "What have I done?"

The trio of friends stood still frozen to the spot, all looking at the name on the envelope, each of them fearing what lay within. Dee was the first to speak. "That's her hand writing. But this doesn't make any sense. She couldn't have written this today. I have been with her the whole time."

"Not when she first woke up, Dee. We were all downstairs when she woke," Marco suggested to her. He was the only one of the three who had the time to digest this latest clue and begin to formulate a theory.

Dee wouldn't believe it. "No, there is no way. She was with me in her house. She was packing her bags to come back here to the mansion. There is no way she could have planned any of this. She couldn't have. This doesn't make any sense."

Their host stared at the white envelope in his hand. "Where did you find it Marco?"

"In the office," was Marco's short and functional reply.

"But we were in the office this morning after breakfast. We would have seen it there surely," his boss added.

"It doesn't make sense, I know," Marco tried to clarify for his dazed friends. "Maybe we were so caught up in the new lead, that we simply overlooked it."

The three friends looked at the white envelope and then again at each other.

"I think I will read this outside if that is ok with you both," he begged Marco and Dee for their compassion and patience.

"Wait! Before you do, there is something that given the circumstances I think you should know," Dee began.

All eyes were on her as she continued. "We met with Doctor Harris today."

She paused to let that piece of information set in. "Kasie was worried because she has been having strange stomach pain." She paused again. "She also worked out that she was late. Doctor Harris took blood to do a pregnancy test."

Her friend let out a heavy sigh. He immediately understood what this meant. Knowing that he and Kasie hadn't had sex, he quickly deduced that the only other option would be Doctor Chris. "Kase, poor Kase," His words faded out. There was no more he could say.

He began to shake his head as if to empty his mind of the horrific possibility he had just heard. He immediately took his phone from his pocket and dialed. "Doctor Harris, I apologise for calling so late."

"That's fine, I was actually trying to contact Kasie. Do you know where she is? She isn't answering her phone," the Doctor replied.

"Yes, I know," he answered, his head bowed in despair. "Doctor, Kasie has gone missing, we don't know where she is."

"Oh no," was all the Doctor could manage to reply with.

"And Doctor, I know about the blood tests and I am aware that you must keep client information confidential but given the situation, I was hoping…" his voice trailed off.

"Of course," the Doctor replied instantly, "I understand. It is only given unusual circumstances and the results themselves that I feel that yes I am prepared to share them with you."

He waited with baited breath.

Dee grabbed Marco's hand and squeezed until her knuckles whitened with the strain. The three of them were silent, waiting for the important reply that would instantly follow.

"The results were negative. Kasie is not pregnant."

He let out a huge sigh, looked toward his friends' panicked faces and mouthed the words. "Not pregnant!" He shook his head to confirm the news.

The relief was overwhelming for Dee and her legs finally gave in as she collapsed on the marble floor, sobbing uncontrollably. Marco rushed to be beside her on the ground, sliding to the floor to hold her in his strong embrace.

The doctor continued. "Please, let me know when you hear anything," she begged.

"I will," he promised as he ended the call and placed his phone back into his pocket.

He walked the two short steps toward his friends and bent down to touch Dee reassuringly on her head. "It's going to be ok Dee. We will find her." His words were barely audible over her loud sobs. "Maybe you should take her to her room Marco, so she can rest. And stay with her," he instructed his friend.

Marco took a moment to look at his exhausted employer. "She is going to be ok. You know that, don't you?" He whispered so Dee couldn't hear.

"I hope so Marco. I truly hope so."

"I'll come back down when she falls asleep," Marco reassured his friend. He knew he needed the support as much as Dee, even if he didn't realise it himself.

"No, stay with her. I need some time alone," his boss instructed him.

With ease Marco lifted the crying woman into his arms and carried her up the marble staircase to her guest room.

He watched his friends ascend the staircase to the third floor. For a moment, he felt alone, more alone than he had remembered feeling for years. Once again, he turned his attention to the envelope in his hand. Willing his eyes to read through the paper to spare him the pain of ripping open the seal.

He needed to find somewhere quiet to read the letter. He headed toward the kitchen, quickly exiting through the back door and onto the terrace. He made his way to the daybed and perched himself on the edge.

He placed his spare hand on the daybed feeling the fabric beneath his palm, remembering back to the night he professed his love to Kasie. His thoughts turned to Kasie but his eyes closed to shut out the pain of her. He dared not try to imagine where she was right now. He didn't want to imagine her anywhere but here beside him. He looked at the envelope again.

Sensing that he needed to do this quickly, he tore open the envelope and unfolded the crisp, clean white stationery in front of him. He closed his eyes once more, took in a deep breath, held it for just a moment and let the breath move through his lips into the chilly night air. He held the note between his two hands, moved his eyes to the words and began to read.

I will never forgive myself for doing this to you.
I need to go home. Please don't follow me. I am so sorry for hurting you like this. Please forgive me.

I will always love you.
Kasie

He let out a wail that could be heard from the bedroom above.

* * *

Marco, having already placed Dee gently under the covers of her bed made his way to the window to look down and see his best friend, slumped over, his head in his hand. The letter now removed from the envelope in his other hand. He wanted to go to him, to help him through this unbearable moment in time but he knew that Dee needed him too and she was so fragile right now.

Marco stood at the window a moment longer. He watched as his friend, as if not believing what he had first read lifted his head from his hand to re-read the words before him again.

* * *

He read every word once more, the pain on second reading somehow magically accumulating in strength to create a huge chasm where his heart once was.

He slowly devoured the last few words, "I will always love you." The only words he was choosing to believe from this heartbreaking message. He read on and noticed for the first time, something that his anguish allowed him to overlook on his first reading;

P.S. Always remember… home is where the heart is.

WANT TO BE A GUEST CONTRIBUTOR?

Did you notice that our billionaire bachelor didn't have a name? I have a little confession to make… I fell in love.

While writing THE LIST and the second book of the series, THE REEF, I surprised myself when I fell in love with the island prince. I had every intention of disclosing his name when Kasie wrote her note to him at the end of THE LIST. I had planned for her to start her letter with Dear _____.

When it came time to write it, no name seemed worthy of him, so instead I continued on with the THE REEF, never sharing his name. A couple of times, our couple tease us and we think we are going to hear it, but alas, they keep the secret to themselves.

This is where you, my reader, can play an important role. I want to hear from you all, what name you think our billionaire bachelor/conservationist/island prince should be named.

Sign up to kelliemcox.com or any of my social media contacts. Take a photo of yourself with the book THE LIST or THE REEF or both and let me know what you want our bachelor to be named and why. Add the hashtag #kelliemcox

As the name suggestions come through, I will choose my favourites and those readers will be the very first to receive a printed copy of my novel, THE LAST FIRST KISS. A personally signed copy will be sent to you to thank you for your inspiration.

ACKNOWLEDGEMENTS

This publishing journey is shared with family and friends, so that the end result is something I hope we can all feel a part of. I am truly honoured to have you all play an important role in the creation of this book with me.

My children Blair and Connor, you truly are the brains and business behind my books. Blair, you create gorgeous book covers that attract readers. They are drawn to your designs. Your creative and technical support is invaluable. Connor, you make the engine behind the books function. You inspire me and keep me accountable. You both joked about my endless editing, I hope you are finally happy to see the books coming to life.

The talent behind the words, my editor and proofreader, Nadine Meyn. I sometimes think you are more dedicated to the manuscripts than I am. You make me believe your job is easy until I see the final edit and realise you spent much more than just your dedicated hours to clean up my work. I am so fortunate to have you in my life.

ACKNOWLEDGEMENTS

My alpha readers, Mark Simmons and Melissa Spilstead, the two of you constantly keep me busy, writing and re-writing endings and identifying storylines that can be improved with a tweak here and there.

My beta reader on this book, Margaret Cox. You loved this story and wanted to see it in print. Your enthusiasm for THE LIST and THE REEF encouraged me to tell this beautiful love story.

And to Georgina Winters, for gifting me these gorgeous images that became the book covers. They were just beautiful. Thank You!

To my readers. Wow, you all were incredible with your enthusiasm for my debut novel, MURDEROUS INTENT. I have taken all of your feedback on board. For these second and third novels, I have added more sexy bits (at your request) and a romantic ending. I know you all enjoy the feel-good ending.